EXTERMINATION OF AN EMPIRE

APRIL FELLOWS

BOOK ONE OF THE
EMPIRE SERIES

Copyright © 2024 by April Fellows

All rights reserved.

No part of this book may be reproduced in any form or by any electronic or mechanical means, including information storage and retrieval systems, without written permission from the author, except for the use of brief quotations in a book review.

This is a work of fiction. Names, characters, businesses, places, events and incidents are either the products of the author's imagination or are used in a fictitious manner. Any resemblance to actual persons, living or dead, or actual events is purely coincidental.

Print ISBN: 979-8-9882641-0-1

Ebook ISBN: 979-8-9882641-1-8

Cover design by getcovers.com

CONTENT CONSIDERATIONS

As an author, I am grateful for your interest in my work. It is my intention that this work gives you an escape from everyday life. However, I do not want you to enter this alternate world without a few preparations. Listed below are some situations that happen in this book which may be difficult for some. Please be aware of your limits and the content included within, and enjoy your journey into Delta.

P.S. I highly recommend the use of tissues

<u>Subject matter to be aware of:</u>

Confrontation of grief
On page dead bodies/ Macabre scene
Death of a tender age sibling
Attempted assault
Violence
On page execution
Assassination Attempt

DEDICATION

To my beautiful grandmother Cheryl Nadine. Supporter of Dreams
and lover of the written word.
Thank you for encouraging and believing in me.
Till we meet again.

ACKNOWLEDGMENTS

I have so many people to thank.

My family

My friends in my Facebook group Writer's Sanctuary

My Beta Team- You helped give me so much direction!

My Hype Girls in the Hype Girl Discord!

My Editor Cathy McCrumb

My Proofreader and Formatter Elisabeth Garner.

My ARC Team Thank you so much for reading my novel so voraciously

As I re-release this novel, I also want to thank my beautiful mother, whose proofreading lent itself to finding and eliminating mistakes previously missed. Thank you so much mom!!

CONTENTS

"After having traveled through space at their own peril, all four hundred eighty-seven souls have unanimously elected to establish a monarchy, which shall govern the planet Delta, through time and in perpetuity, and have chosen Wesley Marshall Caprice as their sovereign leader. The throne will be passed from king and/or queen to the eldest child. Where no living child is found following the untimely death of the sovereign(s), the nearest living relative will succeed the throne."
~ Colonization Charter February 25th 4792

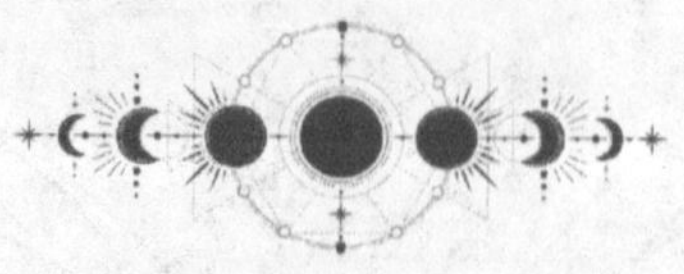

ELAURA

Sugar crystals and flour dust danced a ballet above our heads in the kitchen's controlled chaos. Bakers dressed in white, and cooks with blue aprons over their white uniforms, dashed past one another and escaped collision by mere centimeters. Much of the chaos radiated around the grand tower of the cake that would adorn the ballroom later at Mama and Papa's anniversary party. Candied flowers, dots, and lines embellished each of the cake's seven tiers, woven with patterns so intricate that I could hardly tell where one began and another ended.

I scooted my stool close to the white marble counter and dipped my finger into the bowl of frosting. Anna, the baker's apprentice and my one friend, swatted at my hand and just missed me. I stuffed the frosting coated digit in my mouth.

"Elaura! Don't put your fingers in the frosting! I can't get this cake finished if you keep eating my decorations." A brown curl escaped her hat, and her intense glare would have scared me a couple of years ago. Now it only made me grin wider.

"It's your own fault for making it so good," I argued. "Besides, you know I don't get to go tonight."

Anna rolled her eyes, but her smile was not unkind. She turned back to the cake and used a frosting spreader to carry a beautiful sugar butterfly from a platter to the second tier. I held my breath. She pursed her lips, carefully she slid the decoration atop a frosted flower, and stepped back to study the cake.

With a sigh of relief that nothing bad had happened to the butterfly, I stuffed my right hand into my skirt pocket and fidgeted with the small velvet box. Dropping from my perch to stand as tall as my four-foot-two frame would allow, I pulled out the gift and waited. Anxiety gripped my chest as I held it out for her. What if she didn't like it? Though Anna was at least five years older than me, she was my only real friend, other than my family. As my oldest brother, James had to be kind to me, and three-year-old Greggie was sweet to anyone who offered him a cookie. Anna, however, had no such obligations

Anna finished surveying her masterpiece and looked back at me. Her brows drew together. "What's this?"

"You've been working hard on your apprenticeship, and I wanted to give you something."

Her eyes met mine, then darted to the box. She absently rubbed her apron in a near pointless quest to free her hands of frosting and flour. At last, she reached for her present, and I felt as though my heart might explode. I bit my lip as she opened the hinged box. Her eyes grew to the size of platters.

"Do you like it?" I asked.

Her fingers pressed to her lips, and her eyes glistened when she lifted the necklace. A small crescent moon held a glowing blue jewel on its lower tip, and a small star dangled below.

"It's beautiful," she exclaimed. "You didn't have to do this, Elaura!"

Without hesitation, though, she opened the clasp and fastened the chain around her neck.

She did love it. My heart swelled with pride. "It's the least I could do. You're my best friend, and I wanted to wish you luck."

The kitchen doors swung open, and some of the room's chaos quieted. Anna's back straightened when my brother James strode in, his attention fixed on her. I, however, rolled my eyes and heaved a sigh. Without a glance at me, he slid his arms around Anna and pulled her close. Nothing could have hidden the glee on her face.

I groaned, and the sound halted my brother moments before he kissed her. His eyes locked on mine, and his expression changed in a flash.

"Ella, what are you doing here?" he growled as he released Anna.

"You're supposed to be in lessons right now. Victor's going to lecture you about punctuality again."

"Don't be too hard on her, Jim," Anna murmured. "She wanted to wish me luck on my apprenticeship trial tonight." When he glanced at her, she touched the necklace.

"This time there was a good reason," I added, but even as I spoke, the truth dawned on me, even before James raised a brow. Failure to prioritize my lessons had become such a habit that even the best excuse offered none at all. Tardiness remained tardiness.

"I'll see you later, Anna," James said, then cupped her face and stole a kiss, which made me a little uncomfortable. He turned to me. "Let's go, Ella."

He escorted me out of the kitchen's vanilla-scented chaos, but I stopped to give my friend a brief wave. Anna had already returned to her elaborate cake. The door swung closed. We turned a corner and left the palace's staff section. Paneled walls papered in deep maroon replaced plain beige walls.

"Ella, I wish you wouldn't do this to me all the time," James said gruffly as I trotted at his side. "I only had a short recess from the military council. Instead of spending time with Anna, like I'd hoped, I have to take you to Victor. Again."

I studied the wavy grout between the floor's marble tiles. He was right, of course. It felt like neither he nor I had time and lives to call our own. Secluded as we were from the outside world.

Mama was adamant about our anonymity, insisting we remain isolated until our eighteenth year. James would be free in a month, and I chafed at his luck, even if it came with more duties than just meeting with the council. She said that she wanted our childhood to be normal, so she kept us as far from the fishbowl scrutiny father endured as she could. It also thwarted the designs of anyone who wanted to use us as pawns for political gain. Papa said that it kept us safe in case anything happened to them. If only our mother and father hadn't been so adamant about our anonymity, our lives would've been so different.

Instead of saying all that, I whined, "Do you have to kiss her in front of me?"

"Why would I not kiss my girlfriend? I'm of age, Ella."

"Not until next month," I said.

He chuckled, as though amused at my discomfort.

"You can have any girl in the kingdom. Why does it have to be my best friend?"

"What do you want me to say, Ella? That I chose her because you're friends?" He shook his head, glanced around, then lowered his voice. "She's the only young woman here that treats me like a person instead of some deity."

"I made sure she knows you're normal," I said smugly. "Even told her some embarrassing stories from when you were little. No one can be a deity when they soiled their pants in the garden."

We both chuckled a moment, but humor fled too quickly. He sighed and met my eyes. "Look, Ella, I really care about her. I didn't set out to fall for your friend, or any of it really, but she's special to me. Even our parents approve." Speechless, I couldn't find my way around his admission. He had to be serious if he'd gotten Mama and Papa to agree with his choice.

He took the first step on the grand staircase, and I leapt to match his gait.

"James?" I began, in an effort to break the uncomfortable silence. "I wish we could go to the party tonight."

His answering smile was warm and swift, and he ruffled my hair.

"I'd just be happy to meet our cousins." I'd only seen our second cousin in the throne room a few times when she'd accompanied her father, great-uncle Baron Divo von Grakus, on his official visits. "It'd be nice to have the chance to actually meet Persephone instead of just watching through a peephole."

"I know, Ella. But you know Papa says the same thing every time Great-Uncle Grakus asks to meet us."

I knew. I could hear Papa now: *For the safety of my children, I must decline.*

James patted my shoulder. "Besides, she wouldn't be there even if they allowed us to go. Great-Uncle Grakus sent notice that he's sick or something." He paused at the first landing so I could catch up. "My guess is that he's probably over-training his personal guard again."

I laughed. He didn't.

"Probably. Everyone knows he does that. Isn't that why the palace gossips call him the 'Bloody Baron'?" Clutching one hand to my chest in mock terror and flinging the other against my forehead, I exclaimed, "Oh no! The Bloody Baron may kill us all."

James shook his head at my dramatics. "I wouldn't joke about things like that if I were you. There may be more truth to it than you realize."

My amusement faded into silence, and we continued through the residential hallways to my suite. I reached for the knob, but James stopped me.

"Ella, promise me something." His tone was solemn.

Confused, I searched his blue-gray eyes.

"Promise me that from now on you will focus on your studies." He placed a hand on my shoulder. "I'm the heir-apparent, but I can't do this thing alone. If I've learned anything from my time with Father and observing council meetings, it's that no king can rule well without people he genuinely trusts." His eyes pled with me. "You may be my little sister, and you may be late for studies, but I know I can trust you when it counts. Please study as though *you* were the heir-apparent. Then, when you're ready, you can be my right hand."

I'd never considered the burden he felt until then. The weight of the world would soon settle about his shoulders. Guilt washed over me. I had added to his burden rather than helping him. I couldn't let him carry everything alone. James was my friend *and* my brother. I tried to smile for him, though the corners of my mouth wanted to sink instead.

"I'll be by your side, even if the world should swallow me up," I promised, and finally managed a smile. Our saying always reassured me, and my spirits lifted. It started as a joke when we were playing as children. He'd said it first as he swore to rescue me from the dragon's keep. Now it stood as a reminder that we would support one another

"Thanks, Ella." With a smirk, he pulled me into a hug and muttered our saying back in my ear.

He looked as stately as any prince could as he strode away to resume his council meeting.

I, however, still had to face Victor. Wishing my carved wooden door —or at least the duties before me—would disappear, I traced the petals of ornate flowers with my fingertips. When I could no longer stand it, I pulled the door open.

Victor glared at the pages of a book with an incendiary intensity. Though he certainly wasn't trying to set the book ablaze, his focus was like a magnifier in the sun. More than once, I thought I might burst into flames under his scrutiny.

Eyes never leaving the page, he said, "You're late."

"My apologies, Victor. I'm here now." It was a weak offering, but empty excuses bothered him more.

He closed his book and waved to the open chair across the small table, where I took my seat. After pulling a hand through his brown hair, which was a surefire cue that I was about to get a lecture, he began. I did my best to pay attention, but my notes turned to doodles as I struggled to focus on economic theory.

Despite my best intentions, my attention wandered when a leaf floated past my window, and once it disappeared, Charlie, my old teddy bear, caught my eye from his perch on the edge of my bed. If I was helping James, was I too old for bears? James! I needed to focus. I looked up as Victor pulled his hand through his hair. Did he dye his hair? He had to. His stubble was red. People didn't grow different color hair.

I nearly drifted off to sleep, but a soft popping startled me. Victor stopped speaking, and his eyes riveted on the door. My brows knitted as I tried to place the noise.

Then the screams started. Soft at first, distant, rising and falling in time with the staccato bangs.

A chill ran through me. Victor and I remained frozen in place until his wide eyes met mine. My mouth hung open, desperate questions trapped in my silent plea for reassurance. He took a step toward me, but whirled at footsteps beyond my door. The handle rattled, and my stomach dropped to my feet. My hands raised to cover my head as the door burst open and slammed shut.

Matea, my nanny, leaned against the door, her left hand pressed to her chest. Panic shone like a beacon in her vivid green eyes. Matea possessed nerves of steel; nothing rattled her. Something had her scared, and *that* terrified me.

"What's going on out there?" Victor demanded, an edge to his husky voice.

Her mouth opened and closed a few times. "We're under attack! Soldiers are pouring in and shooting everyone... *Everyone!*"

Fear, like ice, crackled down my spine at her statement. Who would attack us? Why? The questions sprinted through my mind at such a speed, I could hardly touch their coat tails. Finally, one question slowed enough to grasp.

What will happen to me?

Before terror could swallow me, Victor pulled me from my seat at my desk toward my bedside. I stumbled over my own feet.

"What are we going to do?" Matea asked, following close on our heels.

Victor placed my hands in Matea's and began searching around the floor at the edge of the bedframe.

"We can't hide under the bed, Victor!" Matea whispered harshly. "We're trapped! They're pouring through all the exits!"

"Not *all* the exits."

He bent over beside my nightstand. The sharp popping grew louder, pulling my attention to the door. Something on the floor snapped, but I couldn't move, couldn't look away from the carved wood. The screaming and popping grew louder. I stared at my door, terrified that, at any moment, its movement would usher in death.

Behind me, Matea exclaimed, "A trap door? How did I not know? This is—"

"Classified. Get in." Victor ordered.

His command broke the spell holding me captive. He grabbed my arm and spun me around. A square trapdoor had opened by my bed, revealing gaping darkness. Matea had already gone down, but that hole threatened to swallow me. I felt like a swimmer in the Morosian Sea with no direction and no life preserver. Victor's hands on my cheeks directed my attention to his hazel eyes. The strength in his gaze gave me a life jacket.

"Elaura, we have to go now," he said. "You can do this."

I nodded.

He guided me to the small ladder just beneath the opening. Matea waited below and helped me off while Victor slid the door closed. Shadows reached to suffocate me. I heard my tutor land beside Matea and me. A muffled snap echoed, and as a green glow lit the passage, my eyes adjusted. With an arm around my back, Victor held the small light in front and urged us forward.

He kept his voice low. "Hurry. We've got to get to Greggie."

All too soon, the thundering of heavy footfalls pounded above us. Victor pulled me against him, granting me a small semblance of security, and we continued on. We passed another ladder, perhaps leading to James's rooms, and were soon below what must've been my baby brother's suite, for Greggie's whimpers and the muffled voice of his nanny, Fara, reached down into the dark.

Then, the noise of boots echoed. Horror washed over me as Fara's voice sharpened to shrill begging. My little brother's screams were unmistakable. A bang split the air. A thud sounded, and Greggie wailed louder. Victor pulled me and Matea close, shielding us as more bangs followed, and bullets pierced our ceiling, though none touched us.

My brother fell silent, and thin beams of light pierced the gloom.

I pressed my hands over my mouth to keep from screaming, and Matea held me close.

No—my sweet baby brother, who cuddled when I read to him,

who shared cookies with me, couldn't be gone. But the stillness told a different story.

The footsteps thundered away.

Dead. Greggie was dead.

More tears rose, and my feet remained rooted to the floor. It hurt to breathe. I wanted to curl into a ball and let nothingness consume me.

Victor pulled my face into his chest to muffle my mounting hysteria, holding me until I quieted. Matea rubbed my back when he let go and knelt before me, again meeting my eyes in the dim space, this time with a wild determination in his eyes I'd never seen before.

"What kind of monster kills a small child?" Matea's hushed voice broke. "He was only three."

Victor didn't answer her. Instead, he wiped the tears from my eyes. "We need to move."

"No!" I grabbed Victor's sleeve. "James!"

My tutor shook his head. "He's with the army council. He'll be fine."

With his hand firmly on my shoulder, Victor rose and led us further down the corridor. We walked for what felt like forever, at last reaching a staircase. One cautious step at a time, we descended to a dead end. Victor handed my nanny the light stick, pressed his finger to his lips, and pressed his ear to the wall.

Matea and I sat in silence while Victor listened, and the sound of gunfire and screams faded. He pushed the wall open and left us clinging to one another in the dark, waiting for what felt like eternity. With every passing second, my terror grew.

When the hidden door opened, I curled away from the light and pressed my face into Matea's shoulder.

"It's clear if we hurry." Victor's hushed voice felt too loud in the darkness.

I peeked at him, and he waved us forward into a bright hallway with its tall windows and paneled maroon wallpaper. We were in the entry to the throne room, where Mama and Papa were conducting formal business.

"Victor, my parents..." I whispered.

He stooped before me, hazel eyes searching mine. "They're gone, Elaura. There's nothing we can do for them now, except to get you out. You understand?"

The hushed words cut through my heart, hollowing me into a shell.

He brushed a hair from my face and rested his hand over my cheek. "We have to go through the throne room. I checked to see if it was safe, and that's the only way out. It's a terrible sight, so I need you to keep your eyes on me. You need to be brave just a little longer. Can you do that?"

Fighting back tears, I nodded.

He pulled me into a quick hug. "Good girl."

Although I wanted to fall to pieces, I knew Victor was right. We needed to be strong. I pulled away and dragged my hand across my face chasing an imaginary tear. Victor stood, motioned for us to follow, and quietly reminded me not to look away from his back.

I tried to listen. I really did, but my foot bumped something mid-step, and my gaze fell to the floor as I tried to regain my footing. A deep red puddle spread beneath my shoes, and to my right, a hand stretched, motionless. I followed the limb up to the shoulder, neck, and face. He had been one of Papa's staff. His eyes stared up—at me, through me, past me.

Horror-struck, I tried in vain to shrink away, but when I looked away from his blank face and silent scream, the carnage captured my attention. My own heart nearly stopped at the sight. People littered the floor in various crumpled heaps, some atop others.

Then I saw them.

Papa—my dear Papa—sat slumped in his throne, his eyes turned to the ceiling. Red riddled his suit. Head bowed to the floor, my beautiful mother slumped at his side. Her deep brown hair cascaded to conceal her face. Red seeped, staining her teal gown.

Everything else—sight, sound, thought—lost all meaning. My legs buckled, and I dropped to my knees among my fallen people, the ones my family was supposed to protect. My skirt and tights wicked blood from the floor, but I didn't care. Tears coursed down my cheeks, but before more than a half-second of sharp keening emerged, a hand covered my mouth.

"Shhh," Matea hissed in my ear, then called quietly to Victor.

His hand encircled my arm, and I brushed it away.

Mama, Papa, Greggie—gone? I didn't want to leave them, didn't want to escape. Why couldn't Victor and Matea understand? It would be better to join my family now.

Then strong arms encircled me, lifting me from the floor. Matea released me, and they ran, dodging my people's bodies. Victor handed me into Matea's waiting arms and opened yet another hidden passageway. We ducked inside, and he slid the wall back into position.

"They'll find passages soon enough," he muttered. "We have to keep moving if we're to escape."

He had sealed my parents, my little brother, my entire world into a palace-sized tomb.

I wanted to fight Matea's hold on me, but I had no more strength. I had nothing. I was alone in the world.

Once again, Victor took me in his arms. Matea pulled out that green glow stick. They ran again, deeper, farther, faster. Away from home, away from family, away from death.

Even with the glow stick's sickly light, darkness swallowed us whole.

2

It is with heavy hearts that we announce the deaths of King Charles Alistair Caprice and Queen Denna Rae Cartwright Caprice, along with their children. Our sovereigns were killed in an attack on the palace during the king and queen's anniversary celebration. This calculated assault has been linked to an anti-monarchist party based in the southern territories of Delta. A great number of close relations were also slain, leaving a vacancy on Delta's throne, but a thorough search discovered Baron Divo Von Grakus, the closest relative. He has reluctantly agreed to ascend the throne in the memory of his late nephew, the king, and his family. The whole of Delta wishes peace to the souls of those lost as they traverse the expanse of the Ages.

~*Official Announcement, Delta Tribune*

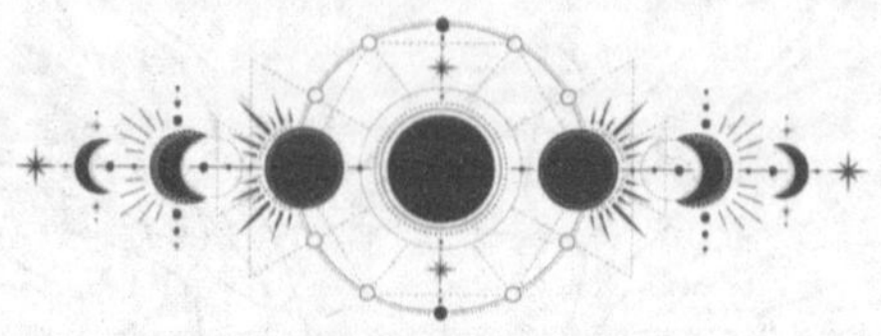

Elaura

Gunfire echoed and screams ripped through the air. My every step slowed as if weighed down by an invisible force, and the very walls of the passage taunted me, stretching further with every step I took. The one thing that drove me forward was finding James so we could escape together. I wouldn't be alone.

Behind me, a *click-click* brought me to a stop. I turned to stare down the barrel of a large gun. Time slowed, and a glow of molten fire rose from the back of the barrel, exploding like a violent volcanic eruption.

NO! Not like this!

The bullet struck me, and—

I bolted upright in my bed, a sheen of sweat caking my skin despite the chilled morning air. Sheets and blankets lay crumpled at my feet, and goosebumps covered my arms. I scanned the darkness for danger, but everything remained where I had left it the night before. There was no gun, no threat. I was safe.

My heart hammered while I chanted, "Only a dream. Only a dream."

Neither Victor nor Matea rushed in to comfort me this time. I must not have screamed, and gratitude washed over me. Their presence would have foiled my plans. Terror retreated, and I glanced at my clock. Not too early, not too late. More than anything, I needed to set out and get this done. Whatever awaited me, my future lay beyond Atha's farming community.

I eased my feet to the stone floor and stood as the slate's chill raced up my legs and spine, waking and sobering me in a beat. Centering me, as it always had whenever memories haunted my dreams. I paused. What would I do when it was no longer there to calm me?

The curtains over the closed windows left the space dark. Shoving that question aside, I tiptoed out of my room. Moonlight spilled through the kitchen windows onto Matea's shawl, where it hung over the back of a chair. She'd tried to teach me to sew once, and the only thing I'd managed with any success was the teal shawl. I ran my fingers across the uneven stitching, remembering how she'd refused the new one I'd offered to buy her at the last festival.

I slipped past Victor's chair, careful not to disturb the book and glasses discarded on the small arm table next to it. I couldn't leave until I confirmed they were still asleep. Stepping over the creaky floorboard, I approached the open door, sticking my head through the opening.

Moonlight danced through their curtains wafting in the morning breeze, highlighting their shapes under the covers. I sighed. After all the tragedy we'd endured, I was grateful they'd found love, especially since their happiness together made leaving easier. Neither moved, and only a soft snore sounded from the mound on their bed.

For a moment, I closed my eyes and leaned against the doorframe. For the past six years, these two precious people—my aunt and uncle, as far as anyone in Atha knew—had been with me every step of the way. They'd taught me and cared for me with love and compassion, even in the midst of their own pain.

Light glinted off the spectacles discarded in the open book. Crossing the space, I picked up the glasses, placed a bookmark within the pages, closed the book, and gently replaced the glasses. I sighed, letting my fingers run along the book cover just a little longer. For a moment, I wanted to take one of his books with me, but I couldn't do that to him.

Determination pulled my shoulders back, and I went back to my room, even while guilt gnawed at me. Neither Victor nor Matea deserved what I was about to do.

I should've made proper arrangements and said goodbye, but it wouldn't work. I had to leave, and Matea wouldn't let me go. She would plead, even beg, for me to stay, though I wasn't sure how Victor would react. No, maybe I did. Since their marriage, Matea had her way. They would have presented a united front, and farewells—if they even happened—would have been messy.

All I knew for certain was that I couldn't handle the idea of losing them, too. Maybe the decision to sneak away before they woke was cowardly, but I would return. This wasn't a final farewell. Only a goodbye for now.

Back in my room, I changed out of my nightdress into a black tunic and gray leggings, pulled the packed bag from the back of my closet, and stuffed my nightdress in. Next, I molded a lifelike lump in my bed. The deception wouldn't give me much time, but it should enable me to make it to Waekfield, the nearest city with a port. I tucked a note beneath my pillow, leaving a meager explanation of where I would go and what I planned to do. Carrying my bag and my shoes, I snuck back into Victor's nook, cringing at each noise, and stood on my tiptoes to pull a small container from between the books on the third shelf from the top.

The smooth wooden box was finer than anything else in the small cottage; it whispered of another life. I eased open the lid and grabbed a handful of bills, hoping I'd left enough for Victor and Matea's needs. Victor's teaching surely offered enough income to make up for whatever I took. My conscience prickled. Shoving that qualm aside, I stuffed the money in my bag and paused at the faint glint of metal in the dim light.

My royal identification necklace. Reverently, I pulled the silver beaded chain out of the box, letting the rounded rectangle pendant swing free before I slipped it over my head. Matea had wanted to get rid of it, but Victor and I had overruled her. Now it hung around my neck beneath my clothes. If it was safe to prove who I was, I would be able to. Again, rising to my toes, I slid the box back into its usual place and crept toward the kitchen door. Its creak gave me pause while I opened it just enough to edge myself outside.

The summer wind beyond whispered an invitation. Ignoring any second thoughts, I eased the cottage door closed and slid my shoes on. The latch fastened between me and my surrogate parents, and the street's silence kept my nerves on edge. Every house enjoyed space between one another with flowers on many of the windowsills. Despite their welcoming facades, each home I passed whispered discovery, and every window reflected retreat.

While the first moon sank behind me with the second moon in close pursuit, sunrise lit the horizon ahead. Though every stride spoke of new beginnings, the crunch of gravel and sand issued a rebuke.

I have to do this, my heart protested. *Victor, please forgive me. I'm sorry, Matea. Don't cry. Surely you both will understand. I have to know.*

I shifted to a jog, then a run, all the while thoughts of James filled my mind.

If I escaped, perhaps he did, too. I knew Greggie and my parents were gone, but more than anything, I had to *know*. Was James alive? Rumors reached even my ears of a surviving heir hiding in a southern province. I needed the truth, and my old home held the answers.

I let the breeze calm my senses. Its wispy fingers caressed my burning cheeks, dried the tears that rimmed my lashes, but nothing stilled the turmoil in my mind.

Victor and Matea suspected Great-uncle Grakus had been behind the massacre, but he had promised swift justice to the traitors who slaughtered my family. I bit my lip. The murderers had not been caught, and the question nagged at me: Were Victor and Matea right? Grakus could easily have taken power by force. He could be the reason...

No, Grakus *is* family, and family would never do such a thing.

I held onto the hope that they were wrong, even while I raced away from them.

The only way that anything might be salvaged from the tragedy of March fourteenth was if James had made it out alive.

Instead of slowing my footsteps, my thoughts spurred me into a run. In no time at all, Waekfield rose into view. The outer wall gates stood open to welcome travelers.

Walls? Had Waekfield always had walls? I didn't remember them when I'd been here last, but I'd been in such a fog when we passed through six years ago, only days after my orphaning. But whether or not the walls had been there before, Waekfield was my first destination. I summoned my courage and strode through the open gates and past the guards who stood as sentries watching my approach.

Smoke and dust marred the once clean lines of the city. Debris. While chunks of brick lay abandoned in the street, crumbled from a windowsill or geometric decoration. In the few alleys I passed, faces peeked from piles of what I imagined were blankets. Atha was nothing like this. The angry glares of every face I passed suggested no one had time to give a stranger directions to the closest transport hub, but undeterred, I pressed on past several scattered soldiers overseeing the citizens on the streets. Had conditions always been this bad?

I finally managed directions to the center, booked my passage to Havenwood, and took a seat in the crowded waiting area. I counted my lucky stars that my bus would leave within the hour while scanning the crowds, terrified that Victor and Matea might try to stop me.

A voice announced that it was time to board, and tearful farewells sounded all around. While friends wished one another well, lovers clung to one another, and children held to their parents, I looked away, uncomfortable with the displays of affection. No loved ones were present to wish me a safe journey.

My stomach clenched in guilt as I climbed onto the bus ahead of the other passengers, internally cringing at the residue from the handrail that clung to my skin. Staggered wear on the seats revealed the pale brown the seats had once been. I realized as I settled into my window seat that I should have bid farewell to my loved ones. Received words of wisdom from Victor or pried myself from Matea's embrace. I took a window seat and tried to get comfortable, distracting myself from impending tears by scanning the crowd, while the other passengers boarded and filled in the remaining empty seats. As the last person boarded, the door closed and the engine roared to life while I settled into staring out the window.

The flash of a familiar teal coat beneath a mess of auburn hair caught my eye, and my heart stuttered. *Matea?* Blinking in disbelief, I looked again but couldn't place where she had gone. Then Victor pushed his way through bystanders. Our eyes met briefly, and he turned back, motioning with one long arm. Matea appeared at his side. I pressed my hand to the glass. Surely they couldn't stop the bus from leaving or, worse, join me? A hiss of steam, a soft jostle, and the bus began to move.

Matea stepped forward, sorrow tracing wet lines down her cheeks. Victor grabbed her shoulder and held her back. He never once took his eyes off me, only tucked her under his arm, smiled, and waved. My heart tightened at Matea's panicked and pained gaze. The bus pulled away from the terminal, and Victor and Matea disappeared into the crowd. My heart splintered inside my chest.

I slid back into my seat and dropped my face into my hands. How could I have been so selfish? They'd loved and cared for me over the last six years, as if I had been their own child. Not once had they complained that they had abandoned their hopes and dreams, even their independent lives, for my protection. What did I do to thank them? Left in the middle of the night without so much as a hug.

Tears coursed unrestrained between my fingers.

What I wouldn't have given to take back the last twenty-four hours and have that discussion with them both. To tell them face to face that I would leave. To give them the closure of a goodbye. I, of all people, knew time could not be undone. Things I could never change had shaped my life. The people around me ignored my quiet sobs, and finally, this new grief spent, and I wiped my face. I stared out my window but ignored the scenery racing by.

Our journey to Havenwood lasted the rest of the day and through the night. Even after the moons rose, we stopped only long enough to change drivers. I tried to rest, but insomnia, my old adversary, kept me from getting more than an hour or two of sleep. Instead, eyes closed, I listened to conversations around me. While some travelers shared stories of ailing family members and business dealings, I also overheard hushed whispers of discontent and still quieter tales of a royal heir who had survived the massacre, one who might rise and take the throne back from Grakus. Even as the thought of survival gave me hope, uncomfortable questions rose. How long had the people felt this way? Had the seeds of discontent been sown by my own family, or by Grakus?

Night faded into morning, and our destination rose on the horizon. The closer we came to Havenwood, the more small businesses and houses rushed by the window. A frown crinkled my forehead. Much of the outlying town resembled ancient ghost stories, with buildings boarded up and abandoned. Plants pushed through the cracks in the pavement in front of the empty structures.

At one point, the bus stopped at a crossroad while stuck in congested traffic in front of a tired, faded house. The front door stood open, and a breeze wafted through decaying, tattered shirts, pants, and dresses on a clothesline. In the yard, a rusted tricycle awaited a ride that never came. Everything sat as though the occupants of the house had simply vanished amidst their daily routine. Goosebumps prickled my arms.

Soon, however, the vacant buildings gave way to a teeming metropolis. Crowds of people weaved between market stands. When the bus paused at another intersection, I watched goods and currency change hands so quickly that I wondered how no one summoned law enforcement to investigate theft. Even on the busiest of holidays, shopping in Atha had never been this boisterous. There, people preferred to take their time and converse with the merchants and traders.

The voices of the crowd merged together into a din that penetrated our windows over the bus's rumble. We finally stopped in the main square, and my fellow passengers wasted little time disembarking. I waited, not at all concerned about being the last one, and when I stepped off the bus, the scents took me back to my childhood. I found a bench and sat for a while, just enjoying the familiar air.

So close, and already home called to me. A long-dry fountain caught my eye, and for a second, I was back in the palace's southern garden with Papa. I was young, perhaps five, and I leaned against his chest and listened to his heart.

"You are the stars, the sun, and the moons, my little princess. And I love you more than all of it."

I crossed to the fountain and ran my fingers over the rough stone. The sweetness of the memory chased back doubt, but even so, weight settled on my chest. Pain rushed back as if the loss were new. Never again would I hear Papa's voice or feel his embrace. Not in this life.

With a breath to steady myself, I set the memory aside and turned toward the palace. I had no way of knowing what I would find. Great-uncle Grakus should live there, and I could finally meet him and his daughter. Though, perhaps it had become a memorial for the lives lost that day, the walls covered with the memorial cards for those lost.

One thing, though, was certain.

I had to find James. Dead or alive.

3

The bodies of any souls, having died, shall be cremated in accordance with Interspace Accord 25623-85d, which requires that all remains to be cremated. The ashes thereof shall be used in the creation of ink with which to make cards of memorium, which are to be given to family members and/or loved ones of the deceased and posted for the general public for up to seven years.

a. Allowing the decay and decomposition of any deceased soul rather than cremating in keeping with the Interspace Accord is a gross violation of human rights, both of the living and of the dead.

~ Colonization Charter Act 548.B385

ELAURA

ura

The sun began the latter half of its journey across the sky as I walked down the lane leading to the palace, dodging potholes and debris. The larger cracks sported weeds, some sporting more greenery than the lawns, which were no longer pristine. Though the scattered stately homes seemed empty, the hair on the back of my neck stood on end as though I was being watched.

When I left the neighborhoods and crossed the parks to the wall separating the palace grounds from the neglected lawn. Vines crept over the walls and many of the access doors barely hung on their hinges. In spite of myself, the poor state of the once grand monarchal home brought an ache to my chest.

Judging the state of the grounds, I bet that my great-uncle would not be in residence, and I could walk the halls alone and grieve in peace. He would never let his home fall to this level of ruin. Perhaps the events which transpired prevented him from taking our ancestral home as his own, but even a mausoleum ought to be better kept. Great uncle Grakus should have fixed it up even if he intended not to live there. I had to see what else had become of my home. Perhaps the interior was better kept.

Beyond its still thick barrier, ivy hid the service entrance along the ground's wall, making it difficult to find the door. Hard, but not impossible. I had to shove through several layers of vines to find the door and took refuge in the shade it offered. Still, I couldn't shake the feeling of eyes on my back. It was a ridiculous thought. I hadn't seen a soul for at least a kilometer or two.

The door creaked in protest as I shoved it open and slipped through it, hoping that only the exterior had seen decay. My hopes were ill-founded. The grounds between the wall and the kitchen door lay neglected.

Unfamiliar shadows swelled, though I should have known that the kitchen would not have been lit. With a deep breath to steel my nerves, I climbed through the weeds, but paused just past the threshold as I waited for my eyes to adjust to the dim light filtering through the dirty, shattered windows. A strange and unmistakable odor—like musty decay, and something I'd never smelled before—pinched my nostrils. The word 'death' whispered in the back of my mind as I pulled a small pen-light from my pocket.

"It must be the food," I told myself. "They forgot to clear it away."

My hushed rebuttal fell flat in the stagnant air, but the hair on my arms stood on end. Stomach sinking to the floor, I reached for the handle, pulled the kitchen door open, and gagged. I pressed a hand against my nose as death's decay washed over me. My eyes adjusted to the dim light, and my hand moved to cover my mouth instead.

They were all here.

Every person who had been shot lay on the floor. Mounds, some atop others, with black crusted rivers stretching to the drain in the center of the floor.

Horror crashed over me.

If these people had been left, then my family would probably be here, too. There would be no memorium cards to look through. No names to read, no registry to mourn at. Everyone who'd died that day had remained where they fell to rot.

Bile clawed its way up my throat and falling to my knees, my stomach emptied. I steadied myself on the door frame. Tears clouded my vision, and I dashed them away, ignoring the ones that took their place, and wiped my mouth with clenched fists. After a few steadying breaths, I stood. No matter what else, I had to make my way to the council room where James had been. I needed hints to find my way to where he was. After only a few steps, however, something caught my foot, and I fell forward. A cloud of dust mushroomed around me, and I coughed. I shoved myself onto my hands and knees and came face to face with empty eye sockets.

My limbs could not move fast enough to get me up and away from the remains, but I landed on my backside in an unceremonious heap. The stained, formerly white uniform of a kitchen staffer tangled with the blue apron of a baker. What little remained of the face stared, dark and paper thin, some sharp facial bones exposed to the open air. I tried to shove myself away, but a glint of silver and blue caught my eye, drawing me closer despite myself.

Fingers trembling, I reached out and lifted a chain from beneath the collar of the uniform. In the dim light, the necklace I had given my dear friend Anna six years ago still sparkled. The crescent moon, the dangling star and glowing blue jewel that rested on the lower ledge of the moon.

Anna?

It was! My dear sweet Anna lay before me, dust dulling her hair. So much promise, talent, and love to give to the world. As much as I had struggled to admit it years ago, she made a perfect match for James, and he adored her.

A wave of sorrow washed over me, bringing with it a fresh batch of tears. I crept closer, and stroked the top of Anna's head, then snatched my hand back when my stomach threatened another upheaval. I recoiled, rubbing my fingers against my pants. Scrambling onto my feet, I raced for the door to the hallway, dodging around the large tables, evading the bodies that littered the floor, and pushing through the bullet-ridden door as sorrow overtook me.

I dashed through the expansive hallway beyond the kitchen. Fewer bodies littered the ground here, and when I reached a space with no corpses, I dropped to my knees, trying to gain control. Eventually my sobs subsided, and I rose to my feet and proceeded with caution. I had come to find evidence about James, but now that I'd seen the bodies, I had to make sure that it was an isolated oversight.

How could Great-uncle Grakus leave people in such a state? Such a callous disregard for the dead rocked me to my core. Mankind had dispensed with such vulgarities on the first voyage from earth so many millennia ago.

"Not even criminals receive such treatment." I whispered aloud, the sound too loud in my ears.

The words fell like lead in the empty hall, and my steps were heavy as I turned to the great hall. The doors stood ajar, and I caught a glimpse of a strange contrast of still-colorful clothing, rotted flesh, and bone. Squeezing my eyes shut, I wished against all hope that the sight might disappear, but when I looked again, it remained.

Across the dimly lit space, the gold-leaf scrollwork of the throne room door caught my attention. An invisible tether pulled me silently to its ornate decoration. If I crossed the sea of people littering the floor, I would be in a place I'd once imagined myself taking a seat by my parents. I can't say quite how long I stood there tracing the designs carved into the wood with my eyes.

No. I wasn't ready to see what had become of my parents. I had come to see their memorium cards, not what remained of their bodies. After the kitchen and the great hall, I had little doubt of what I would find beyond those doors.

I would discover that awful truth in the morning. First, I needed to find James. I couldn't let grief distract me from my initial mission. I had to know whether or not he survived.

Turning on my heel, I crossed to the base of the grand staircase. My fingers gripped the banister's polished wood. With each step I climbed, I recalled sliding down this very banister in my attempt to run from Matea and the way she would catch me at the bottom without fail. Fresh grief and guilt hit me, as my trusted companion wasn't here with me. Because I'd run away.

Once atop the third-floor landing, my gaze turned to the left. To the council room. I sniffed back as many tears as I could and strode down the dark hallway. The small pen-light I'd brought did little to combat the darkness. Numbed by the corpses I'd seen in the last hour, I threaded my way to the council room, avoiding the bodies as best as I could. What more could I weep for these people, whose identities I did not know?

Ahead, the hall turned to the right, and although I couldn't see it yet, the room's carved mahogany door called to me. Ten more yards. Then five. Almost before I knew it, I had turned the corner, and the door loomed in the semidarkness. Black holes peppered the door upon the first sweep of my pen-light.

I hesitated, almost dropping my small light. Was my brother alive, or was he lost to the Ages?

No. I knew what I would find. Men caught unaware, unable to escape. I would have to check each person in the room for his tags. If I didn't find James here, maybe he had escaped—or maybe I needed to check every fallen body in the palace. Was it so bad to go on hoping? Was it awful to believe he might be alive somewhere?

Determination gripped me, and I pushed open the heavy door and blinked. Sunlight filtered into the room through a tall window, washing over two of the bodies. I stuffed the light in my pocket to have both my hands free.

The first had fallen face up, allowing easy access to the faded collars of his uniform to confirm the absence of an ID necklace like mine. I had to roll the other over and did so with care. This one was not James, either. Two others lay in the back of the room by the window, one atop the other.

I turned the first body over and, after a check for ID tags, turned my gaze to the person below. My stomach sank.

Fragmented light shone on the clothing, highlighting the faded red cuffs around the wrists, and the fringe on rigid shoulder pads. A deep breath in the dank air, and I pulled back the collar. Time slowed when I saw the beaded chain.

"No." I breathed, pulling it from the uniform despite the tremor in my hands. There at the bottom of the chain hung a small piece of metal with an engraving.

James Edward Caprice
Born 4/20/5224
Son of Denna and Charles II
Heir Apparent

The world gave way.

Oh, my brother. He hadn't made it out. Hadn't survived, as I'd hoped. My whole family was dead. All of them. Every friend I had ever known, save for Victor and Matea, had joined the Ages. I was wholly and utterly alone in this world, as I'd feared.

Delta seemed to shift on its axis, and the planet spun and twisted beneath me. I tried in vain to fill my lungs. Grief overtook me, and I dropped to the floor. Tugging my knees to my chest, I pulled the matching necklace from my own neck.

Hysteria seeped into my blood, and I gasped out, "You idiot! You weren't, you weren't supposed to die... You shouldn't..."

No one answered me.

The tears began, drenching my face, my neck, my shirt. "You shouldn't have teased me so many times. Shouldn't have suggested that I would have to take charge of the kingdom if something happened to you." I drew a shuddering breath. "You spoke it aloud, and the Ages listened."

Empty eyes seemed to stare at me, and I shivered.

"You were the smart one, and here you were surrounded by our top military leaders. They could have helped you escape. They should have."

The squares of sunlight from the window edged past the table. Night was falling.

Escape...

I needed to get away from this. To be alone. To be away from the dead surrounding me at every turn. They couldn't speak or see, yet I felt their presence as though they stood over me. Blinded by tears, I dropped my necklace at James's feet, pushed myself from the floor and made for the door, desperate to put some distance between myself and the awful truth.

My haste made me clumsy, and I tripped over a shriveled limb. Once free of the room, I ran as hard as my weary legs would take me. Again, I stumbled over someone, or something, with no chance of recovery. The ground rose to meet me, and the low-pile carpet scraped my hands and knees on impact. My energy spent, I lay there without the strength to rise.

Without a visible audience, I shattered on the faded crimson rug. For years, I'd prayed to see James again, but not like this. When my tears, at last, ran dry, I sat up to take stock of where I'd fallen. Motes of dust danced through beams of light that towered like guardians around me. I sat in the mouth of the residential wing.

Oh, sweet boon. Something familiar.

My room was only three doors down, two doors shy of Greggie's room.

Greggie—

My whole being recoiled at the thought. I couldn't. I knew, had heard. I'd had enough cruel truth to last me a lifetime. No, I wouldn't check. Greggie would remain in my heart as the sweet bubbly toddler that gave wet, sticky kisses. Resolving to keep my memories of him as pure as I could, I hoisted myself from the floor and rose to my full height.

My room would be a haven. No one had lost their life there since Victor, Matea, and I had fled. I might even manage some rest. The very thought made me keenly aware of my exhaustion.

Holes riddled the door, and I was relieved to find my room as empty as I had left it. There was no one to mourn here amongst the upended furniture. Without the strength to right my bed, I made do with sinking into the dusty mattress on the floor. I shook out the blanket from the floor and curled into a ball on the mattress. As I lay there, images of the kitchen, the great hall, and the council room flooded me. Murder, compounded by rampant disrespect for the fallen.

As the sole surviving child of the king and queen, it was my responsibility to atone for this neglect, but how would I go about identifying and cremating everyone after so much time had passed? The very idea both overwhelmed and depressed me. Everyone here deserved a proper cremation, and their loved ones should have had memorium cards. My mind raced in fruitless circles. There must have been a registrar of staff, but would there be a guest list? Most likely every relative I had, save Grakus and his daughter, had been in attendance for my parents' anniversary celebration.

Try as I might, I could find no rational reason to allow hundreds of people to rot where they fell, even if a rebel faction had carried out the massacre, as Great-Uncle Divo Von Grakus had claimed. If the crown came to me after a tragic loss of life, my first order of business would be to identify and to process the dead to give their families a chance to grieve. This had always been the Deletian way.

But even as I resolved to make things right, doubts crept through my mind like shadows at dusk, growing ever larger as the light faded. Could Great-uncle Grakus be behind the massacre, as rumors on the bus had suggested? As Victor and Matea suggested? I'd believed in him before. Even denied the whispers in the markets of Atha. After all, he was family.

But...

I'd seen the mounting evidence with my own eyes, and it was damning.

An edict of no entry has been issued for the property wherein stands the palace governed by the late King Charles II. Having been the scene of a heinous attack, this property shall remain closed as investigations continue. Any member of the public crossing the threshold shall be charged with trespassing, the penalty thereof shall be either life imprisonment or public execution. The burden of proof of any soul's innocence lies with the soul so condemned.
~ Official edict, King Divo Von Grakus

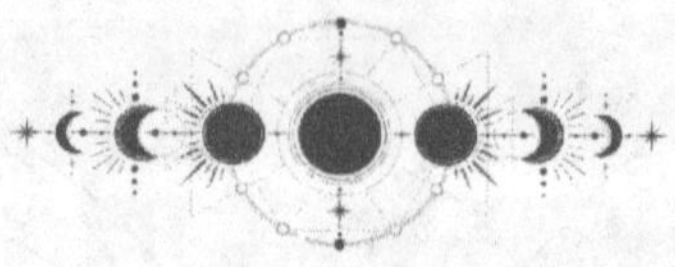

Elaura

Morning light crept through the room and across my face. I opened my eyes to a familiar ceiling and lay there, halfway between dream and waking. Vague terror hung over me, like the remains of a nightmare I would tell Papa later. Just a bad dream. When I rubbed away the sleep, however, my vision snagged on my upended furniture. Reality crashed around me like a vase on the stone floor.

It had been a nightmare, just not the kind I could wake from.

Dust from my mattress on the floor billowed when I stood and made me cough. My reflection stared back at me in the mirror, over the vanity, over the delicate chair on its side. Gone was the little princess, and in her place stood a young woman. I knew that face, had seen it often enough in mirrors before, but this time, in the shattered familiarity of my old room, the mussed mahogany hair and blue-green eyes seemed strange. The tear-streaked cheeks didn't mask the determination in the jaw.

No matter the circumstances of my birth, no one would give me what I needed to make things right, but I was a Caprice. The last of my father's children. I refused to allow anyone finish the job begun in the massacre six years ago. My fists tightened. I would live up to my father's legacy to stand for what I believed in. I would fight for my people.

If Great-Uncle Grakus got away with what he'd done to my family, friends, and our people, their blood may as well be on my hands. If he treated family in such a fashion, how much more so would he mistreat my people? If he treated the dead with the disrespect I'd witnessed last night, he didn't deserve any power over the living.

Leadership had never been a mantle I wanted, and I didn't know if

I was yet ready for it, but I no longer had a choice. Maybe my people would follow me, maybe they wouldn't, but they deserved more than what they had now. I stood as the only legitimate threat to Great-uncle Grakus's claim to the throne now, and he didn't know I lived.

I lifted an old hairbrush from the floor and cleaned the dust from the edges of the emblazoned royal crest. While closing the two steps to my bag, I pulled it through my unruly hair. After pushing the brush into the bag with my other possessions, I opened the vanity drawer and grabbed every item that might fetch a price. By the time I'd put the last item in my bag, the drawstrings struggled to close.

A memory prompted me to check the drawer again, and in the very back, my fingertips brushed a smooth box. Even with the lid still on, I knew what it held: a pendant on a black ribbon. My fingers curled around the box.

Mama's anniversary gift. I'd been so excited to give it to her. I had designed it myself, and the jeweler had allowed me to craft the crude pendant with clay and sealed it with epoxy. I slid it open and held aloft the rough pendant to read my juvenile writing on the front: "I will always love you. For thru and thru."

The words echoed the ones she had whispered over countless hugs and bedtimes, and I could almost hear her, even now.

"I'll always love you, dear one. For through and through."

The ache in my chest grew, and tears pricked my eyes, threatening to escape. I replaced the lid, slid it into the bag, and with a deep breath, turned to leave, but a soft brown lump caught my eye. My little Charlie bear peeked at me from under a bullet-riddled table. I knelt down. Even now, just touching him chased the shadows away. I brushed some of the dust from his fur and pressed a kiss above his beaded eye. I would never be too old for his companionship again. Carefully, I stuffed him down into the sack with my clothes and pulled the strings closed.

With my bag filled with trinkets to both sell and to keep, I closed my bedroom door behind me. I had one final stop to make. My steps were deliberate as I walked down the hallway, trailing my fingertips over the raised fleur-de-lis wallpaper. I carefully descended the grand staircase, entered the great hall, and approached the doors to the throne room, weaving my way between the fallen and avoiding the stains.

It was time to say goodbye to my parents.

Eyes squeezed shut and hands trembling, I pushed open the door.

A handful of skylights offered the only light in the large room, highlighting small windows of horror. Bodies still littered the floor as they had six years ago, but now their faces resembled a ghastly paper mâché that did little to obscure the bone beneath. The once glossy white marble had dulled to muddied black that absorbed the surrounding light. But none of that mattered as ice splintered through my veins when my eyes found what remained of my parents.

Their bodies still slumped together, supporting each other even in death, but they no longer resembled the people I remembered. The greatest king and queen of Delta, reduced to rotted corpses. Every step toward them was heavier, as though I trudged through a mire of mud, until I reached the ancestral thrones and fell to my knees.

For long minutes, I knelt there before summoning the courage to reach toward Mama's hem. A hiccupped sob tore through me before my fingers brushed the fabric, and curling my fingers into a fist, I wrapped my arms around myself and crumpled to the floor.

"I want you back," I keened, and with every breath, a new crack splintered through my facade of strength, bringing a flood of grief.

Finally, I rose to my knees and, sliding my bag from my shoulder, gingerly pulled the little gift-box, let the bag fall to the ground, and tried my best to smile, even knowing their eyes would never see.

"I wish I could have saved you. I wish I could have done something, anything, to keep you with me. James, too." The finality of those words stung like a fresh cut. "I hoped that he'd made it out like I had, but I... I was wrong." A breath, a pause, and I drew what courage I could from my mother's presence. "I couldn't look for Greggie, Mom. I heard him crying. I heard what they did, and I just..." A lump formed in my throat. "He was so little. I wish I could have..."

I coughed, a futile attempt to dislodge the thickness in my throat.

My gaze fell to the floor before I managed to look at what remained of my mother's face.

"I... I made something for you. It's a necklace. I thought I would have time to give it to you before..." I paused, unable to complete the thought. My fingers tightened around the box. "I hope you and papa are happy where you are. I hope... I hope you're all happy together."

Kneeling, I moved to set the gift at my mother's feet, but a silver glint caught my eye—the necklace I'd grown so used to seeing her wear. It held a picture of James, Greggie and myself. Whenever I asked her about it, she'd tap my nose with a sly smile and say that she kept her greatest treasure right inside this locket, over her heart.

To have that part of my family...

With clumsy fingers, I opened the box and lifted out the crude necklace. Several deep breaths did little to calm the churning of my stomach. Still, I had to do it. Despite the tremor in my fingers, I untied the ribbon, stood, and reached cautiously to tie it around Mama's neck.

Tremors shook my hands, but I managed to undo the clasp on the silver chain. Recoiling from the film crusted to the locket, I dropped it into the waiting box, replacing the lid. My hands curled around it, pulling it to my chest as I failed to choke back another flood of tears.

Mama and Papa had taught me that death was only the end of a chapter, not the end of the book. With every fiber of my being, I believed I would see them again on the other side of mortality's veil. I had to. Though a life beyond death removed the sting, the ache remained as a hole in my chest.

But while I cried, a peace embraced me like invisible arms in silent comfort to my grief, enabling me to turn my attention to my father. Everything within me shuddered in my pause.

"Papa, I'm not sure I have the strength to be who you want me to be. I'm not sure I'm strong enough to lead the people." There was no way I could live up to his mantle. "I need your strength to let you go, and... and to carry on without you. Papa, you were always—" I struggled to breathe through the strangled sobs "—my hero."

Slowly, I extended my hand toward his, wishing with everything in me that he might grip my hand, stroke my hair, and tell me to put my worries to bed. My hand pulled away of its own accord, fingers curling inward.

"I'll keep both of you in my heart," I whispered. "Always with me. I love you both. For through and through."

Rising to my feet, I pressed two fingers to my lips and reached them towards Papa's forehead and Mama's; unable to bring myself to touch them as we used to. Lips pressed tight, I squeezed my eyes shut against the moisture. Despite my efforts, however, another tear escaped the gated veil of lashes. I lifted my bag, secured it over my back, and dashed for the door, dodging corpses on my way out. At the door, I paused long enough to look back at them before I ran for the exit. Tears refused to cease.

My bag bounced against my lower back as I ran, the drawstring straps digging into my muscle. Desperate to be free from the throne room turned mausoleum, I raced through the main doors and ran headlong through the main gate—

Right into a passing soldier.

The impact threw us both on our backsides. My gaze met his as I tried to recover my wits about me, and for a moment I saw myself reflected in his steel-blue eyes. Good manners required an apology, but the need to flee overpowered the need to be polite. If Great-uncle Grakus were in fact behind the slaughter of my family, he would punish anyone found snooping around the evidence of his crimes. Sorrow turned to panic, and horror laced through my veins. I launched to my feet, and my tears dried as I ran for my life toward a grove of trees.

"Hey! Halt! Stop right there!" the stranger shouted.

His voice was too close behind me and drawing closer. I couldn't keep this pace for long. Hiding was my best option. He yelled something I couldn't understand over the thundering of my heart, and a second voice answered.

He's calling for reinforcements!

In the space of a ragged breath, everything shifted from a game of cat and mouse to a more sinister hunt. I had to put an end to it soon, or my great-uncle would win. A single tree offered shelter like a kind innkeeper to a wandering traveler, but I had no time for such luxury. I ducked past the leafy embrace into the waiting grove. Trees rushed past me, and I dashed in a jagged line. My eyes swept back and forth for a good place to hide, and I found a tree wider than its friends not far away.

Taking shelter beneath its foliage, I slid my bag from my shoulder and let it hang between my feet. I would have one shot. The forest hadn't slowed him much, and he would overtake me soon. He was a big man. Incapacitating him was out of the question. Stunning him would give me the opportunity I needed to escape. Pins and needles danced along my skin, down my arms, down to the tips of my fingers. I closed my eyes and listened for him to come close enough to swing.

His boots thundered closer through the brush. When it seemed he was just behind the tree, I swung my bag with all of my might, opening my eyes just in time to see the bag connect with his throat. His eyes went wide. He crashed onto the ground with a strangled gasp and clutched at his throat, spittle dangling from the corner of his mouth.

I hoped I hadn't mortally wounded him, but there wasn't time to ponder the repercussions. His reinforcements would arrive soon, and I needed to be as far away from him as possible. Without a second thought, I took off, still unsure of my destination. There had been an inn or hotel in Havenwood near the bus stop. It might be a good place to lie low. It would take everything I had to make it there in time. Mr. Blue-eyes wouldn't be in any shape to follow me so soon, but his reinforcements might.

Almost as soon as I had thought it, sirens split the air in the distance with the faded roar of heavy engines rumbling beneath. Panic compelled me to push my limits even harder as danger began its encroachment. The crunch of leaves beneath my feet did little to drown out the sound of my heart pounding in my chest. Buildings sprang up around me, the grass and leaves giving way to gravel, which gave way to pavement, and my footsteps quieted enough that I could no longer hear them over the pounding of my heart. The sirens had faded to a low whine in the distance, allowing me enough peace of mind to slow my gait to a jog.

The inn I'd seen yesterday came into view on the edge of the square, and I pushed my numb legs just a little further. The steps were almost too steep for my aching limbs after the marathon I'd just finished. With a great deal of effort, I struggled up the steps, every muscle burning with a hollow ache. My lungs cried to squelch the fire, eating them away, but the flames made my throat raw. I barely opened the door, then my legs gave way, and I crumpled into its opening.

A young girl with brown hair raced to my side and tried to push me out of the building. A deep green gown came into view and the girl fell away. Hands helped me to a seated position, lifted me from the floor, and carried me somewhere. Words spoken nearby sounded far away, and I couldn't decipher their meaning. Someone laid me on a soft cushion-like surface.

My mind raced. I had to do something for the people in the palace. I had to make James proud of me. I had to do something for our people...

A sickly-sweet smelling cloth pressed over my nose and mouth. Every hair on my arms stood at attention. My eyes shot open while my intuition screamed of danger. The dark figures over me gave only a small view of the dim room.

This journey couldn't end in a dark room I'd never seen before. I'd come too far to lose now. My fingers curled as I reached for the hand over my face. Hands held my elbows to my sides and the holder of the cloth pressed my head deeper into the pillow. Weight settled over my extremities. My fingers brushed someone's arm, then fell to my side. As my eyelids followed suit, one last image came to mind.

The soldier.

His dark brown hair, steel-blue eyes haunted me.

I hoped that I'd not mortally wounded him. Even his image faded as darkness pulled me deeper into her clutches, binding me where I lay.

5

The monarchy shall task the military force of Delta with keeping the peace on the planet. As the peacekeepers of the planet, it shall be their duty to maintain order and oversee commerce through trade routes. Any soul having received a direct order from a soldier shall be required to obey under penalty of imprisonment. Disobedience of a directive shall result in imprisonment for twenty-four to thirty-six hours without further cause.
~Monarchal Code 388264-294b

TOURELLE

She got away! I thought bitterly as I coughed and struggled to fill my lungs. It was my duty to catch the fugitive, and I'd failed. Time lost meaning as I writhed. The hands that lifted me from the ground remained my only cue of time passing. Every time I managed a word or two of explanation, another bout of hacking consumed me. A medic shadowed my every move, anxiously waiting to examine me. I continued to wave him off until I'd given the young responding captain what intel I could.

"Waste of time," I muttered as the medic directed me to the nearest bumper of one of the twenty rigs that had arrived while he checked my eyes and examined my aching throat.

I didn't want or need to play a victim right now. There was a criminal on the loose, one who had broken the edict of no entry, failed to obey the commands of a peacekeeper, and had assaulted a soldier. The young captain who'd taken charge of the response was green behind the gills, and I wasn't optimistic about his handling of the search, but there was little I could do until the medic finally let me go with some comment about a bruised larynx.

The young Captain Fritz had set up his command center on the hood of one of the vehicles, a map held down by rocks on the corners. He'd drawn circles around the palace ruins, the grove, and nothing else. A quick scan of the area confirmed my suspicions. Infantry men searched tree to tree using flashlights under the foliage. The very sight of them searching where I had explained she wouldn't be, made my blood boil.

Fritz chose that very moment to appear by my side. "Major Breckenridge. No sign of your fugitive."

I pinched the bridge of my nose. "Captain, did you not hear my recommendation from the beginning?"

"Sir?"

"She would have put as much distance between us as possible. Is this the sole perimeter of your search?" When he nodded, I scraped out the words through a raw throat, "Then you have wasted valuable time searching the very places I told you she would *not* be. At this rate, your men will be eating MREs for breakfast in the woods." My voice cracked. The damage she'd done licked my throat like flames, and a short fit of coughing overtook me, shredding it further.

The young officer's cheeks flushed, but he threw his chin up in defiance. "I felt it prudent, sir, to check for your assailant nearby. She couldn't be too clever, if she was breaking the edict."

Pompous, green officer. I clenched my hands into fists, and he took a step back.

"You heard my report, Fritz. A young woman, about five-foot-six, slender build, with long mahogany hair and blue-green eyes, wearing a black top and gray leggings, raced out of the front gates of the ruins and right into me. She ran. I gave chase. She had the presence of mind and the training to assault me."

"Yes, sir."

"The question is—" the gravel in my voice threatened to produce another coughing fit, which I swallowed down "—do I seem like a man who would make up a story of a young woman besting me to boost my ego?"

"No, sir."

"Then get to work. Expand your search," I growled, in part due to the injury, but also to irritation at incompetence and disobedience to both orders and commonsense. "Find the person who defied the king."

Fritz raised his hands in surrender.

"Now."

He immediately turned to his maps, but I studied our surroundings. The former palace's wooded gardens had run wild, and saplings extended past Havenwood's boundaries and abutted three towns within running distance. With Fritz and the others intent on the maps and the nearby underbrush, I rubbed the base of my damaged throat.

Someone who had ventured into the ruins might have planned to flee to Asher, which was the furthest place from the ruins. If she'd had a vehicle, I could have missed it while seeing stars. Springfield lay to the west, but the base just beyond its borders made it a poor choice for someone fleeing the army, unless hiding in plain sight had been the plan all along. Then there was Havenwood. At least a kilometer behind the ruins, it was geographically the closest of all three. It was the easiest, most obvious choice, which made it the last one I suspected.

"Captain," I tried to bark, my temper flaring when he continued to ignore my directions. He finally looked up, and something in my expression or posture straightened his own.

"Major Breckenridge?"

"Send Morrison and a team of four to Asher. They'll overtake her on the outskirts if she's on foot. Assign a few men to patrol the perimeter of the ruins, since there is a possibility, however unlikely, that she circled back for shelter. Cover every exit for the next forty-eight, or until Major General Ancoupe calls off the search. Havenwood is unlikely, so send the rest to Springfield under Locke's command." I tapped the map. "Remind the men that entering the ruins, even to the end of capturing a fugitive, carries with it a court martial."

The color drained from Fritz's pale, freckled face. "Yes, sir. But Havenwood?"

"I will take Havenwood, myself, and keep in regular contact with Major General Ancoupe and General Schmidt. Be certain to send updates while you and your teams investigate."

He saluted and marched away, already calling to the men, and my impatience at his slowness abated.

The image of my father rose in my mind. How would the honorable Admiral Breckenridge have handled the situation? Father had no patience for insubordination of any kind. Had I kept my temper under control, as he would have demanded?

When I was a child, he'd little patience for my youth. Mother had been an angelic buffer between us, but after she passed away, I'd learned to toe the line quickly. As soon as I was of age, I enlisted, just to be away from him. My little sister, however, had him wrapped around her little finger. Although I missed Lunette, I wouldn't trade my military life for anything at home. The military was in my blood, and service had been the one thing that made my father proud of me, especially since he'd retired to take up his responsibilities as Grand Duke.

That, however, was immaterial to the present. I gave myself a mental shake and took a moment to check my sidearms and comm, then hopped into the vehicle's driver's seat. A quick whistle gained the attention of the private, who snapped to attention and tossed the keys to my waiting hand. The truck roared to life and I headed out.

Cool air whipped through my hair as the trees gave way to cacti and dry brush, which rushed past. A few minutes later, I parked in the central square, and when a quick search of the hotels showed no new female arrivals, I entered a shop and interviewed the merchant.

To my surprise, he seemed eager to help, pointing out which building an unfamiliar young woman matching the description had stumbled into, adding an obscure remark about the girl not being a regular. She'd evidently made quite the spectacle, running through the streets and straight to this door. I thanked him and approached the building in question. Something about the entry made me uneasy. I climbed the three steps, slowing when I saw faded ink in the symbol of a hen just above the door handle.

Prostitution?

No wonder the merchant had been eager for a soldier to discover the business under this roof. I grimaced in disgust. The act was illegal, but hens popped up when officials looked the other way, usually for receipt of certain "services." The thought sent a chill down my spine, and I wiped my hands on my pants. An unconscious attempt to rid my hands of imagined filth.

A stray thought suggested that my assailant deserved her fate, but as soon as it came, the voice of my mother rebuked me. Everyone deserved the benefit of the doubt. With Mother's memory firm in my mind, I opened the door and strode in.

Despite my uniform and the authority it should have carried, idle girls swarmed me in the foyer, leaving barely enough space to close the door as each one vied for my attention. Their faces showed clearly in the light from the window, and my stomach twisted. Some looked too young to be in such a place, younger even than my sister. Three sharp claps sounded just behind them. Every girl darted back five paces, their hands clasped before them, eyes to the floor.

"Ladies! Remember decorum." An older woman in a gaudy green gown advanced through the crowd of girls, her skirt sweeping back and forth. She patted her loose bun, dark brown marred by streaks of gray, and bent in a wholly unnecessary bow. "How may we be of service, my lord?"

I squared my shoulders. "I'm looking for a young woman seen entering this establishment recently. About five-foot-six, slender build, red-brown hair, black top, gray leggings. A witness placed her within this building." I felt a scowl darkening my features. Being in the presence of this woman who traded in the lives of young women was unmistakably reprehensible.

She drew back a step. "No, there's been—"

"She's here," said a skinny brown-haired girl from the back of the group, her quiet voice loud in the sudden silence.

Color heightened under the older woman's rouged cheeks, but another one, barely out of her teens, raised her chin. Was that a bruise on her temple? "Madam saw to her."

I narrowed my eyes. "Where is she?"

The matron deepened her obeisance and cleared her throat, but nothing hid the anger that flashed in her eyes. "We did, in fact, have a young woman stumble through our doors today. Poor thing was in awful shape. So, I stepped in to help."

A swift pang of guilt cut through me. I hadn't considered the option that she might've chosen this place by mistake. "I said, where is she?"

The woman waved her arm towards a hallway. "I helped the poor dear to a room in the back."

"Take me to her at once."

A couple of girls paled and shrank back, and the woman hemmed and hawed before adding, "And sedated her for her own safety."

"Sedated for her safety?" My slow boil of disgust grew into outrage tinged with fear for the young woman's life. "This is a brothel, not a medical clinic. You have no right—moral, legal, or medical—to sedate anyone."

Her smile became even more forced and artificial as she turned and led me down the hallway. "We used chloroform, sir. I keep it on hand to protect our girls from violent callers and the occasional jealous would-be lover. It's for their protection." She fell silent for several yards. "She was extremely agitated, and I—we thought it prudent to allow her to rest. To be sure."

She stopped at the last door in the hallway and produced a key.

"You chloroform her, then lock the door?" I demanded through clenched teeth. "To what? Leave her to die? Your actions are nothing more than criminal endangerment."

I caught myself before I spat out that this viper's den would be shut down immediately. I needed to be certain the young woman was alive and any innocents this poisonous female held prisoner could escape before summoning the authorities. The idea of other girls, some even younger than Lunette, trapped in this slavery, then punished for violating the law turned my stomach.

The vile woman's eyes widened a split second, but she recovered herself quickly. "I can't have any of my girls bringing clients to an occupied room, now can I? It is bad for business, and unsafe for the girl." She huffed in false indignation. "All my girls choose this life. I have no way to know if this one does, so I locked the door to keep her safe. To be sure."

Liar.

If anything, her falsehoods clenched my determination to protect the others.

She flung open the door and squinted at me over her crooked nose.

My nostrils flared as I stalked through the door. The girl who'd attacked me lay completely still on the bed atop the covers, so still that for a moment, I feared she was dead. A closer look showed that she was, in fact, breathing, but the short and staggered rise and fall of her chest concerned me.

I spun back to the woman at the door and demanded, my tone curt, "How long has she been out?"

She looked up at the ceiling for a moment, no doubt trying to plan her lie. "Only about twenty to thirty minutes, to be sure."

"Give me that key. Now."

Her expression soured as though she'd eaten something rotten, though she quickly complied, then bowed again with that false smile painted across her face.

"As you wish. If you need anything, just ring one of my girls." She gestured at a deep red and gold braided cord hanging from the ceiling before slipping out of the room.

I looked back at the girl on the bed. She seemed like a shell of the fiery young woman who had taken down a six-foot soldier. Her now-ashen complexion gleamed with sweat, and her brows knit and released as though she were fighting a nightmare. Her respiration, however, was what frightened me, every breath seemingly more hoarse and ragged.

"How much chloroform did she give you?" I whispered, knowing there would be no reply.

How had this small woman been so bold as to challenge the king's edict of no entry and then take me down?

As I stood there, fingers on the comm to call for backup, another memory intruded: sitting beside my sister's hospital bed. Guilt washed through my veins as readily as if the events of several years had happened in the last few minutes. I shoved it away. Now was not the time to allow it to distract me.

The young woman on the bed before me gasped and stopped breathing. For a split second, I, too, struggled for air before her chest rose weakly.

Flames flashed through my veins, and I dropped beside the bed even as I rummaged through my cargo pockets for the medical kit I always carried. Surely it held an antidote?

It did. I skimmed the instructional leaflet to make sure I had the right vial and the correct dose. I only had moments to save her. If I waited for an ambulance to arrive, she'd be dead before they arrived. My own heart pounding, I placed my thumb on her chin and pulled her lower jaw down, parting her lips enough to drip the contents of the dose onto her tongue, careful it didn't drool down her throat.

All I could do was wait.

The girl inhaled, then fell quiet. I pressed two fingers to her throat, laid my head atop her chest—

Nothing.

I hadn't administered the antidote soon enough. Her heart had stopped.

"Damn it!" I cursed as I ripped the pillow from beneath her head and began chest compressions. Fugitive or not. Life was too precious to let slip silently into the Ages if I could help it.

I paused to check that she'd begun breathing. She drew a desperate breath, limbs flailing for a half-second. Each breath was a little stronger than the last. Relief washed through me. With a heavy sigh, I sank into the chair. I'd have to add a trip to a hospital before I could take her in.

Just as I settled, the sound of retching launched me to my feet. I rolled the girl onto her side just in time for her to vomit all over my clothes. For a moment, I froze, as though stillness might prevent it from seeping through my uniform. Then nausea grabbed hold.

My assailant's heaves stopped, and after wiping her mouth and moving her away from the vile liquid, I shifted back.

Bile soaked through the fibers of my uniform, and my skin recoiled from the sticky wet material. The briefest temptation hit me. I wanted to tear into the matron and make her pay for the girl's near-death experience and trauma, as well as for my soiled uniform. That action, however, would leave me exposed. My first goal had to be to get my prisoner to medical care, even though it meant her likely execution.

No, I would deal with this myself.

I rolled the girl over, pulled out the ruined quilt, and slid her under the sheets.

Once she was propped up, in case she vomited again, I removed my sword, sidearm, and all other military paraphernalia from my belt and pockets, piling everything on the small bedside table next to an untouched glass of water—one I didn't trust in the least. I peeled each layer of clothing off at a speed I'd not done since basic training. Thankfully, my undergarments were untainted by the sickly beige stain, and a small sink near a lavatory provided a place to remove as much of the disgusting liquid as I could from my jacket and shirt. I hung them to dry, then unlocked the door to shove the soiled quilt into the hallway, where the odor was sure to attract attention.

That matron would face the legal consequences, I decided grimly. Human trafficking, kidnapping, attempted murder. Oh, she'd suffer alright.

The lock again secured, I settled in the lone chair, and my thoughts sped through what I knew of the drug that beast of a woman had used to subdue my former assailant. The antidote usually took some time to work through a person's system. Chloroform had been a nuisance drug for millennia, and I was appalled that anyone considered such an archaic drug safe. Safer alternatives had been invented over three thousand years ago, long before the exodus from Earth. My thoughts stumbled, then. There was a reason the medical kit held an antidote. It was cheaply manufactured and used by criminals and terrorists.

Still, it'd be a while before the young woman awoke.

Not to mention the trauma her body had just been through.

At the thought of physical trauma, I touched my throat and tested the tender flesh. The area was tender and swollen. The potentially drugged water mocked me, so I had a drink from the sink faucet before sinking into the seat by the bed. Next came the waiting game. I would remain by her side until she woke, then she was going to my superiors for further questioning.

My watch ticked on, and my eyes drooped, despite the situation as adrenaline wore off.

A chime sounded from my belongings just when I'd grown comfortable in the chair.

Just my luck.

I sighed and pulled the comm from my bag and checked the ID. General Schmidt. I'd forgotten to update him.

Well, there was no helping my attire, or lack thereof. A quick press of a button and General Schmidt's likeness appeared.

I snapped a quick salute to the camera. "Evening, General, sir."

"Major." He nodded. "Captain Fritz informed me of his team's status in the search for the fugitive and that you've instructed him to station men at the ruins while you've begun a solo investigation." His salt and pepper eyebrows rose in question of the decision, his eyes flicking down to my attire.

I'd leave that topic alone unless directly asked. Instead, I said, "Yes, sir. An inspection of the neighboring villages and towns was warranted based on their proximity to the ruins. Locke and his men went to Springfield with instructions to return to the barracks if their search proves unsuccessful. Morrison and his men have gone to Asher with the same instructions. I took Havenwood myself. I apologize for not having brought a second man. Time was of the essence, and there weren't a lot of candidates close by." I paused for a moment, collecting my scattered thoughts. "I didn't feel someone brazen enough to gain access to the ruins in broad daylight would be stupid enough to stick around the ruins."

Schmidt threw his head back and laughed. "My boy, that intelligence is why I want you promoted." He sobered. "You were right. There was no sign of her on the palace grounds."

Of course, there wasn't. She lay in front of me.

But I said nothing about her, just as I said nothing about accepting the promotion I hadn't earned. I suspected my latest advancement had less to do with my competency than it did my betrothal to Princess Persephone. Her voice rose in my mind, repeating her desire that I take advantage of my title and status. That I purchase the rank she wanted me to have. "You should think bigger," she'd said more than once.

I finally opened my mouth to protest his offer, but General Schmidt held up his hand, halting me before I could give voice to my thoughts.

"I've given Captain Fritz and his men twenty-four hours before they're allowed back on base. Have you made any progress?"

"I'm following a lead from a few merchants who saw a woman running through the square. I'm confident I'll have her cornered soon…" It wasn't quite a lie, but the explanation stuck in my throat. I paused, then added an actual lie, "Sir, I checked into an inn. I'll pound the pavement on the bright."

"Good." His brow rose a millimeter before the image fragmented, then restored itself. His eyes flicked down and back up, no doubt making an assessment of my condition. "Captain Fritz said the fugitive attacked you. You deserve a bit of rest. Are you alright?"

"Nothing rest and salve won't fix, sir." I curled my fingers in my lap, resisting the urge to rub the sore tissue on my neck. I didn't want to give him any ammunition to order me back to base. The added gravel in my voice already betrayed me enough, and I'd had enough of playing a patient with the medic. Besides, General Schmidt remained in contact with the princess, and I didn't want her to receive a report she'd worry about.

"You are a tough nut, Breckenridge." He leaned forward at his desk, a smirk peeking through his facial hair. "I have every faith that you will find the fugitive. I've spoken with his majesty, the king. He has authorized the use of deadly force. Bring her in, dead or alive. Preferably in a body bag. Less paperwork." He chuckled, a sound which made me sick. The flippant way he spoke about life never sat well with me.

"Understood." I saluted as the general leaned forward and touched a button to end the video call. The moment the screen went black, I leaned against the small table and rubbed my forehead.

Following a lead, huh? What on Delta's sandy hills possessed me to omit the fact that I had the fugitive lying unconscious mere feet from me?

Calm down, Tourelle. Less is more with Schmidt. Always has been.

If Schmidt knew the full truth of the situation, there was little doubt he would order me to dispense with the pleasantries and bag her up. And that, I would refuse to do.

The girl's chest rose and fell much more rhythmically now. She looked so young and delicate. She should have been in a hospital. It wouldn't take much to find the nearest hospital, but again, something stayed my hand before I made the call.

Admitting her to the hospital would seal her fate.

My presence at any point in the process would draw interest, interest that would bring with it the body bag the general had told me to use.

Fingers flexed around the slim rectangle in my hand as I let the comm drop to the floor. I had to trust that she would be safer recovering here in this den of vipers. She would be safer admitting herself once she could travel. For now, I was all that she had.

Guilt rose like a flood and pulled like a mire. Once more, I found myself by my sister's hospital bed as she lie there helpless and broken under thick, scratchy blankets. I heard the monitors' rhythmic beeps and the whir of an oxygen pump that kept time with the rise and fall of her chest. I hadn't been there for my sister until it was too late to undo the damage that had been done. Although I knew full well that being there for this girl would not reverse, or compensate for the past, a small part of me saw my sister in this girl lying prone in the ostentatious bed before me. Maybe I could be enough for her in a way that I hadn't been for my little sister.

Her mahogany hair splayed around her head like a halo, and color was returning to her cheeks. I was no doctor, but it seemed that she was recovering from the chloroform, though only time would tell. I struck my head with my fist, trying to free myself from any imagined connection to a young woman I didn't know. None of my actions would keep her alive for long. I had my duty to fulfill and my oath as a soldier. I had promised to uphold and safeguard the laws of the land.

Even so, I couldn't help but feel for the young woman who lay there recovering alone in a room with the man who'd just been told to kill her for the convenience of saving a little paperwork.

f. *All sale of physical acts of intimacy remains illegal under the Interspace Humanities Act. Those who willingly engage in such acts, whether for sale or receipt, shall face a fine of 1,000 dilerens and up to one year in prison, followed by six months of community service.*

g. *All found to be operating any such facility, where such sales and acts are promoted and performed, shall have all assets seized, face a fine of 1,000,000 dilerens, and serve five years in prison for each person found to be working therein.*

~Monarchal Code 542704-64f-g

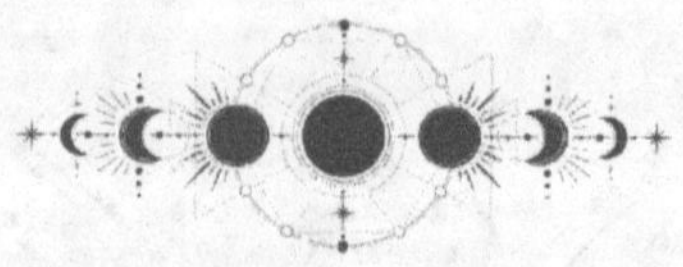

ELAURA

Darkness abated slowly, and an ornate ceiling came into focus above. The deep maroon trimmed with gold spoke of extravagance, and for a moment, I thought I had woken in one of the palace's guest rooms. Dust tickled my nose, however, contradicting my initial thought. I pulled in a breath, wincing at the sharp pain in my chest. Everything from my collar bone down my sternum ached. I reached to rub my eyes, and the weight of my limbs surprised me.

What on earth had I done?

With the small crusts caked in my tear-ducts removed, I tried to place the smells beyond the odor of dust, which grew stronger with each breath. A hint of bile underlay something savory but sweet, with a hint of wood. It reminded me of Victor's aftershave, but it had a deeper musk to it, if that was even the right way to describe it. With a painfully deep breath, I rolled to my side and came face to face with a sleeping man.

Confusion swelled. The pain in my chest indicated I was awake, but this dream felt more pleasant than most. Perhaps my mind had conjured ideas of a life free of the crown. Wisps of light brown hair fell across the man's forehead, and his lashes flitted as his eyes darted side to side beneath his lids. His firm jaw reminded me of a picture of the fabled Adonis from ancient Earth tales. He sniffed, his nose wrinkling. Somehow that slight movement registered something I should have realized already.

There was a man on my bed, his face inches from mine.

On sheer instinct, I screamed as I struggled to move when every muscle in my body felt like lead, and his eyes snapped open. I rolled back, crashing to the floor and pulling the linens with me. A thud and crash on the other side of the bed followed my unceremonious tumble. I snatched a stray shoe from beneath the bed and as I struggled to my feet. The man stood, his palm on the side of his forehead and eyes closed.

My eyes grew wide as his identity registered. The soldier from the palace! Without another thought, I launched the shoe at him, which struck his face with a schlap.

All thought beyond escape ceased. I tried to run, but a pair of boots at the foot of the bed tangled with my steps. The heels of my hands absorbed the brunt of my fall, but the carpet scraped my palms raw. I struggled against the foreign ache in my muscles to right myself and make it back to my feet. I only made it up to my hands and knees.

He was at my side a breath later, hauling me to my feet, his firm hand gripping my arm. Refusing to allow pain to conquer my spirit, I yanked my arm from his grasp, twisted around, and slapped him. His nostrils flared as he grabbed me again and squeezed my wrists together, tugging me toward the table and chair. The more I fought, the tighter his grip around my wrists became until pins and needles spread throughout my hands.

"Let me go," I demanded, my words coming out raw and cracked.

His silent glare blazed with an intensity which threatened to make me shrink.

I can't give up now! My family's counting on me.

He pulled me toward the overturned chair where his sword lie in its scabbard. My energy ebbed. I wouldn't last much longer. Despite the pulsating fire in my ribs, I took a deep breath and screamed with all of my might.

He crashed into my back, knocking me to the carpet before I could draw another breath. Stars danced through my vision. Cold metal replaced the warmth of his hands, and with the subsequent solid click, a shiver racing down my spine.

No one came.

There was no way out.

My energy spent, I dropped my face to the carpet beneath me.

Every breath and movement burned and ached. A chill crept up my fingers when a tremor took hold. I heard his footsteps as he walked across the room, then returned to my side. I waited for the death blow. His blade through my back. Maybe a gunshot to my head. Moments stretched to minutes until I felt gentle fingers on my wrists. Just moments before, I'd been prepared to die, but I hadn't expected his soft touch. He sighed.

"Come on. Let's get you up." He rolled me to my back and lifted me slowly, making allowances for the pain in my muscles. Once on my feet, I tried to yank my arm free. The movement only threw me off balance. He righted me and pointed to the bed. "Have a seat."

Lifting my chin, I looked him right in his steel-blue eyes. "And if I refuse?"

His jaw clenched and unclenched while his eyes met mine, as if he meant to bore into my very soul. "If you refuse, we will go straight to my base, where I will turn you over to my superiors. You will face General Schmidt before being sent to King Grakus's court where you will, undoubtedly, receive a death sentence. To be frank, my superiors would rather me bring you in a body bag. Less paperwork." His eyebrow rose in a silent question I didn't understand. When I didn't answer, he went on. "Look, it's not my fault you're in this mess. You broke the law. I'm just doing my job here."

"Is it your job to climb into a young woman's bed?" I challenged. "Or is that just what soldiers do now?"

His eyes grew wide, and his ears turned a shade of scarlet. He pulled in a deep breath, lowering his hands to fists at his sides. "You trespassed on forbidden property, hit me with your bag, and fled the scene. When I found you here, almost at death's door, I saved your bloody life, got puked on, and still made sure you survived the night. Forgive me for being exhausted and resting my head. I was sleeping in that chair, not in your bed." He stuck his finger to an upended chair, and his voice lowered to a growl. "Get. Your. Facts. Straight."

The intensity in his words bespoke a temper barely under control.

Still glaring, I relented. I walked over to the chair, waited for him to right it, and plopped myself onto its cushion.

"Is it seriously a crime to visit my... the old palace?" I caught myself before calling it my home. "And who are you, anyway?"

"Major Tourelle Breckenridge." He crossed his arms, not amused by my tone. "Yes, it is a crime. The king has issued an edict of no entry upon pain of death or life imprisonment. You also assaulted an agent of the law and resisted arrest. What on Delta's sandy hills made you think you were exempt from the king's edict?"

My brows knit together as his words reached their mark.

Great-uncle Grakus had placed an edict of no entry on the palace grounds? How had the citizens of Delta not seen that as the evidence of his guilt? I couldn't dispute the charges, but the edict still shocked me.

"I never heard about it." I allowed my anger to slip away like water from a duck's back. "To be honest, I... I didn't know. I didn't realize there was an edict." I nibbled my lower lip. "I didn't suppose it would really matter much."

He shook his head and looked at me as though he could see through any lie I told. Goosebumps rose on my forearms. I had a brief flash of gratitude that my discomfort was discreet beneath my sleeves.

"Well, the King certainly feels that it matters a great deal. So much so that patrols inspect the perimeter at regular intervals." He pulled a chair from the other side of the bed and sat before me, almost relaxing against the decorative backing. "It also matters a great deal to me. It's my job to preserve the rule of law." He paused a moment more, looking down, his eyes darting from side to side before returning to mine. "What exactly were you doing in there?"

What could I tell him? That before him sat the rightful heir to the throne of Delta? That Grakus had murdered my parents in pursuit of power? If the Grakus did that to my parents and had every living soul within those walls killed with them, would I be safe admitting my true identity? No. The risk was too great.

I no longer doubted that my great-uncle's reign must end. I would have to remove him for my people, and for my family. But to do that, I had to answer this man as truthfully as I could to have any hope of survival. No matter how small that hope might be,

"I needed to find my parents. They..." I swallowed hard against the lump in my throat as their images raced to mind. "They never came home when King Grakus took over." Though I tried to be strong, tears fought desperately to be free. "I needed to say goodbye."

That much was true.

The major sighed, pulling me from my memories. His hand rubbed across his mouth, and his gaze dropped to the floor, almost as though he were trying to decide what to say. "Miss, like I said before, defying the king's edict of no entry is a crime punishable by life in prison or death. Though I don't think anyone has escaped execution yet." His blue eyes rose to mine as he rested his elbows on his knees and leaned closer. "One of the king's first acts after taking power was to issue the edict of no entry concerning the palace ruins. How could you not know this?"

"I had been visiting my aunt and uncle in Atha. They don't believe in using technology in the home. My uncle is a teacher at the local schoolhouse. When my parents didn't come to get me on time, a neighbor told us about the... the..." My words failed. I didn't know what else I could say that might explain to him my ignorance. I couldn't tell him that when my great uncle issued his evil edict, Victor, Matea, and I were on a bus traveling to Atha with only the clothes on our backs.

The major let the silence be.

Closing my eyes, I summoned the strength to appeal to his humanity and continued, "If your parents disappeared without warning, and everyone told you they were dead, wouldn't you do whatever it took to find the truth? Even if it were a terrible truth? I—" my voice snagged on part of the truth "—wanted their memorium cards."

He sighed again, rubbed both hands over his face, and studied me, his eyes softer than before. Had I gotten through to him?

"Miss... I don't think you understand the gravity of the situation. Just crossing the threshold of the property is a serious crime. Even the soldiers of my company face the same penalty should they venture into the grounds."

My eyes dropped to his feet, the weight of his words settling across my shoulders. Every word from his mouth cementing the reality that I might not get out of this. I looked for patterns on the carpet as I tried to reconcile my fate.

"I've investigated several militant factions threatening the peace, and almost every one of them spins a story like yours. Life in some remote region, like Atha, not knowing the law. If you want any hope, I need full honesty. I'm not an unreasonable person. Do you have any proof?"

That small demand, however small, ignited my indignation. My fingers curled into fists behind me, the back of my neck burning. Before I knew what I was doing, my words came tumbling from my lips. "How about my ticket stub from Atha? Or the names of my aunt and uncle? My neighbors? But why stop there? Perhaps you'd like to search my bedroom looking for ties to this supposed militia?"

My bravado would get me killed if I couldn't get it reined in. I bit my tongue.

After a moment, he cleared his throat, though frustration tainted his even tone when he spoke. "What's your name?"

"Elaura." My given name tumbled from my lips so effortlessly, but I couldn't admit my last name. "Carpe. My name is Elaura Carpe." I hoped the shortening of the name wouldn't create more suspicion.

Again, I waited while he sat, watching me, then his attention fell to his hands, clasped loosely on his knees. When I couldn't stand another second of the uncomfortable, silent limbo, I whispered, "Are you going to kill me?"

While not an inflammatory question, it drove to the heart of my deepest fear. At the moment, waiting was worse than a quick execution. He said himself that his superiors would rather skip the paperwork. His head snapped up, confusion coloring his features.

Might as well get it over with. "I mean, if it's going to be execution either way, I'd much prefer you to be the one to do it. Here and now..."

I dropped my gaze to the carpet's patterns. "You seem the type of person who wouldn't torture someone or drag it out. The sooner I can see my family again, the better."

Even without looking, I felt the weight of his eyes on me. Perhaps death was a mercy. If I died here, it was a sign I lacked the qualifications to lead. I remained unbothered by his heavy gaze as a cool peace washed through me and I released an easy breath.

My people needed James, not me. And he was dead.

"What would your parents think of you giving up?" His voice pulled me from my internal reconciliation.

I looked up to find him still staring at me, gentleness written on his features.

Hadn't he just accused me of being a militant spy? If he took me to his base, he would deliver me to my pending execution. That much was clear. What kind of game was he playing?

"Seems a waste to throw your life away so recklessly," he said, his voice reminding me of the way James challenged me to be better and to try harder.

Pushing my reawakened grief aside and focusing instead on the danger before me, I said, "What do you know about sacrifice, major?"

I hadn't meant it the way it sounded, for no matter how I'd meant it, my life was in his hands.

His mouth opened and closed a time or two before his jaw clenched, the muscle ticking. Shadows of humor, pain, and chagrin raced across his face. He leaned back in the chair, pulling his hand through his hair. "Please don't test me, Miss Carpe. Your venomous barbs are unnecessary."

A small voice reminded me I should be calmer. Kinder. I should accommodate his investigation, hoping to get out of this. Despite the inner voice of reason, I continued to glare at him.

"I have no plans to kill you. Far from it, actually." His hands rubbed together idly, and he glanced at the glass of water on the table beside me. "Whatever you may think of me, I assure you, if you cooperate and answer my questions honestly, perhaps you can be on your way."

I can't say what expression I wore, but I wasn't ready to believe him. I couldn't think of a single reason for his leniency. Almost afraid to believe in the spring of hope in my chest, I couldn't take my eyes off him, though I saw no sign of deceit. "Aren't you honor bound to take me in? To your king?"

He leaned his elbows on his knees. "Yes. I am supposed to bring you in, and I don't know what I'm going to do when I face my superiors, but I could let you go."

"Why?"

Piercing blue eyes met mine, complete honesty in their gaze. "Because I know what it is to have lost someone dear."

7

All property upon the premises of the Caprician Palace shall be considered contraband; possession of said paraphernalia stands as evidence of defiance of King Divo Von Grakus's Edict of No Entry. Any person in the possession of such property shall be brought before the authorities of the nearest military base and interrogated before facing the King's Council, where a sentence shall be pronounced. The minimum sentence shall be life in a detention facility from whence the convicted shall serve the community which he or she has defiled. The maximum sentence will be death by firing squad with criminal marks added to his or her memorium card corresponding with this most egregious of crimes.

~Judicial code 5308: Amendment 23B

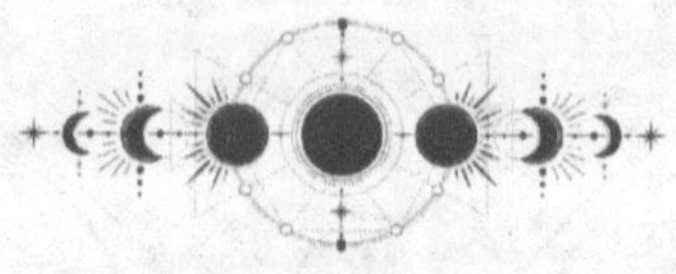

Elaura

"When I found you here," the major continued without clarifying his assertion that he understood loss, "they'd chloroformed you and locked you in the room. You were barely breathing and looked near death."

The look on his face spoke of a pain I couldn't quite place, though I knew better than to question his personal history, but then his meaning struck me. I scrunched my eyes shut. "I remember the cloth on my face. But that woman locked me in?"

"Yes," he growled. He waited until I met his gaze. "With everything they'd told me, I knew I had to act. My medical kit carries antidotes for some more common poisonings, though I'm not a field medic by any stretch. My mother taught me to be prepared, and it paid off this time." His smile was more of a grimace. "The way you were gasping, I believed your lungs were shutting down. Your heart stopped. After that, I administered CPR."

My heart nearly stopped again at his testimony, and my hand rose to my sore chest. I'd not expected the concern behind his lashes while he spoke.

"Thank you," was all I could say.

"Do you know where you wound up?"

"I saw this inn from the bus when I arrived," I said.

"This is no inn, Miss Carpe." His brows drew down. "Didn't you see the hen on the door?"

"The hen?" I shook my head.

"This is a brothel."

I'd unknowingly chosen a brothel as my refuge? *A brothel.* My blood went cold as he described his initial confrontation with the matron. His disdain for the woman was clearer with every word. A sneer pulled at the corner of his mouth.

"Rest assured, Miss Carpe. As soon as I leave, I will make certain this facility," he spat out, "is shut down."

The image of the girl who had tried to make me leave lanced through me, and I was almost unaware that he had shifted the topic from our accommodations to saving my life. He only met my eyes for fleeting moments as he spoke until he reached the point where he'd fallen asleep, his head on his arms while he watched to be sure I lived. His speech stilled, and he looked away, rubbing his hands together.

"I'm sorry that I frightened you. By that point, I was exhausted. I never meant to startle you."

All my focus fastened on this officer who served my great-uncle. It had jarred me to find the face of a man in my bed, and a handsome man at that. I shook my head, trying to focus on my thoughts. This was no time to be thinking of looks. In all honesty, he'd not done anything to harm me, and I couldn't fault him for being human. If I had thought about it, I would've expected a soldier loyal to my uncle to feel superior to the common man. Here I was, a young woman who'd unknowingly defied the edict of no entry, and he apologized that he'd offended my sensibilities.

Despite my fears and physical discomfort, a smile crept to my lips at the respect shown by a soldier of the army. A keeper of the peace. Even if they might be few, there were still good men serving in the military under my uncle's tyranny. The major was proof.

"I am breathing thanks to you. To do anything other than accept your apology would deserve an apology in turn. Thank you for saving my life."

He stood and pulled on his uniform shirt and jacket. I blushed at the faint odor of vomit, but he didn't even grimace. "Well," he said while buckling on his sword and adjusting his other weapons, "since you have no affiliation with any militant group, least of all the Caprician army, I'll escort you past that matron to make certain you are safely out. Make sure you keep out of trouble. Not many soldiers will be as merciful. Remember that."

I collected my bag and followed him to the door, and with a single nod of farewell, he pivoted on his boot heel to confront the horrid woman who kept girls for illegal services. A young girl started when I approached the back door. She was younger than myself with a similar build to mine, albeit thinner, with brown hair, and an inch shorter than me. Her expression spoke of a jealousy that I could leave so easily. She looked like the girl who tried to make me leave before.

"Can't you leave with me?" I asked.

Sadness overtook the envy in her expression. "I have a debt to pay, miss, and can't leave until I pay it, or my family will suffer even more."

I would've given anything to have my family back. I had to do something. My heart ached for her. If I couldn't have my family, I could help hers. I pulled a gilded broach with my family's coat of arms from my bag and, after a glance over my shoulder, pressed it into her hand. "This will fetch a good price. Free yourself and help your family."

"Miss," she whispered, and I hugged her.

I knew, to the bottom of my heart, that Mama would've been proud of the action. It wasn't a grand act, but the small gift seemed a fitting epitaph to her legacy.

I slipped down the back steps and dashed into the scrub oaks outside the town. My plan was to travel to Springfield and pawn or sell some trinkets I'd collected from my room. No matter how much money I'd started with, it would run out. I needed to make sure I had enough for my needs until I gained employment, and I wasn't sure how to go about it, either. Then, I would find the Caprician army and join them.

The distance between Havenwood and Springfield was not one I could traverse in a single day, though I tried. I made camp after the sun went down and the first moon crested the horizon. When I woke early, at first moonset, I walked the rest of the way, and to my surprise, the once sleepy town had become a bustling metropolis.

The market stalls sat vacant in the early light, and morning dew sparkled, making the mundane almost magical.

The very knowledge of a group still loyal to my family gave me hope. Such a statement of loyalty to my father's reign almost brought me to tears. The question became, then, how to find them. I paused just outside the market stalls to consult a map before turning down an alleyway. My conversation with the major played through my mind as I navigated past the community burn barrels.

The edge of the alleyway opened, and I found myself on the road out of town. I had overshot my goal. A man stepped out of a home along the street and reached within to kiss someone within before darting off on errands. I paused at the exchange, recalling the look in the major's eyes as he recounted how I'd started gasping, the raw emotion, the need to protect—

No, that wouldn't do. I pushed the memory away.

I returned to ask about a place where I could sell some belongings, but like my earlier experience in Waekfield, no one listened, let alone answered me.

One person scowled, muttering, "Stupid tourists," under his breath.

Hours later, exhausted, I found a bench near the edge of town and gratefully took a seat beside a sandy-haired man with a five o'clock shadow. My poor feet welcomed the relief, and I sank backward with a sigh.

The man looked up from his paper, curiosity painted across his features. "Long day?"

I nodded, grateful that a stranger might be kind enough to begin a conversation without being asked or pressed. "Since I got here this morning, I've been trying to find someone who could point me toward a market or a pawn house. I have some old belongings to sell," I explained. "So far, everyone I've met won't give me the time of day or calls me a stupid tourist."

He continued to look me in the eye while nodding while I spoke, his hazel eyes clear and tentative. Oh, how I'd missed that show of common respect.

"Yeah. Some people around here got a big head. Think they're better than everyone. What are you trying to sell?" He grinned and extended his hand. "Maybe I could help."

The bag slid easily from my shoulders, and elated that someone might care, I quickly pulled out my hairbrush and gave it to him.

"You're really pretty when you smile," he said before closing his fingers around the brush.

Unsure of how I felt about the compliment, I pulled my hand back quickly.

He took his time inspecting it, as if he'd said nothing. "I know just where you can take it." He returned it back and stood. "It's a bit of a trip, but I'd be happy to give you a ride. My truck's parked nearby."

Something sank in the pit of my stomach. His generosity felt out of place when everyone else I'd met in this town seemed to have more important things to do, and he'd already taken enough time out of his day. Still, I didn't want to be ungrateful. "Oh, thank you, but I shouldn't impose. You've been kind enough already!"

The man laughed. "Nonsense. I'm headed that way myself. Besides, if you're new here, I couldn't live with myself knowing I let a pretty lady wander around alone with all the Neanderthals roaming this place. Someone might take advantage of you."

I couldn't argue with his logic, and despite my uncertainties, I was grateful for his generosity. It wouldn't do to spend all day looking when someone could take me there faster. We walked down the busy block and across the street to a small parking lot. Time and caked dust obscured the sign on the chain-link fence, and I tried not to read too much into the situation as we walked into the parking area.

Like a gentleman, he held open the passenger door for me, waiting for me to climb in and secure my seatbelt. I placed my bag at my feet and pulled the shoulder belt across myself.

"Actually, you'll want to put on the full harness. It gets really bumpy. The road is really old."

He pulled a stronger harness from the side of the seat. I nodded and eased into it, and then he helped me with the clasp at the waist and the collarbone. But when he reached over to secure a strap over my thighs, that sinking in the pit of my stomach morphed into a full chill.

"Excuse me, isn't that a little overboard?"

His smirk resembled a triumphant cat that had caught a canary. "Of course not. We want you to get you there safe now, don't we?"

Every hair stood on end, and my stomach twisted in knots. I scanned the area for someone—anyone who might rescue me this time. No one. The search for assistance blinded me to his next move. In a flash, a wad of cloth was in my mouth being tied behind the headrest, unhindered by my cries. Then he tied my right hand to the armrest. My feeble attempt to yank the gag from my mouth was short-lived as he caught and tied my left hand as well.

He disappeared from sight, only to reappear in the driver's seat wearing a soldier's uniform. Starting the vehicle, he put it into gear and drove out of the city walls. I very much doubted we were even on a road after the first five minutes. Unseen forces threw me to each side and back; testing the strength of the nylon cable webbing. A gag tied in my mouth secured my head to the seat. The restraints did little to soften the ride as we raced through the desert expanse. Each bump sending a wave of fire through my chest.

The driver lifted a comm to his ear, wind whipping through his hair.

"Hey, Banks! Yeah, it's Carlsen... Yeah, let General Schmidt know I've apprehended a spicy little thing selling contraband." He chuckled. "With the Caprician seal and everything. She even tried to sell it to me."

Major Breckenridge had warned me not to find myself in trouble with the law again, as few soldiers would be as lenient as he was.

What had I done?

"Just tell him, would'ya?" the man continued, then added, "Got it."

The hair on my arms stood on end in response to both the fear coursing through my veins and the chilled air whipping around me. Something rose on the horizon like a mirage from the sand, distant and hazy at first, but looming larger with each passing moment. We barreled headlong toward the structure with no sign of slowing. Just as the terror of the impending collision sent chills through my bones, I was slammed against my restraints as the truck skidded to a halt parallel to the wall. Stars danced in front of my vision as the flames in my ribs exploded.

My eyes darted to the gate, a mere meter from the truck's door. I pulled in a shaky breath, unable to stop the tremor in my fingers, the only part of me free to move, or to calm my heart's thunder.

It wasn't simply fear and pain, though. The sound from the driver's seat filled me with white-hot rage.

The soldier, whose name I still did not know, was laughing. What or who he was laughing at was unclear, but his jubilation was unacceptable.

"Carlson, you *idiot*!" shouted a voice from the gate. "How many times do we have to fix the gate, the wall, or that rig before you realize it's not your toy?"

The man who'd yelled at my captor stomped forward. His thick build spoke of nothing but strength, his muscles bulged visibly through his uniform.

Carlsen, however, seemed to think they both were in on a joke. "I didn't hit anything, did I?"

The bulky soldier approached, but when he saw me in the passenger seat, his features twisted with anger. "Are you kidding me? You bring someone in for questioning and you almost kill her? The general is going to have your head!"

The driver smirked. "Only if he can catch me."

The large man sighed in mock defeat, maybe frustration. I couldn't really tell which.

"I'll drive from here." The large man announced. "Someone needs to make sure your suspect reaches the general in one piece."

He waved a hand at Janson, who grudgingly climbed to the backseat. I would've rather he walked the rest of the way. The large man climbed behind the wheel and looked me over. No doubt he saw my trembling hands, because he leaned over and whispered in my ear.

"I'm sorry about that lugnut. Really, he's a good soldier. He just likes to horse around too much." He looked at Carlson from the corner of his eyes, then looked back at me. "General Schmidt ordered everyone on base to treat all suspects with respect. Up until execution." He put the truck in gear, and we rolled through the gate and down the street.

"Yeah, right," Carlsen scoffed. "You're mixing up Breckenridge with the general. All General Schmidt cares about are the pretty faces, and this one's just so-so. Eh, she'll be heading for the king's council, anyway. Might as well have some fun."

The large man yanked the steering wheel hard to the left and sharply to the right. Behind me, a clang sounded from the roll cage.

"Damn it, Nick! That was my head! What happened to you being against horsing around?" Carlsen groaned and mumbled a few more curses.

It was the burly driver's turn to laugh. "*She* wasn't in any danger. You restrained her too well for that. You deserved it."

Well, if I were to die, at least this idiot faced some turn of karma.

The maze of buildings and scattered soldiers offered little hope of escape. At length, we pulled up to a large building, where a flurry of activity milled around us.

"Sorry, ma'am, standard procedure," Nick muttered as he loosened the restraints, and any hope of running fled the moment a pair of handcuffs clicked around my wrists. Without a key, there'd be no way out of this.

Dread only thickened in my veins when he pulled me from the vehicle and led me inside. I stumbled a time or two as I struggled to keep up with the men's ridiculously long strides.

A few hallways down, we turned to the left, got on an elevator, and then climbed a flight of stairs before arriving at a desk in front of a dead end and a door. A young, bulky soldier looked up from his work at us and then back at his hands.

"Is this the suspect?" he asked, his eyes trained on the task before him.

"Yeah. I brought her in. None of these dimwits lifted a finger till I got here." Carlsen announced, his chest puffing out a little. "I didn't need any help with the arrest."

The man behind the desk didn't seem to find the announcement interesting enough to shift his focus from his task. He just kept scribbling away at the document.

"There is no question of who brought her in, Sergeant Carlsen. You called my desk with the information less than an hour ago and I haven't forgotten. I've already apprised General Schmidt of the information."

This must be Banks, then.

I wasn't certain, but Carlsen appeared to stand a little taller on the tail of the reprimand, strange as it might seem. A loud buzz sounded. The man behind the desk nodded to us, and the men on either side of me pulled me through the door into an office.

Certificates and awards adorned every inch of the far wall. Behind the impressive desk, the general, dressed in a dark blue uniform, reclined back in his chair, boots resting on the desk. He had to be in his mid-fifties for all the gray which salted his hair and beard. I blinked. Most military men were clean shaven, or at least they used to be when my father was king.

The soldiers beside me snapped to attention, saluted, and chimed, "Sir!"

The general looked up from his reading material, and the corners of his mustache crept upward. His boots disappeared from the desktop, and a folder of papers slapped across the wooden surface in their place.

"Ah. The little black-market dealer. Please sit down." He looked me up and down, a strange look in his eyes that made my stomach tighten. "Leave the evidence, then you men are dismissed."

Nick took my bag from Carlsen and dropped it on the general's desk, and they left, closing the door behind them. Rooted to the spot, I stared at the door, wishing they could've stayed and kept me safe, though I had my doubts that they would be useful as buffers where their general was concerned.

The general's chair creaked as he stood. I pivoted back to him, unable to shake the feeling that he was a predator circling a caged animal. He made his way around the desk toward me, and I stumbled backward to preserve the distance between us.

"Now, now. I was going to remove those handcuffs for you, but if you'd rather keep them on, I'd be happy to oblige." Something in his voice sent shivers down my spine.

Silently, I thrust my imprisoned hands before me. The brief moments where his hands brushed the flesh of my wrists made my skin crawl. As soon as the cuffs were loose, I snatched my hands to my chest and darted a step away.

He chuckled and waved to the armchair facing his desk. With a flick of his wrist, he tossed the handcuffs on the corner of the desk and rounded the wooden structure in favor of his own cushioned chair. Once seated, he again leaned back, watching me all the while. Again, he motioned to the still empty chair before him.

Rubbing my wrists, I remained rooted in place, but chanced only a momentary glance at the door behind me. The rumble of his muted laughter pulled the full weight of my focus back.

"My dear, if you wish to run, you are welcome to do so. I won't get in your way." He sat straighter, leaning forward and resting his elbows on the desk.

For a moment, I entertained the idea, but suspicion screamed of danger. The door's brass handle all but called to me. Prudence and suspicion held me where I stood.

"I am compelled to inform you that, should you flee, we will treat your actions as an admission of guilt and an act of hostility towards his majesty, King Grakus, and the military under his direction. Your execution would be swift, and without mercy. I can't promise that you would die quickly or without a great deal of pain. Some of my men have rather unscrupulous morals."

My horror seemed to please him to no end.

"Now, tell me, my dear, what you are up to. Your own words, if you please."

I sank into the armchair, and my mind raced as I tried to recall the story I'd told to the first soldier. The kind one who'd saved my life.

"Sir, please understand, I didn't know any of this was contraband. My parents worked in the old palace. I went to visit my aunt and uncle in Atha six years ago, and when my parents didn't come to get me, we were told to assume the worst. We moved on as much as we could, but my aunt... She is ill, sir, and we don't have enough money to pay the doctors for her care." The lies tumbled from my lips without thought.

The general leaned forward, a singular eyebrow arching as he studied me with the intensity of a wolf measuring its meal. "What made you think you could get away with defying the king's edict of no entry just to save your aunt?"

Fear iced my veins. What could I say that might help me through this?

"I didn't enter, sir!"

He huffed and waved a hand at the contraband—at my brush and the rest of it.

"My parents had left me some trinkets they'd been given. Gifts, sir, ones I had in my possession already. No one would buy them back home, not as poor as Atha is, so I traveled to find a buyer. No one told me. We just need enough for her care. My parents had joined the Ages, but I didn't know I couldn't sell these. We're often left alone in the northern region. Sometimes news misses us. Almost no one leaves, so news of the outside world doesn't concern most people." Another lie. News had concerned Victor a great deal. If he'd known, he wouldn't have kept something like that from me... Would he?

After a moment, the general nodded. "I'm willing to be lenient with you since you're so young. It would be a shame for you to face execution. I'll even let you keep your little keepsakes and send them on for your aunt and uncle to sell for her expenses. As long as they are the ones selling them for the medical expenses."

He must have known I couldn't do that. He would track them down.

The man's smirk deepened. "I will, however, be sentencing you to eighteen months of labor in the base mess hall."

My face wrinkled at the idea. "Eighteen months? But sir, I just told you I knew nothing about the edict."

"My men could use a little variety." He seemed amused by his own joke. "Your ignorance is the only reason I am choosing such generosity. In fact, one of my men just had a run in with a young thief from Havenwood who broke the edict. He's bringing her here as we speak." He paused a moment before adding, "In a body bag."

Ice raced down my spine and goosebumps across my skin. I counted myself lucky that the major was the one to find me. Surely the major, who had risked his career to save my life, was better than the man who had killed the young thief to save paperwork.

The corner of the general's mustache seemed unwilling to descend from the ghastly smile he wore. "Make no mistake, young lady, your ignorance will not serve you long. Some people simply die ignorant."

Three beats sounded on the door.

I jumped in my seat.

The man I'd seen at the desk poked his head through the now open door. "Sir, Major Breckenridge is here for you."

General Schmidt's mustache reached for his eyes. "Ah! Speak of the devil. Bring him in already."

The door swung wide, and the man from the desk re-entered the room backwards, carrying one end of what appeared to be a body bag.

But it wasn't Sergeant Carlsen at the other end of the bag.

It had to be a fever dream. I knew that man, but the only acceptable possibility was that he had a twin.

No. Ice splintered through my veins as my eyes reconciled with my heart and mind.

This was the same man I'd considered my savior just a day prior. The general had just told me how fortunate I was not to have met him, and yet I had. His eyes found mine, not a muscle betraying his thoughts, and Major Breckenridge helped Banks place the body bag atop the general's desk.

b. In the event that the deceased soul broke an established law of the land in life, a thick mark shall be made in the center of the memorium card to identify his or her crimes. The mark shall be in the shape of a "C" for common crimes, but a "D" or an "E" for any offenses serious enough to incur the death penalty.
~Criminal Act 548.B.85

TOURELLE

After my attacker, Elaura, had left, I strode through the back hall, grappling with the best way to shut down this atrocity of a business and the fact that I'd just granted a fugitive clemency that wasn't mine to give.

It might still be alright. I had never said I had her in custody, only that I was following promising leads. Returning empty-handed was not unacceptable.

Lost in my own thoughts, I made my way down the hall. A thud sounded from the lobby, followed by screams. Gripping my sidearm and the hilt of my sword, I ran. Girls crowded in a circle, and I had pushed my way through to see the source of their concern. A young girl, no older than sixteen, convulsed on the ground, her eyes wide and unseeing. Bubbling saliva coated her lips, and her hands trembled, stiff and contorted, against her chest.

"Out of my way!" I dove to my knees by her side and pulled her head to my lap, holding either side of her face, while I looked around the assembled group. "What did she take?"

Only sobs answered me.

I demanded again, louder and with more authority.

"She doesn't take any drugs," a dark-haired girl said. "I don't even think she's eaten since this morning."

Satisfied at least one person hadn't frozen in fear, I ordered her to gather any medications the girl might be taking and to call for an ambulance. She darted away.

As I had the day before with Elaura, I rolled this girl to her side, then singled out a young woman to my left, demanding a pillow. She quickly obeyed, grabbing one from a small chair. The girl in my arms convulsed another minute or two, then stilled. I slipped the pillow under her head.

Her wide stare remained vacant as her muscles tensed. Bubbles of saliva emerged through pressed lips. I leaned down, told her that all would be well. Her eyes found me somehow, and she grabbed at me with a frantic strength. Her fingers found purchase on my sleeve, and one of my front buttons snapped off against the force.

"It's going to be okay," I promised over and over.

Her wide and frantic eyes held desperately to mine, but not a word passed between her lips. Her shallow breath hiccupped a time or two, then stopped. Her body relaxed.

I rolled her onto her back and began CPR. After half an hour of solid compressions and still no change, I reluctantly stopped. She was gone. Even though I'd taken action, I'd still failed.

The girl had been diabetic. The dark-haired girl told me her name was Emma and produced a vial of insulin from her room. Then she told me that the medics never came to the brothel. Even told her as much when she called.

I hated my ignorance. Indecisiveness and ignorance always led to death. Always.

I spent the next night and day looking to find her family, but they weren't local, which gave me an opportunity; detestable as it was. This girl, Emma, could be Elaura's saving grace, as well as my own. Her personal effects contained a broach clearly belonging to the old royal family, and that alone made my falsehood plausible.

I resolved to send her family her memorium cards once this business was complete, if I could find them at all. I did my best not to think about the black mark that would mar the cards her family would receive. The mark of a criminal.

Well, I had a few favors I could call in. I'd do my best about that, provided the individuals were amenable.

I opened my comm and called the general's office to let his assistant know I was on my way with the deceased fugitive. When I arrived, General Schmidt's personal assistant, Banks, met me at the front door to help me with the body bag. I was grateful I didn't have to drag her. We made it up to Schmidt's office, and Banks knocked three times before opening the door and announcing me.

Banks and I carried poor Emma into the room, setting her bag down on the general's desk. It was then that I noticed the room's other occupant.

Elaura.

What on Delta's sandy hills was going on? She was naïve, but I refused to believe she was willfully stupid enough to risk betraying my leniency.

I nodded at her and tried to sound indifferent. "Who's this?"

Schmidt waved his hand dismissively in her direction, more concerned with the bag on the desk than the girl in the chair. "Carlsen caught her selling contraband in Springfield. She's a country bumpkin, so I'm giving her a break. The mess hall needs some new decoration, so she'll be the kitchen maid for the next eighteen months." Pausing his inspection of the bag, he waved his fingers at Banks. "You're dismissed."

Standing at attention, I squeezed my fists behind my back. Hadn't I told her to stay out of trouble? I let her go so she could be free of this place, and yet here she was. Caught selling contraband, and by just anyone. By one of the biggest goof offs in the company.

Boots clicked together as Banks saluted and left, pulling the door closed.

Schmidt clapped his hands together, rubbing them in anticipation. "So this is the little minx who attacked you, eh? Well, let's have a look."

I pursed my lips. His revelry and disrespect—even for a purported criminal—was beyond distasteful. Nevertheless, I pulled the zipper from the edge of the bag down to its midpoint before stepping away, my hands behind my back.

Elaura rose slowly from her chair, her eyes locked on the girl who had taken her place. I tried to brace myself for her reaction. There was no way of telling how she would react. She and I both knew that, despite my claims, the girl in the bag was innocent of breaking the edict.

She peered at the pale, ashen face within, and one hand flew to her mouth, while the other curled around her middle.

"I'm impressed, Major. To be honest, I thought you'd bring her back for questioning. You're rather predictable that way." He came around the desk and clapped me on the back. "This is certainly a first."

I tried to shake off the disgusting comment. I'd sooner trade places with the girl in the bag than receive commendation for senselessly taking a life.

"It wasn't my choice, sir." Even the truth felt like a lie on my tongue, perhaps because it was a partial lie. I had not chosen her death, but I had brought her in Elaura's place, selfishly, to save my own skin.

Perhaps the words were a symptom of cowardice. Up till now, I had done it all to save my family, but now, standing before my commanding officer and a near stranger, there was no such excuse for this falsehood.

In the corner of my eye, Elaura swayed. No longer caring if Schmidt caught me staring, I turned my attention to her. Color had drained from her face. Instinct drew me to her side in time to catch her as her unusually wide eyes rolled back in her head. I sank to my knees, holding her tightly against my chest.

"Get that body out of here," I ordered, though it was not my place to do so.

Schmidt may have been crude, but he wasn't intentionally cruel. While I turned my attention back to the girl in my arms, General Schmidt zipped the bag shut and summoned his assistant's help.

Elaura's eyes fluttered open again, but stared, unseeing. I'd lost one already, and I refused to lose her, too. I couldn't feel her moving. She hadn't taken a breath since her eyes had opened.

"Breathe," I muttered, stroking her hair like I'd done with my sister, Lunette, so many times before during panic attacks.

For a moment, she clung to me in silence, taking one shallow gasp, then another, and another. Her breathing slowly improved while I shifted to rub small circles between her shoulder blades. When she pulled herself away from me a few minutes later and met my eyes, I suddenly realized what it must look like to her. What I must look like.

I would just have to be a monster for now.

She launched herself away from me like a cat from its bath, and General Schmidt laughed, clearly amused at the sudden change in demeanor.

I had no words, not here, in front of my commanding officer. Any explanation would be the death of us both. So, I stood and moved away, giving her the space she so desperately wanted.

Schmidt clapped me on the back again. "Well, my boy, it seems you went from monster to hero and right back again. Quite a feat, especially for you!"

I squeezed my eyes and my jaw shut, suppressing the urge to put him in his place. Doing so would undo everything and put Elaura in more danger than she was already in. Given my betrothal to Princess Persephone, I was certain that even if discovered, I'd receive little more than a reprimand. Still, I had my pride and my father's legacy to safeguard. I held my tongue and stubbornly clung to both. Schmidt re-took his seat at the now-vacant desk, his hands folded. I looked back at Elaura and found her still studying me, pale-faced and shaking.

"Major Breckenridge," the general said. "You've impressed me today, son. There is no one I would trust more to oversee this young lady's work here on base."

The request caught me off guard, breaking through my careful control.

"Excuse me?" I looked at Schmidt, eyes wide, mind swimming in search of some way out of the appointment. When he nodded, I managed, "Sir, with all due respect, such an assignment would suit someone of a lower rank. Surely you don't mean to saddle me with her?"

It wasn't that I couldn't trust myself around her; it was that I didn't trust my temper. As a soldier, a good temper was a worthy weapon, but somehow, I knew Elaura could break that control.

"Nonsense," General Schmidt replied. "This assignment is an assurance of trust; one I am wholeheartedly placing on your shoulders. Are you unable to oversee her work release?"

Just like that, he set my orders in stone. He knew I'd be unable to offer a reason against the assignment. If I did, he would see through the lie and that put everything in danger. True, I'd successfully presented someone to the general in Elaura's place, but I wasn't proud of it. A ruse, like this one with Emma, was unlikely to succeed a second time. At least, I hoped it would fail. My inability to save the girl's life would haunt me till the day I died. I couldn't bear the idea of another innocent's death.

Elaura leapt to her feet. Her narrowed eyes met mine, issuing a silent challenge as she launched herself into the discussion. "I won't go anywhere with him!"

Her venom gave me the push I needed for one last try. "Sir, we have more pressing matters to attend to without saddling me with babysitting a prisoner."

"Assign that muscle bound soldier," she demanded. "What's his name? Nick! Assign Nick to oversee my sentence. Anyone but this murderer."

That last word stung, though I knew that in her eyes I deserved the jab.

The general bellowed, *"Enough!"*

Elaura and I fell silent.

"Major Breckenridge, this will take precious little time from your tasks, which at this moment are already being reassigned." General Schmidt held his hand up, again silencing my response, before a single syllable escaped. "In recognition of your victory, and on Admiral Nasser's recommendation, you are being promoted to Major General and will oversee half of Ancoupe's men as your own."

"Sir!"

He waved a hand. "His company has grown too large. This is not up for discussion."

There it was. The unwarranted promotion that I'd been dodging for a year now. Persephone had complained about my wish to advance in the ranks based on merit, saying that everyone who could, purchased their rank. Many of my peers, Ancoupe included, had allowed their father's purse strings to aid in their advancement, but I'd refused such shortcuts, even though my father was a retired admiral and presently a Grand Duke. But merit-based promotion had vanished with the general's announcement. My hands fisted behind me of their own accord. Everything I did to make my way on my own abilities went up in smoke, and there was no way to fix it. The official engagement would come close on the heels of this promotion, and I was running out of time.

General Schmidt turned to Elaura, his demeanor turning as serious as stone. "You, young lady, will get used to having no say. I pronounced your sentence, and if you don't like your supervisor, I'm happy to send you on to his majesty for execution. Now..." He resumed his seat and picked up a pen. "What was your name?"

"My name is Laura Carpe," she blurted.

I turned to her before she finished the last syllable. She'd told me her name was Elaura, not Laura. For half a second, I questioned my memory. Had I heard it wrong? Wrote it wrong? Then her eyes met mine in a silent demand that I remain silent. I hadn't been crazy after-all. She had told me a different name.

General Schmidt said something to her, then turned to me.

"Please show her to the kitchen and to the staff so they know to expect her tomorrow. Then get her settled in C block. One of the single bunks should suit well, considering."

I snapped to attention, acknowledging my orders with a crisp, "Yes, sir."

He dismissed both of us. I opened the door, and she snatched her bag from the floor where it had fallen when Banks and I had set down the body bag. Elaura—Laura—stalked past me. I followed, the door clicking behind me. She threw her bag over her shoulder, crossed her arms, and glared.

"Well, after you, Major General." Her lips pursed, but her eyebrows rose in challenge. If I hadn't grown up around polite ladies of court, I wouldn't have believed that eyebrows could be sarcastic, but hers nearly dripped with the same venom in her words.

I set my jaw. I needed to get out of earshot of the office. The explanation could wait until we were outside, away from listening ears.

"Follow me."

I led her out and across the compound to the mess hall. Her silence ate at me. The sun's glare morphed the windows into looking glasses, but I found my chance just before we reached her new work assignment. I pulled her into a quiet alley and dipped my head close. "What in the hell are you doing here?"

She ripped her arm from my grasp and shoved herself away from me. "Me? What am I doing here? How about, what is that girl from the brothel doing here?" She pointed back the way we'd come. "You tell me I'm free to go and then turn around and murder an innocent girl?"

The deep breath I took wasn't enough to calm my churning emotions. My words emerged in a deep growl. "You weren't there. I tried to save her!"

My hands shook. I couldn't even form the words to say more. I stepped back, lowering the finger I'd pointed at her face. Her eyes glistened, jaw trembling.

"You tell that to her." Her voice broke. She rubbed the heel of her hand across her face as tears streamed down her cheeks.

The raw emotion in her voice gave me pause, and my burgeoning anger would do nothing to assuage her fears. In fact, it likely cemented them. "I didn't kill her." My hands shook, and I squeezed them into fists. *Keep it together.* "I tried to save her... I did everything I..." My words no more than a soft ache spilled from my lips; the consequences be damned.

"Right. Then what happened?"

I stole a glance at the mouth of the alley, the back at Elaura. Even now, I hated myself for not saving the girl. "I'll have to wait for the autopsy, but the others told me she was diabetic. I suspect it could be related." She was quiet a long while before I looked up and caught the tears trailing down her cheeks. I reached for her shoulder, slow enough not to jostle the poor girl's clearly sore ribs.

She recoiled, clasping her hands protectively against her chest. "Don't touch me."

Her words threatened to reignite my anger, but I tried to keep it under control. Tried. "Look, you had one job: to stay out of trouble with the law. But no, you had to get picked up by Carlsen. Carlsen! And now you're handpicked by General Schmidt to be my personal nightmare."

When at last I came to myself, I found her furious, staring wide eyed at me. I straightened my posture and my appearance, and motioned toward the alley's opening. "Shall we?"

She stalked past me out to the street, where she, once again, waited for me to take the lead.

I kept it strictly business once we entered the mess hall. I pointed out the kitchen and staff areas where she would spend most of her time. The head of the kitchen was absent, but a pair of privates were rushing around the dining area to clean up the dinner mess. Their eyes followed us as I showed Elaura—no, I had to remember her as Laura—the simplest of the duties she'd have the next day.

Scuttlebutt would begin flying before we'd left the building, but I tried to push that from my mind. Rumors in a mess hall wouldn't reach the princess. If they did, I'd have other problems.

C-Block was, thankfully, close to the mess hall. Laura was silent while I informed Sergeant Brays of the general's commands and Laura's needs. I wasn't familiar with Brays, but he was intelligent and efficient, a pleasant change of pace from most of the desk jockeys I'd interacted with.

It didn't take him long to produce a key and a folder with the printed mess schedule for her. I thanked him and escorted my charge to the lift. Once inside, we both faced the door. One question still plagued me. I'd tried to brush it aside, but it remained an itch I couldn't scratch.

Sneaking a glance at her, I asked, "Why did you give General Schmidt a different name?"

She crossed her arms, refusing to look in my direction. The lift jostled and began its climb.

"I don't trust him," she finally whispered, never taking her eyes from the door.

"But you trust me?"

"I'm not sure." She paused for a moment. "What was her name?" Her voice barely rose above a whisper.

"Emma. Her name was Emma." I stole a glance and found her gaze firmly on the floor before us.

The door of the elevator opened, and we walked out into the hall.

"I could tell General Schmidt your actual name is Elaura." The words flew out without forethought. I hadn't actually considered doing so, but once I'd spoken the words, I wanted to gauge her response. "He is my commanding officer, after all."

She threw me a wicked glare. "Then you'd have to tell him how you know I gave him the wrong name, which means you'd have to admit that you brought the wrong girl in that body bag."

I halted for a moment. Somehow, more than disappointing me, her reply only highlighted her ability to stand toe to toe before a challenger, which both surprised and impressed me.

I sighed, walking past her down the hallway. "Let's get you settled."

Once we'd located her room, I opened the door and stepped aside to let her in. It was smaller than most. Folded linens and a pillow had been stacked on a single bed. A narrow desk and chair, as well as a locker for clothing and personal items line the wall opposite. The walking space was so narrow, one could reasonably sit on the bed to work at the desk. She slipped past me, dropped her bag on the desk, and took a seat on the bed.

I held the folder and key out for her. "I'll be here to escort you to the mess hall at 0500. Be ready. Brays, the sergeant at the desk, said you'll find uniform shirts and pants in the locker. Lock your room if you leave it, and don't lose your key."

She didn't respond, but simply pulled her knees to her chest, eyes fixed on the floor. I set the folder and key atop the desk, and my heart twisted in knots. I was so used to sitting next to my sister and rubbing her back until she was ready to talk. Something told me that any attempt to do such a thing here would only make things worse.

She didn't trust me, and I couldn't quite blame her. As I eased the door closed, I was sure I heard her sniffle. I rested my forehead on the wooden door, wishing that there was something I could do, but tonight, space was the greatest gift I could give her. After all, I would see her in the morning.

Tonight, however, I needed to see what strings I could pull to help prevent a criminal's black mark from being added to Emma's cards. Locating her family to deliver her memorium cards was the only way I could thank that poor girl for her part in this whole mess.

The one benefit of my promotion would be the resources I needed to make things right.

As right as they could be.

Heart heavy, I took the stairs to the first floor and turned left for the mortuary building.

In the event that the general in question finds the suspect to be guilty of a lesser crime, he may sentence said soul to indentured servitude under the direction of any lieutenant or major to be overseen by an officer of any station. For more serious offenses, after the individual soul's guilt has been determined, the general shall send him/her to the King's Court for sentencing.

~Judicial Code 1686843:684 Amendment:23B

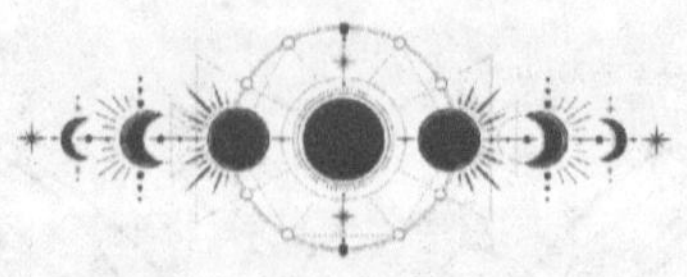

ELAURA

I never imagined I might be grateful for the rescue of an alarm clock, but after a night of dreams haunted by the girl from the brothel—her hand stretching for my help while I was never able to reach her—the high-pitched wail was welcome. I awoke more exhausted than I'd been the night before, even more exhausted than from nightmares in Atha. This time, neither Victor nor Metea was here to comfort me.

Throwing aside the thin blanket, I lowered my feet to the cold floor. At least the chilly surface was similar to the cottage where I'd spent the past six years. A photo of Grakus hung on the wall just above the desk. His eyes followed me wherever I went. Others might see a sincere, gentle smile, but I saw sinister glee in that face. I stepped into the wash closet and grabbed a washcloth, which I hung on the frame to hide that stare.

It only took a couple of steps to cross the room to the narrow locker and its supply of uniforms. I pulled on the smallest one, but the stiff, starchy clothing still hung loosely on my frame. Fortunately, the belts on the top shelf offered a solution, and the third one finally fit. My pants were secure. I stepped back to look in the small mirror over the desk. Small puffy bags hung below my eyes, evidence of the tears I'd shed the night before. I doubted anyone here would notice. Matea would have. She would ask me why and insist that I tell her about the brothel girl.

Her name had been Emma. That was all I knew. But the fact that she had taken my place, my guilt, was still a bitter pill. The past few days held so much grief, so many dead. In the palace, most people had been hollow remains of their former selves, but the brothel girl, Emma, wasn't changed from when I had given her the brooch. That gift had cinched her guilt as the major's attacker. I tried to shake myself free of that line of thought while I pulled my hair into a ponytail.

At 04:58 precisely, a knock sounded at my door. Major General Tourelle Breckenridge was probably glaring holes through the wood. With a roll of my eyes, I smoothed my shirt and brushed a hand over my hair before turning the knob and opening the door.

Piercing blue eyes met mine. "Ready to go?"

I nodded, wishing I could run and hide rather than walk into my sentencing, but retrieved my key, followed him out into the hall, and locked my door. He didn't insist on talking, and I was grateful.

He led me back to the mess hall, where he introduced me to Fredericks, the man in charge. After the major general left, Fredericks and a few of the staff provided me with very basic instruction and put me to work washing and drying dishes. When I'd finally exhausted the first round of dishes, they sent me to the dining area to collect more in an endless cycle. A sea of eyes followed my every move as I walked through the dining hall. By the end of the day, I was better at suppressing the urge to look over my shoulder, especially with the copious number of catcalls

The major general made routine visits throughout the day to ensure I was being compliant. He never sat to eat, only checked in, then left. Though he was, perhaps, my only ally, his presence was another reminder that escape would be nigh on impossible, especially in the middle of this sea of sharks.

The next day offered the same routine. The same nightmares, morning pickup, and work. Each day, hungry eyes followed my every move, never failing to make my skin crawl. Banks and Carlsen appeared regularly. Sometimes together and sometimes individually, so I learned to ignore men trying to get my attention.

By the end of that first week, my hands were chapped, and I was exhausted. After the major general escorted me back to my quarters, I sat on my bed and stared blankly at the wall. I had promised my parents to do my best for our people, but had already failed. Even awake, the images of the people in the palace and the girl in that black body bag on the general's desk tormented me. I had to do better for them. All of them. My fate would be the same if anyone discovered my true identity: a black bag, dropped unceremoniously on a general's desk. The major general couldn't protect me then, if he even could now.

My thoughts shifted to Major General Tourelle Breckenridge. He appeared the epitome of a true-blue soldier, bound to his code and opposing treason. Papa would have liked him. My crimes, to his knowledge, were a desperate act to aid my family. Still, his lenience gave me pause. Why had he let me go? I couldn't shake the feeling there was more to him and his behavior than met the eye.

And how on the sandy hills of Delta I was going to get out of this, for my own life and that of my people?

I leaned my head back against the wall. In an attempt to dismiss the circular questions, I turned my mind to Atha. What would Victor and Matea be doing right now? I could almost see them in my mind's eye. Victor, in his reading chair with a book in hand, chewing on the earpiece of his glasses, oblivious to the world around him, and Matea, milling around the house or preparing the evening meal. If they knew what was happening right now, Matea would work herself into a panic, and Victor would pace a hole in the floor. It had been almost two weeks since I left, and like a flash of lightning, the question struck: what if they decided to follow me, to see how I was doing?

I needed to write to them.

Jumping to my feet, I snatched my key from the desk and headed to the attendant's desk in the lobby. As soon as I turned the corner, I realized I'd get along with him perfectly. The young man reclined in his chair, knees pressed against the desk and book in hand, his brow furrowed under black curls. I watched him for a moment, almost feeling guilty for having to tear him from his book.

"Excuse me," I tapped my knuckles on the wood of the desk, startling him. *Just like Victor.*

"Yes, miss?" he blurted, pushing his rounded glasses up his freckled nose. "What can I do for you?"

"I'd like to post some letters," I said. "Where can I get writing materials? Do I need postage, or does the military stamp the mail that gets left here?"

He turned and shuffled around in a few drawers in the wall behind the desk. Within moments, he set a couple of notepads and some writing utensils on the desk.

"You can have these. I'm afraid we don't keep any postage here, so you'll need to go to the central office for postage. It'll be open for another hour." He pulled out another small memo pad and scribbled away. "Once you're inside, turn left at the first hall and take a right at the second. It's the second door on the left." He ripped off the page and held it out. "Tell them Sergeant Otto Brays sent you, and they'll set you up."

I glanced over the directions, which were fairly legible. "Thank you, Sergeant Brays. Since the office closes up soon, I think I'll get the postage first. Can I pick this up when I get back?"

He grinned. "If it makes things easier, I'll drop them at your door."

Grateful to have found at least one friendly person, I said, "Thank you. That would be wonderful."

His smile broadened, and I set off into the evening air on my first trip through the base alone. The sun sank toward the horizon, threatening to plunge the world into night, so I kept my pace brisk. There weren't many people out at this time of evening, which made the journey a little more pleasant. Signs pointed me down two different streets before I saw the one atop the building at the end of the road. The central offices.

My goal in sight, the tension in my shoulders eased. I didn't notice the rumble of masculine voices from the establishment on my left until it was too late to turn around. Soldiers sat at tables along the sidewalk, drinking who knew what. One whistled, and all conversation faded away. Once more, my back stiffened. It was one thing to be the object of their attention in the mess, but another entirely while walking past as dusk crept in.

"Hey, baby," an unfamiliar voice called.

"Shake that sweet thing, honey!"

"C'mon, sweetheart," whooped a third. "Lemme show you a good time."

I walked faster, veering as far away as the street allowed. Before coming to this base, I'd only been the subject of such attention once, but he had been a teenage boy back in Atha. He'd learned quickly how much I didn't appreciate his remarks. This, however, was a bar full of trained men. Men who could kill without a thought. The idea chilled me.

One darted from his seat and grabbed my arm. My stomach sank.

His sour breath washed across my face as he growled, "Don't you walk away when I'm talking to you."

I flinched but sneered, "Take your hand off me."

His massive biceps flexed when he shifted his grip. "Now, why would I do that?"

"Let go of me!"

The man's gaze shot to his associates and back. "No, I don't think I will. See, we don't get many dames around here, and lucky for you, you're just my type."

I spat in his face.

The burly man released me to wipe the spittle from his face, and I ran.

"Oh no, you don't," ground out behind me.

Fingers again snagged my arm. The attacker spun me around. All humor had drained from his face. His hand flew, and my cheek exploded with fire. My ears rang. His vise-like grip tightened, and pins and needles stabbed at my fingertips as stars danced in my vision. Behind us, men hollered, egging him on.

He pushed me backward against a wall and forced his mouth over mine. I pinched my lips shut. My skin crawled, but even with no way to aim, I jerked my knee up with as much force as I could muster. The man stumbled away, eyes and mouth flying open as he curled inward. I tried to escape, but someone else pinned my arms to my sides.

"You aren't leaving now, little doll." The speaker's words sent a shiver down my spine.

"Let me go," I cried in desperate hope that one of the men had the moral compass to come to my aid.

He—they—only laughed.

The attacker on the ground rose, his face red. The fire in his eyes chilled me, but I pulled in a deep breath and screamed with all that I had.

The first attacker's fist found my stomach. My arms stretched behind me as I lurched forward. Then came another blow to my face, this time with the back of his hand. I dropped to the ground, gasping and sputtering. I only managed one breath that didn't add to the fire in my lungs while I desperately tried to take in enough air to satisfy.

I curled into a ball there on the pavement, while shouts echoed off the buildings. Though footsteps approached, I only focused on the gravel of the pavement beneath my cheek. I heard a struggle and something that seemed to be fists striking flesh, but I couldn't focus. Everything hurt, from the numbness spreading across my lower lip to the ache along my cheekbone, and my ribs burned. Even the breeze prickled my face. The noise settled, and gentle fingers touched my throat. I flinched. Despite the pain, I tried to push away, to lift myself from the ground.

"Woah," came the familiar voice, and a hand steadied me. "I'm here to help. Let's get you up." He paused a moment and shouted, "Fritz, call the medic!"

Added embarrassment heated my damaged cheeks. I set my jaw and squinted through a swollen eye at Major General Tourelle Breckenridge, who crouched beside me. His eyes searched mine.

"I'm fine," I groaned, finally rising to my hands and knees. Pain shot through me, and the world tilted and heaved.

"I doubt that," he said, his baritone voice low and soft. "Here, let me help you."

His fingers curled gently around my elbow and hoisted me upright. A wave of nausea crashed over me, and I accepted the help, albeit clamping my free hand over my mouth. He slid his hand to the middle of my back, then leaned slid his other hand behind my knees.

"I can walk." When I tried to wave off his help, however, I teetered.

"Sure, you can." He sighed with a shake of his head. "Laura, I'm seeing you to the infirmary. You have two choices: a gurney or me carrying you."

"Neither," I breathed, leaning my weight against the concrete wall. I'd had enough of being the victim for the day. All I wanted now was my bed.

"Fine," he huffed. "But I'm helping you walk." Not waiting for an answer, he lifted my arm, snaking his own around my back. My hand dropped behind his neck.

A large, boxed vehicle pulled up before us and a couple of men jumped out. One came to look at me while the other went across the road. Why, I wasn't sure. The men at the bar silently watched as though entranced. I may have convinced the major general, but I couldn't sway the medic. He insisted that I take the gurney to the infirmary and loaded me into the back of the large vehicle. The major general took the seat next to me.

When the medic left us alone, he broke our uncomfortable silence. "What are you doing out this late?"

I sighed. "I wanted to get some postage. My family hasn't heard from me since I left. They need to know I'm okay."

He laughed darkly. "What about any of this suggests you are okay? You've been attacked, and—" His mouth pinched. "You're going straight to the infirmary."

"I don't need—"

"You could have internal organ damage." He scowled. "Or broken ribs. I saw him hit you."

I blinked against the pain.

He was right.

We both fell silent on the slow ride back to the clinic, where a medic pronounced me bruised but whole, and wrote out a slip to excuse me from duty until he cleared me. The pain medications took the edge off the pain, and I argued until they let me walk back.

Halfway back to C-hall, I said, my words slurring even in my ears, "When I was little, J—" I stopped, concern ringing faintly in my head. *No, don't tell Major General... Tourelle... that.* I recovered and finished, "My brother and I played dragon and damsel. I'd be trapped, guarded by a terrible beast, and he'd conquer the creature. My gallant knight would rescue me, and I would bestow my favor."

"You have a brother?"

"Not anymore." I rubbed my forehead. "But now that I find myself in need of real help, I hate it. I don't like the feeling."

Blue eyes held mine. "It doesn't help that you're in pain."

"That's not the point. I don't want to rely on someone else for salvation. The pain isn't as bad as being helpless. I never want to feel that way again. I won't."

He nodded.

"I want you to train me."

He stopped so abruptly that I teetered. "What?"

I didn't answer, and we crossed the threshold into C-block.

Sergeant Brays jumped to his feet. "Carpe! What happened?"

I smiled and answered muzzily, "Some people aren't very pleasant."

He shoved his hand through his black curls. "Do you need any help?"

Major General Tourelle's free hand rose. "I've got it in hand, sergeant."

The sergeant sat slowly before he nodded, but I thought he watched us as we crossed the floor to the lift.

The moment the doors closed in front of us, I pushed away and leaned against the railing. "You pity me, don't you?"

My guess made me even more nauseous, or perhaps it was the pull of the elevator on my stomach. A look of stern disapproval crossed his face as his eyes met mine. It surprised me since I'd only seen that type of look when Victor was especially upset. I clutched the rail defiantly and focused on the ascending numbers over the door. Just a few more floors to go.

"You will follow the doctor's orders and will not return to work until the medic releases you." His demeanor left no room for argument. No hint of emotion crept across his brow. "Consider your time in recovery a free pass. It won't make your sentence any longer."

The elevator chimed as the lift came to a halt and the doors breezed open. I pushed away from the railing and stumbled forward a few steps, still cradling my mid-section. I made it a few more steps beyond the door before I had to reach out for the wall. He was at my side at once.

"I understand your need to be strong, El—I mean, Laura. I really do, but don't confuse strength with stupidity." He lifted me into his arms without allowing me time to protest, though he kept his eyes forward and missed my indignant glare. "Should you defy my orders to rest, I will have you strapped to a gurney until the doctor clears you, *and* will add your recovery to the tail-end of your sentence." His blue eyes challenged me to defy him. "Are we clear?"

I opened my mouth, ready to say something, anything, to wipe that look from his face, but instead, I pressed my lips together, giving him a silent challenge of my own. He stared me down, his right brow arching higher. At last, I relented.

"Fine."

He set me down in front of my door, where the paper and pens sat to the side. I dug the key from my pocket, opened the door, hobbled in, and took a seat on my bed. He entered behind me and pulled the chair to face me.

I could feel the lecture coming.

"Laura," he began cautiously, "you need to take extra care around these men—"

"Don't you dare put this on me. All I did was walk down the street. Nothing more. I never invited their attention!"

His hand rose. "I am not suggesting anything of the sort. What I am pointing out is that you are the only young woman in a base full of men." A silent storm I couldn't decipher gathered behind his steel-blue eyes. "Some, like myself, will always come to your aid, but others…"

"I get it."

"Did you—" he stroked his chin, then inhaled "—what did you mean, earlier?"

I fought against fatigue and medication to answer. "About?"

"Training. You said you wanted me to train you."

I bit my lower lip, a flash of pain exploding as my teeth grazed the split. "Oh. Yes." I forced myself to sit up straight. "Combat training. Enough to disable any would be attackers. Even a guy as big as the one who attacked me."

He rubbed the back of his neck. "Not when you are injured."

"No," I demanded. "Tomorrow."

For a long moment, he studied me. Finally, he said, "I'll set aside time at the end of your shift once you're back to work. You will have an escort everywhere you go for your safety until you can prove your ability to hold your own."

My ribs twinged, and I groaned. "Fine. After I'm back."

He chuckled, a shallow smile spreading across his face. "Well, you figured me out. I'll check on you in the morning." He rose and turned for the door.

"Major General Breckenridge?"

He turned, looking over his shoulder. "Yes?"

"Thank you."

He gave a wordless nod before leaving.

I tried to do my best to recline on the bed. The pain had eased a little, but still remained ever present. I'd had enough humiliation to last a lifetime, and yet something about this place whispered that it had only just begun.

As agents of the king's peace, all members of the king's army are held to a certain decorum. No soldier shall be found to violate the rights of any person on base. Anyone not measuring up to these standards shall face court martial and disciplinary measures up to expulsion from the ranks, imprisonment, and a monetary fine.

Addendum: A photo of the Sovereign King Divo Von Grakus shall be found in every room of every military installation as a reminder.

~Military Code 651684:54

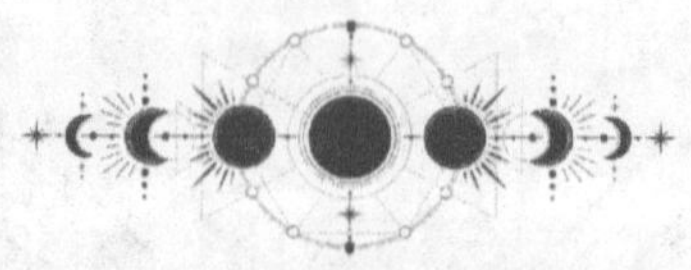

ELAURA

I tossed and turned all night. While the muscle relaxers and creams the doctor prescribed had eased much of the ache, I didn't trust the lethargy of the sedatives. The remaining medication sat untouched beside the sealed letter on my desk. With nothing else left to entertain myself beyond writing to Victor and Matea. I was sick of rest before noon.

The major general walked me to a follow-up appointment, back to my room, then left me to rest, though it was the last thing I wanted, despite how sore I felt. I paced most of the day, avoiding my bruised reflection in the small mirror. Relief came that evening with another knock, and when I peeked into the hallway, the desk attendant, Sergeant Brays, stood with a folder in his hands and a sheepish grin across his freckled face.

"Evening, miss." He paused for a moment, as if he were gauging my reaction. When I smiled, the slight gesture seemed to release the floodgates. "You see,.. the base has been buzzing all day about what happened to you. I... I understand if you aren't interested, but I hope you don't mind, but I brought you the postage you wanted the other night.."

I pulled the door open. "That's very kind of you. Thank you, sergeant."

He set the small paper envelope in my hands. "I hear that the man who attacked you is—"

"Please." My fingers tightened around the packet. "The less that's said about him, the better."

His brown eyes searched mine while his brows pulled together. Confusion coloring his features.

I marshaled as convincing a smile as I could muster, hoping to set his mind at ease. "I'll be fine, Sergeant Brays."

His responding smile revealed a dimple on his right cheek. "Call me Otto."

I pulled in a deep breath, hoping to keep my tears at bay. It was too soon to know whether or not he was genuine, but if he were... Well, I could use a friend.

"Thank you, Otto."

His smile grew even wider at my use of his given name rather than his rank, but before I could ask a little more about himself, the elevator opened. Footsteps drew our attention down the hall. I drew back slightly.

Otto snapped to a salute. "Sir."

Major General Breckenridge nodded, holding a covered tray. "Sergeant Brays."

The younger man blushed, scampered past him, and disappeared into the lift. Major General Breckenridge chuckled and lifted the tray between us.

My stomach growled, and I turned to place the postage on my desk, then swiped the towel from Grakus's picture, in deference to the major general's uninformed attitude. His eyes found mine all too quickly, as stern as they'd been when he'd reprimanded me in the alley when I'd first arrived.

I arced an eyebrow. "Major General?"

He held out the tray. "I thought you might be hungry."

"Oh, thanks. Come on in." I took the tray and sat down at the desk. He took a step into the room and closed the door. The smell that came from the food as I lifted the lid made my mouth water. "Wow, Officers must get the good stuff! I've never seen anything this nice at the mess hall." He said nothing as I ate with abandon and waited until I'd finished eating.

"Don't like the picture of the king in your room?" He asked, a smirk pulling at his mouth.

I shrugged, "I don't really like being stared at. It's like the picture is watching me." Unconsciously, I shivered. "I'd just as soon cover it."

"Fair enough." He nodded and pushed away from the wall he'd been leaning on. "You want to go for a walk?"

Confused, I stared at him. "What do you mean?"

He shrugged. "I thought you might like to get out and get some fresh air. I can't imagine being in your room all day is very stimulating."

"Why?" Of course, I was sick of the four walls I'd been stuck in, but I worried about his purpose.

He shrugged. "The best thing for healing is a calming walk. Maybe even a stop at the chapel?" He stood with both hands perfectly behind his back. When I remained silent, he continued. "The most important thing to do after being thrown from a horse is to get back on it."

The example confused me. "I'm afraid I have no idea what you're talking about. I've never seen a horse, let alone ridden one."

He nodded, rubbing a hand across his mouth. "What I mean is, after something awful happens, it's important to face it head on so it can't cripple your progression."

"And going on a walk will do that?" Even with my limited knowledge of the man, something felt off. He shifted his weight back and forth. When he nodded, I shrugged. "Sure."

"I'll step outside so you can get ready." He smiled, but it seemed hollow somehow. True to his word, he let himself out, and I was left alone. I put on the few things I wasn't already wearing and found him waiting outside my door. He started walking wordlessly and I followed him out of the building. We walked through the streets right through scatterings of men.

Each man set a chill in my blood as they passed. After the first wave, Major General Breckenridge nudged me and motioned to himself standing a little taller. I understood, straightened my spine, pulled my shoulders back, and lifted my chin.

The chapel was a few blocks away, and the sanctuary was thankfully empty. We sat in the front pew in silence for a long time before I broke the silence. "What's wrong?"

He shook his head, his elbows resting on his knees, and gaze fixed on the floor. "They finished the cards."

I hadn't imagined the subject would bother him so. I was wrong. "Oh," was all I managed.

"I wasn't able to keep the black mark from her cards, and I have to deliver them to her family." His voice barely above a whisper.

"I can come with you if you'd like." I offered, finally understanding why he was feeling down.

He chuckled without mirth. "You're restricted to the base. You can't leave until your sentence is over." We both sat in the silence a minute more. "But, thank you."

I nodded, falling silent, staring at the backdrop behind the pulpit. We sat that way for a long while until he broke the silence. "Yesterday, on the way back from the clinic, you mentioned your brother; that he died." He paused a moment. "I'm sorry."

"Thanks." I offered a feeble smile before looking away, uncomfortable. "I wish I had their cards." I started, unable to stop the words from spilling from my mouth.

"Next of kin is always the primary designated recipient. Didn't your aunt and uncle give you their cards after they died?" he asked.

"There weren't any cards. That's all I wanted when I went... there. But there weren't any cards." The truth I'd wanted desperately to tell another human being was out in the open. He didn't say anything. Just stared wide-eyed beyond the pulpit and then at the floor. After a few minutes, I changed the subject, hoping not to bring further trouble down on myself.

"I need to thank you." He looked at me surprised, but I kept my gaze forward for the moment. "You've saved my life several times and I've never once thanked you." I waited a few breaths before I chanced a look at him. "You're a good man. Your parents should be proud of the man you are." I offered him a smile and looked forward again, unable to read his expression.

All recreation facilities shall remain open to all service members at all hours. Every man shall maintain a standard of excellence in all things; Including, but not limited to, their physical health. Each man shall complete a physical fitness test once a month to ensure his ability to serve the sovereign is not diminished.

Any officer may reserve the gym for an hour at a time for company exercises or the planning of such. These shall be posted in advance and shall not exceed two hours.

~Military Code 63560:616b

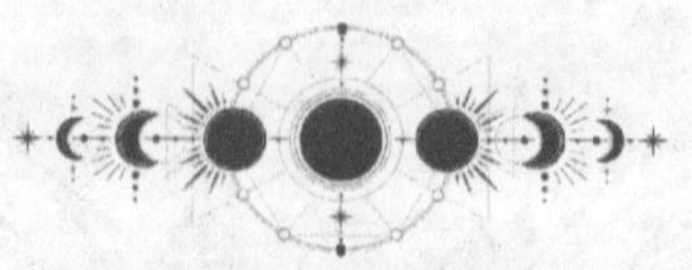

ELAURA

"How soon can you be ready?"

I eyed the major general, wrung out my rag and tossed it back in the bucket. "Ready for what?"

"You wanted to learn a few drills." He leaned against the door frame, holding a duffel bag. "At least, that's what you said six weeks ago."

For a minute, I just stared at him vacantly, then I realized what he meant. "Self-defense?"

He seemed to be hiding a smile when he rubbed his chin, as if he were resisting the urge to laugh. I arched a brow, and he chuckled. "You have a rather expressive face."

I rolled my eyes. "I'm right, then, aren't I?"

His smile shifted into something more serious. "Yes."

"Good. What do I need to wear?"

"I'd recommend light clothing. Sweats and a t-shirt or even tank top," he said.

"I have the clothes," I said quickly. "I just haven't had a reason to wear them yet."

He nodded. "If you prefer to train later, we can make that work. It's only that the gym is empty right now, and I thought you'd prefer to work without an audience."

"Now is definitely better."

"Let's go, then." He motioned toward the door. "C-block is on the way."

"Good," was my only reply.

We reached my room, and while he waited in the hall, I searched the locker and pulled out a loose shirt and sweats, even if I had to cinch the drawstrings to make sure they stayed put. I slipped out, secured the door, and tucked the key in my pocket.

"Shall we?" The major general pushed effortlessly away from the wall, retrieved the small duffel bag at his feet, and started down the corridor.

The lift's doors slid open, and I followed him wordlessly as he weaved down several blocks. The twists and turns disoriented me enough that I wondered if I'd be able to find it again.

The gym was a squat concrete building with little to distinguish it from its neighbors save a sign mounted outside. We pushed through the doors, and I ignored yet another framed photograph of Grakus. The same image mounted in my room. Instead of mocking me, though, this time his image made me square my shoulders.

Exercise machines gleamed on a sprawling expanse of thick mats. He led me past them, motioning for me to wait while he disappeared into a changing room. Movement caught the corner of my eye, and I spun around to see my reflection, wide-eyed, in a floor to ceiling mirror obscured by the machines.

Moments later, Major General Breckenridge, the man in the crisp uniform, emerged wearing a shirt and sweats that matched mine. Though they made me look shapeless, he had no such problem as the material clung to his arms and chest, highlighting the muscle tone everywhere.

"This way."

I blinked.

He tossed his duffel onto a vacant chair and led me to a large oblong leather bag hanging from the ceiling.

"We'll start with punches," he said. "Learning the right way to punch is more important than how hard you hit. I have gloves if you'd like to use them. The bag may look soft, but until you get used to it, it'll feel as soft as a brick wall."

My gaze drifted back to the pile of towels and gloves on a table against the wall. The idea of using communal gloves was about as appealing as walking through a men's locker room.

"I think I'll take my chances," I said. "Who knows where those have been…"

The major general grimaced. "Suit yourself, but I'll need to tape your hands." He waved me over to the table and pulled a roll of tape from a small white box. "Taping is standard when punching a bag or boxing without gloves. It allows you to get the training you need while reducing the impact and protecting your hands."

I raised my right hand and watched as he started taping my arm six inches above the wrist, then down toward my fingers. He worked with only the smallest direction to open my hand wide, to close my hand into a fist, or to switch to my left. Only after pronouncing himself satisfied did he lead me back to the punching bag.

All business, Major General Tourelle Breckenridge said, "Your turn. We'll begin with spurts of three, alternating sides with each strike. Start with your dominant hand, and remember to lead with your first two knuckles."

He folded his arms and stepped away, and I hit the bag as hard as I could, three times in a row.

"Left," he ordered.

I did.

"Again!"

Right—*right, left, right.*

Left—*left, right, left.*

Over and over.

"Again!"

I began to hate that word. My newly healed ribs ached, and my hands throbbed. I wanted to crawl back into my bed. Finally, nearly spent, I paused my assault on the bag and rested my hands on my knees; hoping to catch my breath. Sticky sweat coated every inch of me. Even my eyelids felt sticky. I could only hope that the exhaustion might help me sleep dreamlessly.

"If you want to succeed, you need to push through the exhaustion," came his voice. "You must be able to strike your opponent just when he's counted you out."

I waved my hand at him. Wherever he was. "Give me... a minute... to breathe."

I'd expected a protest, but he held his tongue. When at last I'd gathered the strength to rise, Major General Breckenridge appeared at my side.

"We're building muscle memory right now," he said, his baritone stern but soft. I glanced up, and he continued, "When you are in the middle of a fight, there won't be time to think. Only time to react."

He was right, and I knew it, but I groaned all the same.

"Let me help you for a moment." His brows bunched together. "If you don't mind."

"That's why I asked you to train me," I said.

When he positioned himself behind me and took hold of my hand, his breath tickled the crook of my neck, sending a shiver down my spine. A hint of musky cologne penetrated the gym's smell. Acute awareness of his proximity made every nerve tingle.

"Time your breathing with the strikes," he said matter-of-factly in my ear. "Exhale with every attack. Ready?"

"Yes."

He launched my fist toward the bag.

It happened so fast, all thought of exhaling with the movement fled my thoughts.

That dreaded word: "Again."

Twice more, my fist launched.

Then Tourelle stepped away, leaving my back a little colder. "We need to work on your breathing. You need to internalize the breathing pattern." His fists rose and turned his focus to the bag, bouncing side to side on his toes. "Every time your fist connects with the bag, I want you to yell."

"Are you serious?"

"Absolutely. Do what I do." Without a second's hesitation, his fist flew. As it connected with the bag, a yell accompanied the strike. The two following punches finished out the sequence, and his voice echoed in the wide space. Each subsequent volley brought corresponding shouts. He stepped back and motioned for me to try.

Exhaustion rooted me where I stood.

"Let me guess," he said with a quirk of an eyebrow. "Not lady-like enough?"

I narrowed my eyes. *More like too embarrassing.*

He shook his head. "Alright then. One last thing."

Last thing. The words sounded magical. Thankfulness spilled over me, and I closed my eyes. All I wanted was a hot shower and sleep.

"Hit me."

I spun toward him, eyes and mouth open wide. "You want me to *what*?"

"That's what this is all about, isn't it?"

"No," I sputtered. "It's about—"

"Self-defense." His tone was gentle. "Hitting a person is very different from hitting a bag. Just like muscle memory, you need to be able to put a punch into practice."

"You can't be serious."

His blue eyes twinkled, but his face was serious. "Completely."

He led me to a large, elevated mat with a yellow painted circle marking out the center. Halfway between the center dot and the circle's edge were a pair of parallel white lines. The major general pointed to one and stood atop the other.

Taking my place on the line, I studied him for a few moments, keeping track of every movement, then brought my fists up before my face, just as he'd shown me. The words spilled out, unintended: "If I'm supposed to hit you, maybe you should try to hit me too."

"We haven't gone over that yet."

"I'm ready."

He sighed, and the corner of his mouth rose. I waited for him to assume the same readiness stance he'd taught me. He didn't. Instead—

"Evade."

One word. One word was all the warning he gave before he launched himself at me. Shocked by his speed, I barely ducked the fist directed at my face. I sidestepped, avoiding him by only the narrowest of margins. He jabbed again.

Desperate to stay clear, I didn't pay attention to my surroundings. My foot crossed the mat's edge. The uneven foothold disrupted my balance, and gravity took over. Eyes wide, I flailed and, in my terror, grabbed his wrist.

We fell. I landed on my back; the wind knocked out of me. Somehow, the major general braced himself so his weight didn't crush me when I pulled him after me. His musky aftershave and my desperate need for air were overwhelming.

"You okay?"

His words somehow snapped me back. I inhaled and opened my eyes to find his eyes searching mine. Every breath brought with it more of that savory–sweet musk. We were so very close.

I couldn't answer, only stared back into his steel-blue gaze.

The door to the gym rattled open.

The trance which had held us both captive shattered.

He was on his feet, offering me his hand. A furnace must have exploded in my cheeks as he helped me up.

The thought of what had happened... We'd been so close...

What on Delta are you thinking? Stop it, Elaura!

I shook my head to banish the rogue thoughts.

Major General Breckenridge cleared his throat. His ears practically glowed scarlet, and he didn't look at me. In fact, he seemed interested in looking at anything—and everything—else. "I think we should call it a day. We might have overdone it for the first lesson."

Weights clanked as whoever it was began his training circuit. I tried not to listen.

"I'm sure you have a lot to do," I murmured. "I won't keep you."

What else could I have said? *Sorry I pulled you over? Sorry you fell on me?*

"Yes, I've got some paperwork I've been putting off." He paused and finally met my eyes. "Practice what I showed you. I'll be there to escort you to the mess hall in the morning." He straightened his shirt and turned to leave, but stopped in the act of retrieving his bag. "First, I'll escort you back to C-block."

I almost missed his meaning, but once my brain caught up, I nodded, then jogged across the mat to follow him. More than anything, I just wanted to forget any of this happened.

But I knew I wouldn't.

All military personnel shall be subject to a battle test before their release from basic training into the ranks. The terms of the battle test shall be determined by the ranking commanding officer. All testing shall reflect real-world situations, equipping each recruit-in-training to serve their sovereign king.
~Military code 208205 Amendment:324b

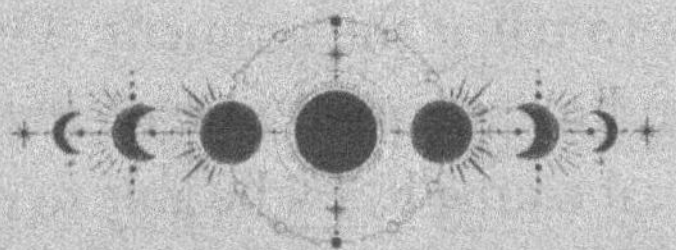

ELAURA

With the fourteen-hour days at the mess hall and my daily training sessions, the next six weeks passed in a blur, and though my muscles ached at first, the change in my energy was an unexpected perk. I wouldn't have expected that training would give me energy, not just take it.

Tourelle—I'd ceased thinking of him as Major General Breckenridge by the third week of training—had informed me at the end of my first week of training that there I would need to pass an aptitude test in order to shed my daily escort. The idea of having a small measure of freedom excited me, but as eager as I was to be free of constant supervision, his lack of details unsettled me.

I worked hard, practicing every chance I had, and after those six weeks, the appointed day came. Although I still knew nothing about the test, I was eager to prove myself. Tourelle and I arrived at the gym at our usual time and instead of suiting up, we waited for an hour. I sat by the main door bouncing my leg aimlessly, while he paced back-and-forth, which made my leg bounce even faster. For the millionth time, he pulled back the sleeve of his uniformed jacket to check his watch. This time, however, instead of sighing and continuing to pace, he straightened his jacket, taking care to brush off imagined specks from his shoulders.

I jumped to my feet.

"I believe we can start now," he said.

"Are you going to tell me what all this involves, or is all the cloak and dagger part of the test?"

He glanced out the window, then back to me. Something in his expression felt just a little off, though I couldn't quite tell how.

"There isn't much to tell at the moment. The assessment has a lot of moving parts, including variables out of my control. Each one is tailored to the individual taking it. I'll be able to explain once it's over." He held the door open for me to exit.

Every ounce of my agitation and irritation was channeled into the glare I threw at him. I hated puzzles, and his cryptic responses were like a pile of jigsaw pieces without a picture. He was hiding something.

I paused long enough to let him take the lead. His normal stride was hard to keep up with, but he seemed even faster that evening, almost as if he were just as motivated as I was to get this assessment over with. Keeping up meant a quick jog. When he stopped dead in his tracks, I ran right into his back.

"Shoot." He turned to face me, barely seeming aware that we'd just collided. "Would you mind a brief detour? I left a classified document on my desk and need to review it before my meeting tomorrow morning."

Was he trying to delay my evaluation? Why? He didn't think I would fail, did he? But no, he'd been exacting and encouraging this whole time. The Tourelle I knew wouldn't betray me like that. Part of me wanted to be angry, furious even, but the stress he put on that classified document took me back to moments in my father's office. Papa had always respected military classifications. Protection of his military personnel was always of great concern to him. If I wanted to be like my father, I couldn't fault Tourelle for wanting to retrieve it, needing to be prepared.

"Sure." In an attempt to be nonchalant, I shrugged. "I've waited this long. What's a little longer?"

A strange smile, one I couldn't decipher, flashed across his face. "Thank you."

And, once again, I fell in step behind him while he led the way through the winding streets to the central offices. The number of men walking the streets dwindled in the fading light. The evening air's slight chill calmed me; there was peace in the twilight, one not available in the light of day. Only the slow journey of the moons, Kipp and Eira, marked the passage of time. For a moment, homesickness took hold. Back in Atha, their ascent was unencumbered by buildings, far from the dangers that surrounded me on every side. The skin on the back of my neck prickled. Every shadow along the streets whispered a secret, and the sound of my footfalls echoed too loudly in my ears.

We neared the last turn, and every hair on my arms stood at attention. A familiar clamor rose into the air.

Our route would take us right past the base bar, the same one where that man had attacked me a little more two months ago. Since then, I'd heard rumors in the mess hall about the men who frequented that bar narrowly missing demotions or being disciplined frequently. The urge to retreat swelled as we approached, but sooner or later I'd have to come to terms with my fears. I clenched my jaw so hard my teeth hurt. I refused to shrink and give them any power.

Spurts of laughter met my ears, and despite my resolve, I stepped closer to Tourelle.

The place came into view. I kept my head held high. When we approached, the men seated outside leapt to their feet, saluting their superior.

"At ease." Tourelle waved his hand at them and continued walking.

It took a great deal of control not to react to their presence or to their every move.

They were talking about me. Whether or not I heard their conversations, I knew it. I was the only woman on base, and I was with the man people called the "goody-two-shoes major general." I glanced up at Tourelle, who'd fixed his gaze straight ahead, his focus set on the mission alone.

When we reached the building, leaving the bar behind us, Tourelle pulled a badge from his jacket and waved it over a small gray box beside the door. A small light flashed green, then a buzz and a click sounded. He pulled the door open and waved me through before entering. Dark corridors seemed almost as menacing as the streets outside.

I stayed close to Tourelle, my attention flitting from side to side. Slowly, his presence calmed me. His office wasn't far from the lift, so we reached it soon enough. The desk outside his office was almost identical to the one outside the general's, but I didn't ask if he had a receptionist as well.

"I'll be just a moment," he said before disappearing through the door.

My arms wrapped around my waist in the dim light. Though I tapped my foot to keep myself centered, it wasn't long until the ghosts of my past emerged. Imagined eyes watched me from the shadows, and every moment felt as though it may be my last. Dangerous men in unmarked uniforms could be hunting me in the dark. Unshed tears threatened to betray my silent panic.

Finally, Tourelle emerged from the now dark office. He paused mid-step, an open folder in one hand, and peered at me through the dim emergency light.

His brows pulled together. "Are you okay, Laura?"

How could I explain why the dark corridors terrified me? I couldn't, so I blinked away any traitorous moisture. He couldn't discover my fears. That would lead to questions, which would lead to discovery. And undoubtedly, discovery led to death.

"I'm fine." I smiled unconvincingly. "Just ready to be out of this place is all. I want to finish that assessment, you know."

His eyes stayed on me for a long moment, inspecting me before at last he nodded and led the way out. He didn't press any further, and my shoulders sagged with relief. We rode the lift in silence, then left the building. Kipp and Eira shone down upon us, and I exhaled deeply.

Tourelle's full attention remained on the contents of his folder. Even the men seated outside the bar noticed. They elbowed each other, pointed at him—or us—and remained seated. Their conversations hushed as we approached, maybe in an attempt to keep his focus away from them.

My fingernails pressed into my palms as we passed. If he wouldn't watch them, I would. My attention was so riveted I didn't see Tourelle stop. Once again, I ran right into his back.

"Why did you stop this time?" I demanded through clenched teeth. The back of my neck flushed with heat.

"Sorry." A frown pulled at his lips. "There's a page missing." He flipped a few sheets back and forth before turning to the office building again, then glancing back at me. "I need to find it. I'll be right back."

Anxiety swelled. The sinister corridors inside that building took me back to our escape six years ago, when I'd lost everything. And yet, the open street contained a slew of drunken men whose eyes were fastened on me. I didn't have to ask what would happen if he left me on my own. Right then, I decided that ghosts of the past were much less dangerous than the predators watching me.

"Then I'm coming with you," I said in an undertone.

Tourelle shook his head. "It'll be faster if I run back alone. Those offices made you uncomfortable. I could tell. It would be cruel to make you go through that again." He smiled and tapped my shoulder. "You'll be fine. I'll only be a minute."

He launched himself down the street at full speed before a protest could pass my lips. In no time, he disappeared inside the building.

In his attempt to be kind, he'd left me to face the ravenous predators on my own. The gathered men leered, and a shiver raced down my spine. Trying my best to ignore them, I folded my arms and inched toward the other side of the street.

Moments passed into minutes, and my heart sped up each second. I could feel the soldiers' eyes on me. Every bout of laughter grew more sinister than the last, but my attention strayed to the building down the street. There was no sign of either Tourelle.

A flash of movement in my peripheral vision pulled me around to see a man approaching, a bottle in his hand. He seemed familiar, but he hadn't been at the bar last time. I shuddered and stepped to the edge of the sidewalk.

"Hey there, why don't you come join me for a drink?"

"No thanks. I don't drink, and I don't have the time." I turned my attention back to the door of the central offices. *What was taking him so long? Tourelle should have been back by now, shouldn't he?* Anxiety weighed like a rock in my gut, chilling my skin.

"Aw, c'mon. The boys and I can show you a better time than ol' straight laces." An insincere smile spread across his face and creased his five o'clock shadow. He waved at a table of men who all raised drinks in near unison. Besides, we'd like to get to know ya better."

"I'd rather watch paint dry." I looked away again, hoping he would take the hint. *Where are you, Tourelle?*

Large fingers circled my arm just above the elbow, pulling me close enough to smell his rancid breath. My stomach soured, but at that moment, something within me snapped. No. Not again. I wasn't going to let it happen again.

I raised my chin and ordered, "Let me go!"

"Don't be like that. That's just rude. We offered a real friendly invitation," he breathed in my ear. "Either you come have a drink like a proper lady, or I'll show you what happens when someone is rude to me."

"Take your hand off of me this instant!"

"Whatcha gonna do? You gonna call for Major General Goody-Two-Shoes? News flash, sweetheart. He can't even take a dump without General Schmidt's go ahead, and anyone wanting to see the general has to go through me." He smirked. "You'd better believe I can sideline that idiot faster than you can say, 'Princess Persephone.'"

The memory surfaced at last. He was the man behind the desk when they brought me here that first day. The one who'd helped Tourelle with the body bag. *Banks!* My temper surged, pushing back some of my fear. No matter what his name was, I wanted his filthy hand off me.

Gritting my teeth, I swung the arm he held up and over his own, breaking his hold. My fist slammed into his nose. He dropped the bottle, which shattered between us, and stumbled backward, sputtering profanities. He pinched his nose in a vain attempt to stop the flow of blood.

"Don't touch me!" I shook out my stinging knuckles and assumed a defensive stance, my fists up in front of my face.

Banks pulled his hand away from his nose and wiped his bloody fingers on his trousers. "That was a mistake, missy."

He launched himself at me, wrapped his arms around my middle, and knocked me to the ground. My head hit the pavement. He pinned me down, but when his meaty hand caught hold of my right wrist, rage and frustration flared. I jerked my knee up. All I received was a grunt in return. I hadn't hit my target. In my desperation, I threw my head forward, hitting his, and a sickening crunch sounded. He disappeared from above me, scrambling to his feet and a guttural howl ripped from his throat. I struggled to my feet.

The man pulled his hands from his face, and his nose sported a sharp curve to the left. Gushing blood morphed his already terrifying appearance into something even more sinister. His hands curled until they resembled claws. I retreated a step. My back hit the wall of the building across from the bar, and he lunged at me, his hands wrapping around my throat. On instinct, my hands wrapped around his wrists, trying in vain to pry his fingers away. All defensive strategies raced through my mind so fast I couldn't catch hold of any.

In the middle of a fight, there won't be time to think.

Stars danced before my eyes as my lungs burned for air. I marshaled every remaining ounce of strength and kicked. My leg stuck him between the legs, and his hands fell away. Without the pressure holding me up, I dropped to my knees, wheezing and greedily gulping for air. Something moved in my periphery, and I cringed away from the stranger. A familiar hand on my back rubbed circles across my shoulder blades, bringing my eyes to its source; Tourelle looked down at me while a large number of the assembled men formed a jagged half-circle around us.

"You're okay." He said in a hushed tone. I nodded.

I rubbed at the ache in my throat, hoping to stop coughing before it started. "Sir. That prick—" I nodded to the man curled in a ball "—wanted to force me to have a drink and whatever else he thought might be a good time. I said no."

Tourelle watched the writhing man. "Banks. Didn't think you'd be the type." He shook his head and muttered, "Definite broken nose, possible genital trauma."

The surge of energy from moments before dissipated. My fingers wouldn't stop shaking. I stood on the sidewalk and wrapped my arms around my waist.

He squinted at me before turning to the men, who stared open-mouthed. "Attention!"

Every man within earshot snapped a stiff salute.

Tourelle clasped his hands behind his back as he stood and strode toward them. "Since you all need a refresher, anyone caught assaulting another person on or off base will be disciplined, per regulations." He paused, his eyes scanning the men before him. "If I don't see at least two men step forward immediately to deliver Sergeant Banks to the base medic, each one of you will spend the night scrubbing every toilet and urinal on base with your own toothbrushes."

A collective "Yes, sir" sounded. Four or five men leapt forward to collect Banks from the pavement.

Tourelle waved his hand at the rest of the men. "Consider your evenings over. Now."

The remaining men slunk away.

I tried to gain control of the tremors in my hands and arms and squeezed my eyes shut, willing the memories to cease their barrage on my mind. *His hand on my arm. Him knocking me to the ground. His sour breath on my face. The blood smeared beneath his nose. My struggle against his hold. The crunch as I broke his nose. Him writhing on the ground.*

It didn't feel real, more like images from someone else's life.

"Laura." Tourelle's voice pulled me back, and I looked up.

His jaw muscle jumped, but he peered down at me steadily and said, no louder than a whisper, "Hey, you're going to be alright."

"I, I, I can't stop shaking." I held up my quivering hands as proof.

"You're in shock." He crouched before me, nearly blocking my view of the men carrying off my attacker, then pulled off his jacket and wrapped it over my shoulders. Tourelle's brows pulled together, and his eyes flicked to my neck. He held out his hand. I took it and climbed to my feet.

"Th-thank you."

He inspected my knuckles and upper arm where Banks had grabbed me. "This will bruise. You should see the medic."

"I'll be okay. Just get me some ice." Though the tremors in my hands worsened, I pulled Tourelle's jacket close. I wanted all of it to be over.

As he shepherded me back toward C-block, I tried taking deep breaths—I really tried—but emotion flooded me, and I wept. We stopped just past a streetlight, and he stroked my hair, hushing me softly until my cries and tremors stilled. He pulled away, holding my shoulders while his deep blue eyes searched mine.

"You know you really did well. Better than I expected, actually." The right corner of his mouth pulled into a half smile. I blinked up at him, confused. It took a few moments to process what he'd just said.

"I did? Thanks, I.... Wait.... what do you mean *better than you expected*?" I demanded with a sniffle. "You knew this would happen?" I stepped out of his reach, my eyes wide.

He remained still and instead rubbed the back of his neck with his left hand, not meeting my eyes.

"You *planned* on me getting attacked?" I stood there, my arms wrapped around myself, trying to understand why. Every way I looked at it, he'd betrayed me. How could he?

His mouth opened and closed a few times, but no words passed his lips. His aversion screamed where his words failed in the tense silence.

Turning on my heel, I stormed away. I needed to get to my room as far away from Tour... Mr. Breckenridge as I could. I'd made it a block when he finally caught up. Of course, he'd follow me. I thought bitterly. "You did it, Laura. You brought down a trained soldier. I'm proud of you." He paused for a moment. Perhaps hoping for some gratitude on my part.

All I could do was stare at him, enraged. "You left me alone on a dark street, expecting someone to attack me. What do you want, some kind of thank you?"

"Laura, I didn't orchestrate it," he protested, his eyes growing wide and hands waving as he spoke. "I was on my way to help, but you finished him before I could reach you."

"You betrayed me."

I fled. I needed to get to my room as far away from Tour—no, not Tourelle. Mr. Breckenridge. He didn't deserve the use of his title.—as I could. Hot tears streamed down my face. I was so tired. Tired of this place, of everything... I wanted nothing more than to take a shower and retreat to my bed to forget about all of this. To go home—if such a place could ever exist again. Even the horrors of my nightmares were better than this.

Not far from C-block, he caught up, but stopped when he saw my face. "Laura, could you at least listen?"

"Fine." I wiped my cheeks dry, then let my arms drop to my sides as I stared pointedly at him. "Let's hear it."

He took a breath, opened his mouth, and closed it again. His hands rose before him, palms out; a conciliatory gesture as the words formed. "The best way to prove a person's abilities is in real-world situations. It had to be organic to be real. I'd prepared for every scenario, and you always came out the victor. No one arranged for those men to do anything. I just..." His eyes searched mine, perhaps for what I wanted to hear. He let out a long breath as though he'd been holding it this long time. "Are you okay?"

"No." I couldn't mistake the way his face fell at the syllable. "I'm not okay. I'm not okay with any of this..." My voice broke. "I trusted you. But now...I just don't know what to believe." I removed his jacket and tossed it at him. "I can handle myself now, so just... just stay away from me."

Without even a nod at Otto, I trudged to the lift, slapped the door-close button, and slumped against the wall.

Sod them all.

13

Reports of troop movements among Caprician ranks have come from Southern territories. General Nasser's men have kept advances at bay. Various scouts indicated a potential offensive against New Brighton, despite the area's public loyalty to the king. All scouts are to keep their ears to the ground for any further confirmation of an offensive strike. Long live King Grakus!
~Inter-office communication

TOURELLE

I caught young Sergeant Brays' attention as Laura crossed the lobby and stepped into the lift. Confusion pulled his brows together, but I shook my head. She wouldn't welcome company right now. He settled back in his seat, his focus on her as she entered the lift. The doors closed, and it began its ascent, offering me a small measure of comfort. Even though I knew she'd be safe enough in her room, guilt and regret pressed me down with their mighty thumbs.

Despite the late hour, home was the last place I wanted to be. I turned away, a single destination in mind, and jogged to the gym. A wave of cleaner mixed with sweat assaulted my nose at the gym entry. I removed my jacket and dress shirt and tossed them aside, paying no mind to the glances thrown my way by the other men. It only took about fifty determined paces to pass the taping table and reach the punching bag. I deserved whatever injuries I might receive.

Laura had so much unlocked potential. She had bested Banks before I even got there. I had been so caught up in 'standard methods and protocols' to see what my test might do to a young woman's spirit. I was an absolute fool.

Her tears drove off my flicker of pride in my student, and I blew out a deep breath as I struck the bag for each bruise, tear, and word, welcoming every wave of pain. The sting of my fist on leather fueled the strikes.

How could I have been so stupid? I wouldn't blame her if she hated me. Why not? She's right. I abandoned her to an impending attack. Might as well have ordered that little prick, Banks, to attack her. Someone would've. I'm just as much to blame.

Each bitter thought drove my strikes harder until sweat caked every inch of me. Still, I punished that bag. Punished myself.

She'd bested Banks, but it was *wrong* to put her in that situation. If it'd been Luna... I paused, breathing heavily.

My sweet sister had been the victim of an attack not four years ago when she'd tried to follow me on horseback. I'd told her not to come. I'd been attacked on the road before and didn't want to take any chances.

I hadn't realized I was being followed until her screams ripped through the air. I tried to reach her, but I wasn't fast enough. I couldn't stop them before they wounded her deeper than any doctor could heal. The sight of her bloody and broken on the ground snapped something within, and I loosed my sword on them without mercy. When they were dead, I returned to Luna's side. She flinched away from me. There was too much blood. When she finally let me touch her, I had to carry her on my horse screaming to the nearest hospital. I'd never been so scared. The doctors healed her physically, but she'd never been the same after that...

I pounded my palm into my forehead to drive the memories away and brought my gaze back to the swinging leather bag. Luna had healed from her ordeal. Laura would, too.

I struck the bag harder and harder, as if spilling its sandy contents onto the mat would solve anything. A rogue bead of sweat dripped into my eye, and one hand dashed it away too late. The salt in my eyes burned, and I stumbled back a few steps.

The gym door opened, and the familiar rhythmic clack of high heels echoed in the space. For a moment, I hoped the feminine stride might be Laura's, but the thought quickly died away. I knew that other than military issue, her only outfit was the one she'd worn when we met. Even if she owned such shoes, it would be absurd that she would seek me now. For any reason.

The clacking stopped. Small hands clasped mine, lowering my fists from my face. The soft blue-green eyes of my sister, Lunette, stared back at me.

"Rellie, what's wrong?" Her soprano voice ghosted back again in the open space. "Your eyes—"

"—are fine." Sighing, I pulled up the hem of my under-shirt to wipe my brow. "Just got a little sweat in them is all."

"Oh?" She snatched my hand, and her hair—the same warm blonde as Mother's had been—fell over her shoulder and half-obscured her face as she inspected my knuckles. "Good gracious, you're bleeding! What have you done to your poor hands?"

"I'm fine," I said before glancing down. She was right. My knuckles were raw, though to be fair, deep down I'd hoped as much.

"How many times must I remind you to tape your hands before you brutalize one of those bloody sand bags? Here, let's clean you up."

She turned to leave, my hand still in hers, but stopped short when I didn't budge.

As I snatched my hand back to tuck my shirt in, her unusual presence registered. Blinking against the lingering sting of sweat, I leveled a look at her. "What are you doing here, Luna? You shouldn't be out this late."

She pursed her lips. "Do I need a reason to visit my favorite brother?"

"Your *only* brother." I folded my arms. "What's going on? You didn't come here to make sure I was taping my knuckles."

Her mouth opened and closed a few times before her back straightened. "Tomorrow is your birthday for one." She drew a deep breath. "And truth be told, the princess invited me to the palace, so I'm stalling."

"Luna..." I sighed. I couldn't fault her for her aversion. If not for my betrothal to her, I'd avoid the princess as well. I opened my mouth to answer, but at that moment, someone dropped some weights. We weren't the only occupants of the gym, and all three soldiers watched us with quiet interest. I nodded to the door. "That is a discussion best had in private."

She followed my gaze, and her eyes widened. In a flash, her amiable smile was back on her face, and she waved at the men, two of whom blushed and went back to working out. I retrieved my dress shirt and jacket, and we left the gym.

Once out on the street, she continued in a lower tone, "I don't want to be her friend, Rellie. I don't care for her manner or her company." She huffed. "Besides, I can't let you spend your birthday alone. Mother wouldn't have it."

I forced a chuckle. "Do you even remember Mother?"

Her glare was instant and fierce. Perhaps a young lady of breeding shouldn't be able to devastate a person with a single look, but Lunette could—and in spades. I smiled. She was every bit the image of our mother with all the fire of our father.

"Don't get all clairvoyant on me," she said indignantly, "telling me what I do or don't remember."

I held my hands up in surrender. Arguing with her was a battle I couldn't win, and we both knew it.

"I'm here for your birthday and that is that."

"Alright, Luna. You win." I pulled her into a hug, then returned to the more serious subject. "I do wish you would try to make friends with Princess Persephone. After the official announcement next year, she'll be my fiancée and then my wife. She'll officially be your sister."

Luna's pout was instant. "Sister-*in-law*," she corrected. When my brow rose at her rebuttal, her words burst forth like a flood from a failed dam. "I do try to be friendly with her. And still, I wouldn't wish her company on anyone, least of all, you." Her hand brushed my elbow. "I wish you didn't have to marry her."

I couldn't admit that I shared her feelings, that I wished for a way to dissolve the arrangement without sacrificing my family's safety.

"Don't, Luna." I cast a quick look around the empty streets and kept my voice soft. "This agreement is the only thing keeping us from disappearing like all the other noble families with ties to the Capricians. Father made a wise move when he retired from the military and betrothed me. Every other member of the late king's inner circle disappeared."

We paused, and she looked up at me, questions in her eyes that slowly faded into horrified understanding..

"Father was the late king's admiral," I reminded her while tucking a stray hair behind her ear. "And whatever else, I will always protect you, little Looney."

She shoved me half-heartedly. "Don't call me Looney."

I couldn't help it. I laughed at the same old protest she'd issued since we were small. She always raised her hackles like a kitten staring down its reflection in a mirror.

She waited for me to finish, hands on her hips and toe tapping. "You still haven't explained why you bloodied your fists. Why are you up so late? Usually, you're sawing logs this time of night. I thought I'd be able to sneak in and surprise you in the morning. When you weren't home, I thought I'd check the gym. So. What did that poor sandbag do to deserve such violence?"

Her question sobered me in an instant, all humor forgotten. We walked to my building in a pregnant silence. She held her peace until we were in my apartment, then perched on the arm of my couch, giving me room to collapse on the cushions beside her. "What shall it be first? Telling me what happened, or a shower and bandages?"

I rubbed my palms up and down my face, then clasped my raw hands in front of me. I couldn't tell her the whole thing, so I started with Laura being caught with contraband and assigned a work detail. About the first attack. Luna went very still. I explained about Laura's training, and my sister's one response was a quiet, "good." Then, I told her about the "real-world test" and how Laura had blamed me, then how she had walked away. "...So I went to the gym," I finished, staring at the ceiling, waiting for Luna's rebuff.

Instead, she slid down to sit beside me, her hand sliding into mine. Her tone was soft and disappointed. "Oh, Rellie... What have you done?"

"I don't know... It's similar to what we do with green men. I just didn't orchestrate someone attacking her like I would with them. It just happened. She doesn't see how competent she is. She learns so quickly, but... Everything's gone so wrong." My gaze lifted from the floor to meet hers.

"Rellie, something like that..." She bit her lip, looking around the room as though the words might reveal themselves on my walls. "She trusted you to protect her... Yes, you did well to train her to fight for herself, but... to do what you did..."

"Is a horrible thing to have done, I know." My head sank to my hands, hiding my face from her knowing gaze. Luna knew more about hurt and betrayal than anyone ever should. A fact that sickened me. "What can I do now, Luna? How do I fix this? I still have to oversee her work-detail. How do I get her to trust me again?"

Silence hung between us like fog. Several minutes passed before I looked at my sister, whose gaze was fixed on something across the room. Her eyes darted side to side, almost unseeing. When she finally met my gaze, her sad smile confirmed my fears.

"Rellie," she said softly, "you couldn't fix me. You can't fix this. Only time and patience might mend the rift." She rested her cheek on my shoulder. "You know how long it took me to find myself again after..." She rose abruptly and crossed to the dining table. "Forgiveness takes time. Trust, once you've broken it, is much harder to earn. Letting go... Well, that takes longer."

My gaze dropped to search the grains in the wooden floor, hoping to divine some answer from their abstract lines.

Luna's hand on my shoulder pulled me from my morose thoughts. "Would you like me to talk with her?"

My head snapped up, hope blooming in my chest. "Would you?"

"Yes." A small smile flickered. "I'll introduce myself, especially since I wanted to anyway, but I won't be speaking to her on your behalf."

It was worth a try. Father used to say, *Tourelle, you miss a hundred percent of the shots you don't take.*

He was right.

Whether or not this fixed things between Laura and me, I had a hunch that Laura and Luna would be good for each other. If I had no hope of rebuilding my friendship with her, at least she could have Luna.

14

Any individual in a position of indentured servitude on a military compound must receive authorization from the officer in charge of their sentence before being released from their daily duties for any reason, including instances of injury, illness, or any other circumstance.
~Military Code 18640/Amendment 688:A

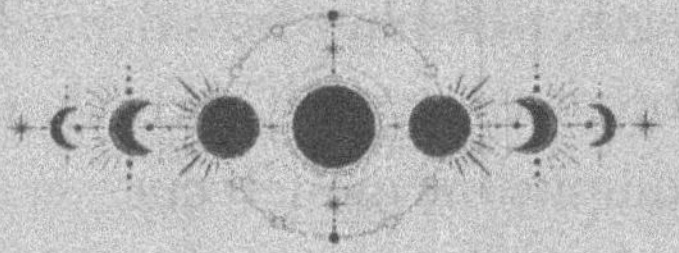

ELAURA

My alarm clock pulled me from my usual nightmares at the usual time, as if last night hadn't happened. I'd demanded he leave me be, but he was at my door like always, right when I opened it to leave for my assignment.

"Morning," he said.

I simply nodded and locked my door. We set off down the hall, and the weight of last night's events pressed in on me.

Silence swelled during the entire thirteen-floor journey in the lift. What was there to say?

When we exited into the lobby, I waved a greeting to the unfamiliar Sergeant at the front desk.

I chanced a glance up at Tourelle in the dim morning light. His expression was tight and measured. Not a hint of emotion betrayed his image of a model soldier. Half a block before the mess hall, he wished me a good day and left me to walk the last stretch on my own. Perhaps it was just as well.

The morning meal passed in a rush, with little out of the ordinary, if one didn't count the hushed whispers as I passed. I had still-blooming bruises around my neck and arms. That was enough to talk about, though I imagined the events of the night before had spread. One or two men stopped me to apologize on behalf of the decent men on base, confirming my suspicions. My heart swelled at the knowledge that good men still served in papa's army. Or what was left of it.

During the lunch rush, though, an audible hush fell over the hall, something I'd not yet heard, not even when General Schmidt dined with the men. Ignoring the pile of soiled dishes, I'd carted in, I poked my head through the kitchen's open door. A slender young woman in a short-sleeved, knee-length, pale-blue dress danced through the hall. Her long, blonde curls bounced against her shoulders, and her dress accented every curve, despite the modest cut.

Every eye followed her. She retrieved a plate and took her place at the end of the line, but every man in line stepped aside to allow her through.

With a bright smile at the awe-struck soldiers, she slid her plate to the head cook, Fredericks, who'd not looked up from stirring the hash. "Good morning, Freddie."

Her melodic voice startled Fredericks, whose spoon clattered to the floor. The metallic clanking echoed in the room's silence.

"Miss Lunette? Wh-what an honor! What brings you here?"

"Well," she leaned forward, her voice dropping to a conspiratorial tone, though I could hear it from my spot inside the kitchen. "I'm here to surprise my brother for his birthday." She leaned back. "That, and I've been missing your bacon cheddar hash. Would you mind?"

The plate in her hands edged closer to the plastic partition dividing them. Fredericks sputtered a moment before retrieving a fresh spoon from a table behind him and scooped a generous helping to her waiting plate. The simple act broke the men's collective trance, and a hushed murmur swept through the room.

As one of the few females on base, I'd come to expect a certain treatment, and couldn't help staring as she walked through the hall without a single whistle or cat-call. I was even a little jealous. She approached a vacant table, and someone from another table pulled out a chair for her. Another man dashed up with a cloth napkin for her lap before yet another scooted her up to the table.

Dumbfounded, I watched soldier after soldier serve her. Each one earned a smile and a gentle thank you.

How on earth had she tamed these reprobates into respectable men with only her presence?

Even as I wondered, though, something within whispered that these men had never mistreated her, else why would she be so gentle and kind with their attentions?

I kept sneaking peeks while I worked on my tasks.

Eventually, the men dispersed one by one, called away by their various duties. Fredericks started dinner preparations, appearing only occasionally to deliver something to the food line. Once the dishes were finished, I returned to the hall to sweep the floor.

The young lady called Lunette caught my eye and waved me over from across the room. Nervous for no real reason, I gripped the handles of the broom and dustpan tightly as I approached.

"Would you mind joining me?"

"I have a job to do, miss," I said.

"Please?" She grinned. "Just for a few minutes. I've heard so much about you, and I have a feeling you make good company."

Though her announcement about having heard of me made me a little anxious, the warmth of her smile made me instantly feel at home, and my concerns fled. No wonder the soldiers were so drawn. Setting down the broom and dustpan, I took the seat across from her.

"I've never seen the men so well behaved," I blurted. "How on Delta's sandy hills did you do that?"

"My brother is an officer, and I'm certain he has something to do with it." She extended her hand. "I'm Lunette, but you can call me Luna if you'd like. All the best people do."

I took her hand, offering a smile in return. "Nice to meet you, Luna. I'm Laura Carpe."

"Lovely to make your acquaintance, Laura." She pushed back in her chair and tilted her head to the side. "So, my brother's busy all day. Would you mind spending the afternoon with me?" Her blue-green eyes sparkled in anticipation.

I cast a glance back at the kitchen doors to make sure Fredericks wasn't glaring at me. "No, but thank you. I... I have to work. To be honest, I shouldn't even be sitting here right now."

For a moment, I thought I was in the clear, but he poked his head around the corner, then disappeared. Quickly as I could, I stood and slid the chair back under the table.

"I can't afford to be in any more trouble than I am already." I offered a contrite smile, hoping her feelings wouldn't be hurt. "Thank you for the invitation, though."

Instead of letting the subject drop, however, she leapt to her feet. "Freddie?"

A clatter rang out, followed by a string of low curses. His balding head reappeared. "Yes, Miss Lunette?"

"May I have a word?"

Fredericks emerged, scrubbing his hands on his apron.

"Freddie," she began, "would you permit me to steal Miss Laura for the day? I bet you don't really need her assistance, but I do. It's my brother's birthday, you know, and I still need to finish his cake."

His brow furrowed. "I'm sorry, miss. If it were my call to make, I'd let you have her the whole week, but it's out of my control. I'd have to get permission."

She frowned a little at that. "Oh, I forgot."

He swallowed hard, looking back at me, his eyes searching mine in what I imagined to be a silent plea for my help. A half-hearted shrug was all I offered. Fredericks sighed. "If it were up to me, of course I would say yes, but—"

Luna squealed. "Oh, thank you, Freddie! I'll be right back!"

She pivoted on her heels and dashed from the hall.

Fredericks retrieved my dustpan and broom and thrust them into my hands. "Better get as much done as you can. You don't mess with Miss Lunette when she has her mind set on something."

Indeed, it was barely twenty-five minutes before she returned and pressed a piece of paper into Fredericks's hands, then skipped to my side, took me by the arm, and pulled me from the building. My broom sat forgotten in our haste.

Once outside, I filled my lungs with the crisp, clean fall air. Even though the temporary respite neither negated the terms of my imprisonment nor shortened my sentence, I couldn't deny that it felt good to be free of the mess hall during daylight hours.

"What now?" I asked.

Luna arched her brow. "Surely you heard what I told Freddie? It's my brother's birthday."

I blinked blankly.

"My apologies. I have assumed too much again. My brother keeps telling me not to, but..." She shook her head. "Mostly, I'd like to get to know you, but I *do* have a cake to bake before long." She slid her arm back through mine and strode forward. "So, how long have you been working for Freddie? You weren't here last I visited, though I'll admit it has been longer than it should've been."

Having someone want to spend time with me felt wonderful. "A few months now. General Schmidt sentenced me to eighteen months of service in the mess hall."

Luna grimaced.

"No, it really is better than what it could have been."

Her eyes grew a size or two. "Really? Schmidt, was it? My brother told me about him. He's not very... Well, I'm so glad you didn't face the firing squad. Although, I have to wonder if that old cad had ulterior motives."

My step faltered a moment.

"Don't worry," she assured me, "if he hasn't made a move yet, it's likely that his men have frustrated his motives. There are still some good men under his command. They just try not to call attention to themselves if they don't have to."

I nodded, hoping to all things holy that she was right, but for the first time since I'd run away from Victor and Matea, I felt I found someone I could trust. Not with everything, of course, but Luna felt like a kindred spirit. Even in Atha I had felt alone. No one was really my friend, in part because friendship wasn't worth the risk.

We walked on in a comfortable silence until I asked, "How often do you visit your brother?"

She hummed a moment before speaking. "Oh, every few months. His apartment has an extra room for me. I stay longer if I have a social engagement to escape, and this time, it's a doozy."

"At least you have social engagements," I said with a grin, motioning to my drab uniform.

"I wouldn't wish these on anyone. I'm afraid I stayed away longer than usual this time. Though, when my brother's intended complained,

I told her I had some work to finish up." She smiled at me. "It's true, but it's a convenient excuse, don't you think?"

"I'd say so. What kind of work do you do?"

Her cheeks pinked a little, and she ducked her head. "I run a charitable organization that looks after the troubled. It took a little more finagling than usual."

A charity. And here I assumed she had a job, if not like mine, then of more importance.

"Are you any good with baking, Laura?" she asked, yanking my thoughts back from whatever unflattering comparison I was ready to draw.

The question caught me off guard and threw my thoughts into turmoil. I'd never baked with Anna, and though Matea had tried getting me to help, I never had.

"Um... maybe? I was friends with a baker a long time ago." I tried to keep my voice even at the painful and powerful memory and achieved moderate success. "Mostly, I just ate the frosting while she worked."

She giggled. "I'm afraid I use pre-made frosting from a can, so it's nothing special." She nudged me with a wicked smile. "But I have a spare canister just for us to enjoy after we finish the cake."

For the first time in ages, I found myself giggling. "That sounds perfect."

She led me to a building near the gym, this one without a desk attendant to greet us, like I'd grown accustomed to. Riding the lift to the third floor, I followed her to apartment 3B. When she opened the door, it looked as simple and nondescript as the rest of the base. The sitting area had a couch and a chair with a bookcase where most homes would have an entertainment screen. There was a small stack of books beside the sofa's arm, their curled corners identifying them as the most loved.

The kitchenette and table surprised me. I'd assumed that everyone on this base ate at the mess hall. The simple furnishings gave the feeling that I might like her brother if I were to meet him. A bookshelf adorned the wall where most would have an entertainment screen. The books were a familiar and welcome window into his interests. I wanted more than anything to explore this entire little apartment, especially the three closed doors along the wall, but the knowledge that this was an unfamiliar man's private space stilled me.

"Is this your brother's apartment?" I wondered aloud, trying hard not to marvel at the sheer amount of space compared to my small bunk.

"He's an officer, so his place is roomier than most. I stay here whenever I visit." She waved me over to the table where she'd begun pulling ingredients out of the mini fridge. Once satisfied, she pulled a pair of aprons from a nearby cupboard and offered me the simple black one. "It's a nice place to hide away from certain social engagements."

"So… These social engagements. Are they really that bad? I used to dream of being able to go to such functions." Pressing my lips together, I stopped before careless words betrayed me. I'd already said too much.

She glanced up at me while tying her apron. "Only when they're with the princess. My father is a Grand Duke and my brother a Marquiss. Though, to be fair, he doesn't care much about society. He much prefers the company of the military." She bent into a cupboard, pulled out mixing bowls and stirring utensils before she straightened. "He and papa don't see eye to eye very often." She set out a few more ingredients and rubbed her hands absentmindedly on her apron. "I think I have it all." She said, more to herself than to me.

I sat baffled at the hand that fate had dealt me. For years I had wished to meet others my age in the polite society I'd heard about, and here I was, a guest of a grand duke's daughter and no longer a princess in the eyes of my people. Well… I might've been, if anyone realized I lived.

"You get invited to spend time with the princess? I… I heard she was rather pretty." I'd only ever seen her through the peephole in the throne room when she and great uncle Grakus would visit. She'd always been so poised and well-dressed each time I saw her. More than once I'd pretended to be her when James and I played make believe.

She passed a couple eggs for me to crack, while she poured flour, sugar, and a few other powders I wasn't familiar with into a separate bowl and began whisking. "I suppose you could say she's pretty. She has a rather handsome face, but I don't much care for her company. I look for any excuse I can to avoid or shorten my visits with her."

The more she mixed the powders in the bowl, the more that floated into the air before me. I struggled to pay attention to what she was saying as I watched crystals of sugar and flour dance a ballet in the light before me. In a moment, I was back in the palace kitchen with Anna while she baked all of my favorite things. Things I'd not had the heart to eat since that horrible day. Luna tapped her whisk on the side of the bowl, ripping me from the scene which had overtaken my mind. Disoriented, I turned my attention back to my new friend, who seemed confused by my sudden preoccupation.

"Laura, are you alright?"

My breathing sped as my mind made comparison after comparison between the two. I stepped away, rubbing my hands on my pants, unable to rid the feeling of something caked on my palms, despite their being clean. "I... I..." I fumbled, unsure of what words even lie in my comprehension.

"Oh dear, you're white as a ghost! Here! Let's sit you down on the sofa!" Her project forgotten, she took me by the arms and steered me to the living area, planting me on a cushion close to the pile of books I'd eyed on my way in. "Sit right here and collect yourself a moment. Alright?" She watched me for a solid minute before going back to making the cake.

To calm myself, I pulled a book from the stack at my side and thumbed through the pages. I didn't see the words, but the paper on my fingertips slowed my heartbeat. Something about the pages of a well-loved book took me home to the little cottage in Atha, with Victor by my side. Pausing on a random page, I reached for my mother's locket, clinging to memories of lullabies she sang to calm me. Next I knew, Lunette was by my side.

"Are we feeling better now?" She touched my shoulder, watching me closely. Before I could answer, her attention shifted to the necklace in my hand. "Are you wearing a necklace? Oh, I love jewelry! May I see?"

The question caught me unaware. I'd scarcely realized I'd had it out before she spoke. I glanced down at my fingers curled around the locket like a bird protecting its chicks from the rain. Was it safe for her to see? Would she recognize it? If I refused, would that raise more alarm? So many questions swirled through my mind with nary an answer beyond a cautious chance. Perhaps it would be alright to show her.

Slow as a sloth, I opened my fingers, revealing the jeweled locket. Lunette crouched closer, drinking in its beauty.

"Oh, my stars! Wherever did you get such an exquisite piece of art?" she marveled, sliding a finger across the beveled edge. "I've seen nothing quite its equal. And I see a great deal of jewelry."

I bit my lip, pausing a moment for the courage to speak aloud the truth I'd wanted to bury. To deny its existence.

"It was my mother's," I confessed. My voice scarcely crept above a whisper, hating how the words felt on my tongue. If Lunette had never seen its equal, she must not know my mother. I couldn't remember a time she hadn't worn it. "I don't remember giving it to her, but I was really little when we did. She never took it off..." My voice died out, too thick with emotion to find the right words. Memories of Mama showing the necklace off to friends and new staff danced through my mind. As much as I wanted to remember her, losing myself in memories with someone I'd just met was dangerous; I might slip and say the wrong thing. No matter how many years divided us, I would not allow her death to be in vain. Or any of the others I'd lost.

"How long ago did you lose her?" I met Luna's soft eyes, my mouth falling open. I'd not told her she was dead. How could she know? The corners of her mouth pulled up in a sad smile. "I know what it's like..." she admitted, holding up her right hand where a beautiful diamond ring adorned her index finger. "I wear my mother's jewelry, too."

Then I understood how she'd read me so well. Another reminder that I was not the only one to have lost someone dear. My teeth drug across my lower lip for a long moment.

"It's been around six years..." I choke out, my voice low. She stroked my shoulder, my sleeve bunching under her palm.

"Your father must love you a great deal to give you such a precious piece of her."

I looked away, my fingers curling back around the locket. "I lost them both the same day. They... They're all gone." I left it there, my voice too thick to say anymore. For better or worse, the truth was out. Time had yet to ease the gaping hole in my chest. Speaking about them made it too real. If I didn't say it aloud, I could almost convince myself they might still be alive somewhere. Like I could wake from this awful nightmare and run to my mother's arms and weep. Putting verbal words to their loss was akin to a public memorial. A eulogy sealing the crematory ink to their memorial card.

"I'm so sorry," she began. "My mother passed away when I was little. I don't know how I would have managed it without Rellie or papa by my side. I can't even imagine how horrible that must've been! To lose them all at once. Why, that's just awful! I'm sure it must've been a terrible accident." Her arms were around me so fast, I'd hardly realized what was happening. There was a warmth and a kinship to her embrace that eased a little of the ache. Whatever hesitations I might've had melted away, and the tears I'd held hostage over the years broke free of their dam unrestrained.

The bond of our shared grief created a silent understanding. Holding one-another, grieving together until at last my eyes had dried.

I pulled away with a smile, opening my mouth to speak. The click of the lock stopped me. Being as she was visiting her brother, it was likely that he was back from his assignment. We both turned to see the door open where a tall, crisply dressed soldier stepped through. I couldn't help wondering what kind of man her brother might be, and if he was someone I knew. He kept his eyes turned down to the small side table by the door, where he dropped his keys and deposited his sidearm into the small drawer before he turned to greet us. When he met my eyes, realization slapped me across the face with as much force as any man on this base might. It was the last man on Delta I wanted to see, and here I was in the apartment of Major General Tourelle Breckenridge.

Luna leapt from her seat to greet him with a hug while my jaw fell slack. My thoughts raced at such a speed that I couldn't comprehend more than the color of the emotion flashing through my veins. Red. Pure, unadulterated red. Had this all been a ploy to earn my forgiveness? Trot out the little sister to gain my trust and convince me he wasn't a complete sodding jerk? No!

I shot to my feet, fingernails biting into my palms. "YOU!" I spit, my lip curling. All attention turned to me. Lunette eased away from her brother a step or two, her eyes darting between us. "Did you really think I would forgive you that easily? Send in your little sister with the sob story and all would be well?"

A muscle in his jaw bulged. When he opened his mouth to say something, my hand shot out between us. "No! You don't get to say a word." I snapped, turning away, with my hands pressed to my face. "UGH! How could I have been so stupid? Of course, you'd want me to think I'd found a friend. To think I almost fell for it!" I spun back to them, pointing my finger in their direction. "I don't want to see or speak to either of you right now. Do me a favor and just leave me be."

I allowed myself one last look at Mr. Breckenridge's measured expression and pushed past both of them through the door. My chin trembled and tears flowed freely down my already damp cheeks as I slammed it behind me. I didn't stop till I was safely in the confines of the lift. There I leaned on the railing, willing my hands to stop trembling and the tears to stop flowing. I don't know how many times I rubbed them across my thighs before the lift arrived at the ground floor. I took a deep, quavering breath and freed myself from the vicinity of that monster upstairs.

15

Of the ills which humanity fled when leaving Earth, the Five Councils recognize unregulated possession of weapons to be one of the most grievous sins. Therefore, to protect the citizens of Delta, no civilian shall be in the possession of any firearm.
Any such possession without license shall warrant a one hundred thousand dileren fine, along with a year in prison for each charge.
Any crimes committed with a firearm in possession will receive an immediate life sentence. If the crime involves any loss of life, the convicted will receive an immediate death sentence.
~Colonization Charter 61961948:94

TOURELLE

After Laura left, a disappointment I had not foreseen shot through me. With a deep sigh, I pulled my sister into a hug. "Forgive me, Luna. I should've seen that coming."

"I expected as much, but it would be disingenuous if I said it didn't still hurt just a little." She sniffled and pulled away. "I like her. She's very much your equal, you know."

The oven timer broke through our sullen fog, and Luna dashed to the kitchenette faster than I'd seen her move in ages. Donning the gray oven mitts, she pulled out a pair of round cakes and set them out to cool. She deposited the mitts and apron in a heap atop the kitchen table.

"I'm not giving up," she announced.

"On cake?"

"No." Determination was written on her face, and she placed her hand on her hip. "I like her. I'm determined to make her my friend."

Though Laura's departure had dimmed my evening, I knew Lunette's look well. It would be easier to stop a sandstorm in its tracks than to dissuade her once she set her mind to something.

"Just don't go too far, Luna. Not only do I still have to oversee her indenture, but she's had it rough. Be kind." With a kiss on the top of her head, I retreated to my room to change.

"I *am* kind," she called after me.

I leaned against the door in my room, looking up at the dark ceiling. "That's one way to spend a birthday, I guess."

Allowing myself a few minutes to collect my thoughts, I flipped the light switch, stripped out of my uniform, and donned slacks and a nice shirt. After all, Luna had journeyed to see me on my birthday, so a little effort on my part was the least I could do.

When I emerged, she'd finished frosting the cake and carefully spaced unlit candles around the circumference. The abandoned frosting can, with a protruding spoon, beckoned to me. I snatched it up before it could be thrown out and shoveled a spoonful of icing into my mouth. Luna punched my arm.

"Hey, that's mine!"

I chuckled, which made me choke on the creamy chocolate, and lofted the container high above my head. "Finders keepers, Looney."

Luna leapt for the can but gave up after a few tries. She glowered at me, her arms folded across her chest. "Fine. Keep it, you big bully."

Opening a drawer, I grabbed another spoon and offered it to her. "Share?"

Wordlessly, she snatched the spoon and plunged it into the can.

"I'll let you get away with stealing the icing and calling me Looney today, and today only. That will be your gift this year." She sighed. "Maybe next year I can stay longer."

The thought of next year and my formal betrothal to the princess nagged at me. I refused to burden my sister with that concept, so we just finished the remaining icing. After dinner, we shared the cake, said goodnight, and retreated to our rooms.

I stared up at the darkened ceiling, torn between gratitude for Luna's presence and vague dissatisfaction with how I'd handled talking to Laura. Sleep was patchy, and the following day Luna left to visit Persephone while I was at work.

Over the next week, Laura spoke to me only when necessary, and at the end of her workday, she disappeared the moment we reached C-block. I missed our daily trainings, though nothing would induce me to say as much. The week after, she softened a little around me.. Although she greeted me with a silent smile in the morning, she resumed our light conversations while I escorted her home.

At her three month evaluation, she sat quietly while I interviewed Fredericks, who said she was a good worker: solid, reliable, quick. He also said that the men had stopped ogling and harassing her. I glanced at her, but she had no input on that count.

Weary from a long day, I pulled open the front door of my home, eager to see my two favorite people in the world.

The clicking latch must have announced my arrival, for when I bent down to remove my boots, a squeal from the end of the hallway. I dropped to my knees as my two-year-old son dashed into my waiting arms, bright blue eyes alight with laughter. I stood and launched him into the air, catching him and making him squeal. He wrapped his little arms around my neck, and I kissed his sticky cheek and set him back down.

"We've been waiting for you all day, darling." Her soft voice filled my heart.

I ruffled our son's mess of blond curls, and he darted away after some distraction in another room. His little pigeon-toed stride warmed my heart and pulled a smile onto my face.

And at last, I was alone with Elaura. "And how is my beautiful wife?"

She chuckled, and her playful smile took my breath away. I closed the distance in two strides.

"Oh, you know. Playing till the day is through and counting the moments till next I see you."

I pulled her against me with a speed that made her squeak. She looked up at me with her lip between her teeth. She probably didn't know how often she did that, but I'd found it adorable from the beginning. A strand of mahogany hair fell across her face.

"Tourelle."

I reached up to brush the hair from her brow, my palm lingering on her cheek.

Her hands slid up my chest and clasped around my neck. Her

touch sparked like electricity, and I never wanted to be free of it. My eyes closed, and I leaned forward. My lips found hers. She sucked in a ragged breath, and her fingers threaded through my hair. Lost in the moment's magic and the ambrosia that was her lips, I slid my hands down her back, fiddling with the hem of her shirt.

All at once, the world around us erupted in a blaring high pitch alarm, jarring me into adrenaline-laced panic and utter darkness.

I swung my arm wildly and hit a plastic box. The blaring noise stopped as my alarm clock struck the wall, splintering into shards of plastic and circuits. Throwing the covers aside, I sat on the edge of the bed, my heart racing and my breath coming in uneven gasps.

Slowly, reality broke through my fading panic and confusion. I rubbed my hand over my face.

"What in the name of all things holy was that?" I asked the dark.

It was a good thing Luna had left the day before. The crash of the alarm would have brought her out of a dead sleep and into my room. It was enough to wonder alone what tricks my mind was playing on me. I didn't need my sister's questions.

My fingers fumbled across my nightstand to find my watch. 0335? I dropped the watch and flopped back onto my pillow.

I'd had the same dream since I was fifteen, except the woman and child had always been faceless, even though they always felt familiar. It had always ended just before I kissed the faceless woman. At least it had until now.

I groaned. I needed a shower.

Not two steps from the bed, something bit into the pad of my foot, drawing a string of incoherencies from my mouth. In the dark, I made my way to the wall and slid my hand along the smooth surface blindly until I found the light switch. I winced against the sudden light, which left me blinking to adjust. About ten seconds later, I balanced precariously on my good foot so I could remove whatever had stabbed me.

Of all the rotten luck, that blasted alarm clock had its revenge. Once I had extracted the jagged piece of black plastic, the pain receded, though my foot started bleeding.

Great. Plastic, circuits, and blood. The very things I want to clean later.

At least I didn't have carpeting. I stood on one leg for a moment like a resting bird, pressing in on the wound, hoping to stem the blood-flow.

Why, of all people, was Elaura the one to take the place of the wife in my dream? And *why* was that her name in that dream? I'd gotten so used to addressing her as Laura, since she came here, that I'd nearly forgotten her name was actually Elaura, which suited her so much better.

I hit my head against the wall, but even that didn't make the memory of the dream recede. I couldn't allow my mind to wander like this. Relentlessly, I shoved the longing aside, determined to ensure my family's safety. Deviation was a death sentence, and I wouldn't condemn Luna or our father like that. No, I had to find a way to be at peace with my planned future.

Jaw clenched tightly and careful to avoid any more pieces of the clock, I made my way to the bathroom. I cranked the water to the highest setting, and while it warmed, I returned to my room to pick up the remains of the clock, only then noticing the hole in the wall.

Great.

With all the stray pieces disposed of, I returned to the now steaming bathroom, shed my nightclothes, and slipped into the scalding water, letting it course over my face.

Why had my recurring dream changed? I hadn't been sure of the child's gender until now. I would lean in to kiss "her," and the dream would end.

I wrenched my thoughts back.

Persephone. Remember Persephone. Remember your duty. Protect Father and Lunette.

Maybe I was doomed to be a character in a classic Greek tragedy, forever haunted by what could never be.

The water had cooled by the time I collected my errant thoughts and refocused enough to wash my hair, but, no sooner did I have a lather going, than someone started pounding on my front door.

I startled at the sound, a move that sent suds racing for my eyes. I wiped the soap away and hastily rinsed my hair. The pounding sounded again, then stopped.

Who on Delta would be knocking on my door this early?

The warning about insurgents infiltrating military compounds echoed in my mind, and I set my jaw. Last reports indicated an imitation of an early morning emergency and abducted several officers from the base. It was far to the south, but the Caprician attacks were never isolated to a single region.

I stepped out of the shower and wrapped a towel around my middle. When I reached the door, the pounding sounded again. On impulse, I pulled my sidearm from the side-table drawer and loaded it. Ready to deal with whatever waited in the hall, I opened the door.

16

Any female seeking entry into King Grakus's army must first have an officer in good standing vouch for her ability and sponsor her entry into basic training. As this officer has staked his name and career in her favor, he shall sign off on her dismissal from basic training at such a time as she is determined unfit for service to King Grakus and his successors. Proof of disqualification may be requested and stay dismissal until such a time as the female's inability to serve within the ranks shall be confirmed. This provision shall guarantee that all females shall receive a fair opportunity for service to the King.
~Military code 1984 addendum A23

ELAURA

The longer I spent on the base, the more my resolve steeled. Something needed to be done for my people. It was my duty to take the throne back in the name of my slain family.

The citizens of Delta deserved better than the world they had: the repressive laws, the death penalties for minor infractions, the fear. I would avenge Papa, Mama, James, Greggie, and all the many other lives Grakus had snuffed in the name of power.

The question was then, how could I accomplish such an exchange of power? Was it incumbent upon me to eliminate him, as he had destroyed my family? I certainly couldn't appeal in a court of law. But assassination?

It seemed the only way.

If it was, I had to get close enough to retire Grakus and his corrupt regime, and I needed weapons, but the law restricted possession of firearms to the military, under penalty of death. I couldn't see any way to remove Grakus except by force, and it was unlikely that a bow and arrow would get close enough to make a difference, even if I could become proficient enough. Using a sword was even more unlikely.

The questions cycled endlessly through my mind—while washing dishes, training with Tourelle, doing my own laundry—and there was no one with whom I could discuss them. Consulting Victor and Matea by mail would be beyond foolish. Doing so would probably line the three of us up at a firing squad, if we were that lucky, and besides, they wouldn't understand the necessity. Matea would cry, and Victor would counsel me to set revenge aside. This wasn't about revenge, though. It was about duty.

I certainly couldn't discuss this with Tourelle, who was one of the king's officers. Even though I knew he was trustworthy, he was also loyal to Grakus.

After months of deliberation, I couldn't tell precisely when the thought solidified in my consciousness: *if I joined the military and worked my way through the ranks, I would be armed.*

It was the only way, but although the law allowed for women to join Grakus's army, it would be incredibly difficult. I was the only woman on base, unless family visited.

And then, I realized how to accomplish my goal.

I was talking with Otto, and he mentioned how much he admired Tourelle for the way he trained and tested his recruits. He had a tendency to focus more on the real-world applications over the technical classroom learning, which explained my assessment. The men in his service often performed better in combat than their counterparts. That was my way in.

I had to ask Tourelle for a favor, and I couldn't wait any longer. Training would be long and hard, and I only had a few months of my sentence left. If I didn't make it into the military by the time my assignment was over, I would have nowhere to go except back to Atha.

And so, the next morning I woke hours before I needed to and dressed for the day. Otto was off duty, and the young man on night shift had fallen asleep, so no one saw me slip out of the building into the early morning darkness.

I made my way to Tourelle's apartment through the empty streets, and since no desk attendant was there to ask what I was doing, I simply walked to the lift with confidence. My stomach rose and fell with gravity as the lift brought me to the third floor. For several minutes, I stood before 3B, summoning my courage.

Then, I knocked.

He didn't answer, so I knocked again.

And again.

I bit my lip. Perhaps he hadn't woken yet. Or had left already. I knew he rose early for PT, but just how early was early? Or... what if I had the number wrong?

I'd nearly resolved to go back, maybe ask him when he arrived to take me to the kitchens, when the handle rattled. I mustered the best apologetic smile I could.

The door pulled back, revealing the business end of a firearm.

My mouth went dry.

The dim lighting of the hallway contrasted with the bright light from within, accenting the gun's menace. My hands flew up in surrender on sheer instinct.

Tourelle's face appeared above the muzzle, his eyes widening when they met mine. He lowered the gun. "E—Laura? What are you doing here?"

It took a moment to compose my words. "May I come in? I have something I need to ask you."

He hesitated half a breath before nodding and opening the door all the way. I strode right to his couch where a stack of books still lay. The opening of a drawer pulled my attention back to Tourelle, who was returning his firearm to the side table.

Then I noticed his bare shoulders and the towel around his waist. Heat rushed through my cheeks, but as if it had a will of its own, my gaze roamed the bare skin of his back. Well-defined muscle stretched taut across his shoulders, and his wet hair sent staggered droplets of water down his neck and spine. He turned to face me with arms crossed over his chest. Water glistened in the light, holding my attention like a trance.

He cleared his throat, and frustration laced his tone when he spoke. "What is so important it couldn't wait another hour?"

Now my ears burned. Was there any part of my face that wasn't red?

"I, I need a... favor. I..." My gaze followed a lone drop as it slid between the muscles of his chest. Good heavens, had the temperature in the room gone up? My eyes slammed shut, and I turned around, not wanting to dig a deeper pit than I already had. "I'm sorry. Could... could you put some clothes on? I can wait a few minutes."

"Not my fault you interrupted my shower."

Without thinking, I stole a glance back over my shoulder as he pulled a hand through his hair. Beads of water launched from the wet strands, and a chuckle rumbled through him. I returned my attention to the books on the side table.

His footsteps crossed the room. "Hang tight. I'll be just a minute."

My muscles remained taut until a door clicked, signaling his retreat. I sank into the nearest seat and hit my forehead with my fist, but that didn't banish the image of him standing there, half-naked.

Focus, Elaura. Focus! You're here to ask a favor, not fantasize about his bare chest.

Seconds ticked past until Tourelle emerged from his room wearing a beige short-sleeve shirt and gray sweatpants. He stood before me, his arms folded across his chest and his eyebrows raised.

"Alright Elaura, what is so shower-haltingly important that it couldn't wait till I come to escort you to detail?"

I tensed when he called me Elaura. Searching his eyes didn't tell me why, and I forced myself to set the worry aside. The favor I came to ask was more important, so I tried to will the fire raging in my cheeks to cool. Being in someone's debt bothered me, and Tourelle had already done so much for me. He had kept my given name to himself, hadn't outed my crimes to his superiors, had taught me to fight and taken care of my attackers. Concerned that those steel-blue eyes would ruin my resolve, I kept my gaze on the floor and wrung my hands in my lap.

"I... I was wondering what it would take to join you..."

His chuckle piqued my interest. Against my better judgment, I glanced up.

"You want to join me where? My shower? That's a bit forward." He arched his brows, though an odd smile touched his lips. "I'm sorry, but that option isn't available."

Embarrassment and a hint of anger flared. I launched to my full height, looked straight into his eyes, and announced. "I'd like to join the Army."

There. I'd done it.

That statement sobered him, but he only said, "Is that so? I thought you were eager to free yourself from this place?"

"I want to contribute to something bigger. Make a difference in the world." I bit my lip, hoping my words didn't sound like the lie they were. After all, they were true, at least from one perspective. "The best place to do that is here, serving on this base."

He turned to pace back and forth across the room, and his silence felt akin to a refusal.

This had to work. I lifted my chin and squared my shoulders. "I'm not asking for charity, sir. I fully intend to earn my place among the ranks."

Tourelle came to a stop before me, his hands on his hips. "You'd have to pass basic training."

"I know," I said. "That's one of the reasons I came to you."

He rubbed his hand over his mouth absently, and his eyes swept the room before finding me again. "If I give you my approval to enlist—if that's really what you want—you need to manage your expectations. How many women have you seen working on this base besides yourself?"

"None," I admitted.

He nodded. "There are no women on this base because there are almost none among the ranks. Across Delta there are, perhaps, three. The few that try to join fail basic training."

I couldn't lose this opportunity. Not if my plans were to succeed. My voice came out just above a whisper. "All of them?"

"Not a single woman has made it through basic in the past six years, but if you make it through, and are assigned a post, it's a great deal harder to get dismissed." He studied me. "And that's only if you get that far."

I swallowed, unsure of what truths my face might have told on my behalf.

He continued, "For a young woman like yourself, there will be a heavier workload than your male counterparts. Your instructors will look for any reason to dismiss you. Any minuscule infraction, whether real or imagined."

Maybe I was wrong. Could I handle it after all? Still, I said, "If they need your signature for my admittance, wouldn't they also need it for my dismissal?"

Tourelle rubbed his chin a moment or two, then turned abruptly and strode into the kitchen. I waited silently while he set a pan atop the stove.

"I think better on a full stomach." He said, keeping his eyes on his work. "You hungry?"

I didn't answer right away, but my stomach replied with a low gurgle.

He smiled as he pulled eggs and a package of bacon from the fridge. "That's a yes, then?"

"Um.... Sure. Can I help?"

He nodded toward a shelf above the sink while sliding bacon into the pan. "Grab a couple of plates and utensils from the drawer on the right and set the table. I've got the rest in hand."

I wasted little time following his instructions as Tourelle finished cooking and, when my simple task was finished, took a seat at the table. He finished and portioned the food between the two plates before depositing the pan into the sink. As soon as he'd taken his seat, he folded his arms and bowed his head, mumbled a prayer over his meal before shoveling food into his mouth. I followed suit.

After only one bite, I realized why I'd never seen him in the mess hall. His cooking far surpassed anything served on base. The savory eggs and bacon combined with the sweet maple sauce made a symphony for my senses. If I could cook this well, I'd avoid the food at the mess hall, too. My restraint crumbled, and I dove in with abandon.

The scraping of forks across porcelain filled the kitchenette. When most of his food was gone, Tourelle pointed his fork at me. "You're right... I do have to sign off on the dismissal of every cadet I recommend." He took another bite before continuing. "If I agree to help you, it isn't a guarantee that you will pass. It won't make your workload lighter either. You do understand that, right?"

I swallowed a mouthful and nodded. "I don't need easy. I just need possible. I want a realistic ability to determine whether I will succeed or fail. If you could bar dismissal for reasons that have nothing to do with performance, I would be grateful."

He chewed methodically before responding. "If I help you and you can't meet the performance requirements, you'll accept dismissal? No questions asked?"

"Of course."

"I'm probably going to regret this... but, alright. I'll deny any frivolous complaints while you're there. You'll succeed or fail by virtue of your merit alone."

I nearly dropped the fork I'd just lifted. Had he really said what I thought he had? I had to be sure. "You'll really do it? Help me, that is?"

He nodded.

"Thank you!" Without thinking, I leapt from my seat and flung my arms around him.

He gave my back an awkward pat, and my cheeks heated again.

I backed away faster than a cat from the water's edge and sputtered, "I... I'm so sorry... I... should be going."

"I'll be by in a while to escort you to the mess hall?"

"No. No thank you. I'll be fine."

Why did I have to hug him?

Spinning on my heel, I darted from his apartment. From him. I skipped the lift, opting for the stairs. Once free, I raced to the streets.

I was one step closer to taking back the kingdom and avenging the fallen who'd been so savagely cut down that day. My plan was in motion. James. Mama, Pappa, and Greggie would have justice soon.

17

All recruits shall be paired in twos upon admittance to Basic Training. In the event that one man is left without a buddy, he shall be added to an established pair. The three shall be held to the same rules as partnered counterparts. At no time are they permitted to separate while on base. No recruit shall go anywhere without his appointed buddy. Any fault of one is the fault of the other. They will be tested together, sleep together and eat together.
~Military Code 351668

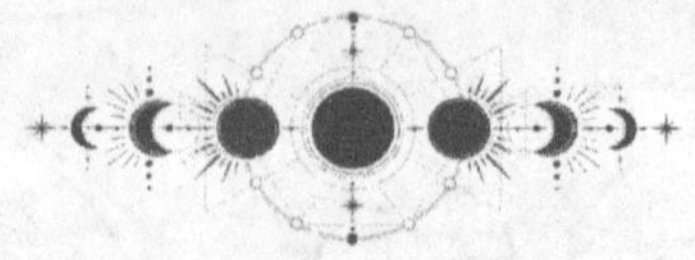

ELAURA

In the months leading up to my departure for basic training, I trained hard. When I arrived, however, even Tourelle's training hadn't adequately prepared me for what I encountered.

The first day, I sat with the men, waiting for some unannounced event to take place. Not knowing when, where, what, or how was draining. The moment the clock struck 1945, a large man in a drill sergeant's uniform appeared and directed us into a single file line with strict instructions to keep our eyes forward at all costs. We all scrambled to our feet and marched outside. After a brief explanation of how to stand at attention, the sergeant ordered us onto a hover-bus and told us to sit with our faces between our knees. I thought I heard him leave, though I didn't dare look.

The bus began the twenty-minute journey to what would be our home for the next eight weeks. Hissing brakes announced our arrival, and another sergeant boarded, shouting to get off his bus and line up single file.

More sergeants shouted instructions while a man walked down the line with a marker, writing numbers on our left shoulders. Another followed him and handed us each a small, numbered box with instructions to deposit all personal effects not allowed on base within. Anything that did not fit would be incinerated with the trash. Thanks to Tourelle's warning, all I had on me was a pack of gum, which I could afford to lose. I'd left all of my personal effects, especially my mother's locket, sealed in a box with Tourelle. After a few minutes, someone collected the boxes and shoved an empty, oversized duffle bags into our hands.

They directed us into a large warehouse and down an assembly line, where we received bedding, toiletries, numbered uniform tees, sweats, socks and shoes. Sergeants barked at us all the way to our barracks, which was a large room with bunkbeds protruding from the walls and lockers staggered at regular intervals. We were to report to our numbered racks, strip out of our civilian clothing, which was to be incinerated, and dress in our new uniforms.

While the other recruits promptly stripped down to their undergarments and shouted, "Yes, sir," I hesitated. After those episodes in front of that bar, the idea of stripping in front of the men was nauseating. That pause brought down the wrath of a nearby sergeant, who bellowed that I was to obey at once.

I cringed away, but shouted back, "Yes, sir!"

I buried my discomfort and stripped down to my undergarments before yanking on the short-sleeve shirt with my number printed on the back and the jogging pants with a matching number printed down the left leg. I'd prepared myself for cat calls or snide remarks about undressing in a room full of men, but with the sergeants' shouts, the other recruits were scrambling to obey.

I stood at attention at the end of my assigned bunk, which the sergeants called racks, until everyone had finished. They bellowed the command to go outside, urging us to move our sorry behinds and speed up.

Even though it was already late, they lined us up, assigned our battle buddies, and gave instructions on decorum, procedure, and the laws surrounding our service. I expected my buddy to at least wince when he got me, but he kept his expression free of thought. We answered any directions or insults with a loud and resolute, "Yes, sir!" or, "No, sir!" We did push-ups and sit-ups, followed by an extended amount of time spent in what they called "forward leaning rest." We were nothing, only a speck of dust on the ground.

Time dragged on, and my muscles quivered as if the very fibers were unraveling. When I thought I could bear no more, they made us run. When anyone tripped or fell behind, the company would do twenty push-ups if no one came forward to assist. Likewise, if someone did in fact assist the fallen man, both would have to do twenty for holding up the company, and the rest of us waited in leaning rest. I felt certain their goal was to make us each vomit.

"Your individuality," the closest sergeant yelled, "died the moment you boarded that bus. You'll only be worth spit on the ground when you're a team—the type of team His Majesty the King expects!"

Any regret I had, the sense of inadequacy to meet this challenge, the realization that Tourelle's training had barely prepared me for this, faded to nothing. The words "His Majesty the King" had me clenching my teeth.

We ran until 0000, at which time they led us to a small mess hall and fed us a meager meal. Our sergeants continued to yell while we ate. My arms and legs felt ready to fall off, but Tourelle's words echoed in my mind: "Show no weakness. Don't give up. Keep going. Even if you're ready to crumble, keep moving."

They allotted only twenty minutes for everyone to get and finish their dinner before taking us to a large gymnasium for even more exercise. While we ran, climbed, and did more pushups, the surrounding men left for another room, returning with their hair cut almost to their scalps. Thankfully, no one touched my hair.

Like before, we only had twenty minutes for our breakfast. Our intake processing continued the moment we left the mess, and after a full thirty-six hours of PT tests, forms, exams, and endless push-ups. At long last, our company returned to the barracks for sleep.

Everyone was grateful, except my battle buddy and I. He and I were the lucky ones chosen to stand watch while everyone else slept. A couple of men chuckled at our plight, but sleep claimed them the moment their heads touched the pillow. My 'buddy' and I took to pacing while we cradled the watch sticks, weariness dripping from our shoulders.

On the last stroke of the second hour, the sergeants strode through the door, snatched our sticks and began beating them on metal trash cans and the shaking of racks to wake the company.

This began a schedule of rising before the moons finished their descent below the horizon for PT, followed by morning chow. We had another round of training before they fed us again. Recruits who kept their food down between meals were the fortunate ones. A variety of specialty classes filled the afternoon before another workout and our evening chow. Infantry, medic, mechanic, administrative, and field ops, to name a few.

As I acclimated to my training in administrative management, I became acquainted with my battle buddy, a buoyant fellow close to my height. His name was David Wilhelm. A popular man, David was well known in the company for his good-natured sense of humor. More than once he'd condemned me to extra push-ups when his little jokes reached the sergeants.

Sometimes, I felt bad for him. Being the buddy of the only woman on base was a stark disadvantage, but he shared in the heavier workload we received without complaint. The sergeants seemed determined to make me collapse under a workload even heavier than that of the average recruit's.

Despite everything, it quickly became apparent how secretly thoughtful David was. He opted to shower late in the evening and would stand watch outside the door so I could have the shower space to myself. No one else seemed to care about indecency, and the sergeants made no accommodations for a woman on a man's base.

At the end of the first week, we finally had some downtime, which the drill sergeants called "liberty." Whatever they called it, the freedom from their oppressive presence and noise was an absolute respite. After attending religious services on base, I sat in my rack, doodling in my little notepad.

I'd tried several times to get the lines of the Caprice family crest right and had erased my attempts enough to question the integrity of the sheet. At last, the lines of the symbols came together. I had managed something resembling an eagle, its head turned, wings spread wide, and a shield guarding its breast. Rough as it was, it brought back memories of my father teaching me about the symbolism behind our family crest.

I was so engrossed in the drawing that I lost track of the room around me.

"You know, drawing stuff like that in plain view is pretty dangerous."

David's voice startled me. I dropped the pencil and glanced up. He watched me, his expression measured and unreadable. A look between him and my pad left me even more confused.

"How is a doodle dangerous?" I set the pad down on my bed. "Is it going to jump off the page and bite me?"

"A doodle that bad just might." A dark look crossed his face, and his brows knitted together. He pressed a finger to his lips, snatched up my drawing pad and waved for me to follow him, then he said loudly, "I gotta get my sheets from the laundry before church services. If we hurry, we can make it."

Confused, I followed David out of the barracks and crossed the compound toward the laundry building. Once inside, he steered me toward a linen closet next to one of the large machines.

The door clicked shut, and he lifted my pad between us. "This 'doodle' of yours is a symbol of the Caprician army," he snapped. "It could get us both killed!"

My eyes widened.

"Our sergeants would see this as an admission of treason."

Confused at his venom, I stumbled back a step. "I'm not drawing anyone's symbol." Before I could stop myself, the damning words had spilled from my lips, "That's my family crest. It's belonged to my family since the founders landed."

I threw my hand over my mouth. I couldn't take them back. Moments stretched for what felt like hours.

"They're all dead..." His voice was barely audible over the loud hum of the machines on the other side of the door. "Everyone there died that day..."

I could scarcely breathe, waiting for the words that would spell my doom.

"Then you—" His eyes snapped back to me, wide with wonder.

"How many…" he breathed, stopping to swallow. "How many survived?"

"Only three—"

My drawing fluttered to the floor where it rested face-down, and his eyes went wide. He closed the space and grabbed me by the shoulders. "Who? Tell me who else survived!"

Shelves pressed into my back. I stared silently into his frenzied eyes before he released me abruptly and crossed back to the door. His right hand rubbed his mouth, and he slid down the door, his head bent between his knees.

When he looked back up, tears swam in his eyes. "There was a bakery intern there. Her name was Anna Whittacre. My older sister." A lone tear slid down his cheek and dropped onto his shirt. "Please … I need to know. Did she make it out?"

His sister. My friend.

The wound in my heart opened again.

I shook my head, and he choked back a sob. His long fingers gripped the sides of his head, while his shoulders shook. At last, he rubbed the tears from his face, wiped his nose, and took a deep breath, then two more. He rose to his feet and straightened his shirt, his gaze finally meeting mine.

"I'm sorry." He pulled out a handkerchief and wiped his face dry. "That wasn't fair. The idea someone made it out… It brought up a lot of feelings I thought I'd buried." Bending down, he retrieved the drawing. "So, you're the legitimate daughter of King Charles Caprice?"

I had no words. I had already betrayed myself, and even though this young man was my Anna's brother, I had already blown my cover. There would be no way to avoid the firing squad, no way to dodge the proverbial bullet.

So I nodded.

His eyes narrowed, and he stepped closer. "Then tell me: what was the name of Anna's boyfriend? Only a Caprice would know."

"James." My chin came up in defiance. "My brother James was dating Anna, even though I begged him not to."

He blew out a breath, then dropped to one knee, his right fist against his heart and his head bowed. "Your majesty."

His obeisance had me at a loss. Unready to be saluted the way my father had been, I pulled him to his feet. "It's okay. You don't need to kneel."

"Majesty." His eyes met mine. "Your people need you. They need to know you're alive. You're the hope for a brighter future."

I studied him. Yes, I could see the similarities to my dear friend Anna, but he was still a stranger. "I don't understand. Your name is Wilhelm, not Whittacre."

A conspiratorial gleam flashed in his hazel eyes. "It's an alias. My given name is Daniel Whittacre, and I'm an undercover agent for the Caprician army. *Your* army. We—"

He turned his head suddenly, as if toward a sound, and when he looked back, his eyes were wide. Without another word, he wrapped his arms around me and pressed his lips to mine.

I pushed against his firm chest, trying with all of my might to shove him away.

The door handle rattled, and the noise of the laundry machines roared through the open door. There was a cough and a muttered, "Sorry to interrupt."

David and I broke apart. A pair of recruits from our company gaped at us. My face ignited in a blaze of embarrassment. David chuckled, which made the whole scene worse.

He eased to the side, and I saw him wink. "No problem, Gibbings. Just wanted to steal a few moments without the sergeants seeing."

Averting his eyes, Gibbings ducked past us and grabbed a small stack of towels, but his buddy just flashed a wide smile and offered a thumbs up. They closed the door, leaving us in silence until their muffled laughter faded away. Then I turned on David. With all of my strength, I punched him in the stomach.

His mouth forming a tight *O*. He sank to his knees, arms wrapped around his middle.

"Who gave you permission to kiss me?" I demanded. "Just because your sister was my friend, doesn't give you any right! You, you, you *jerk!*"

He coughed a moment before bringing his right fist to his heart again. "For—forgive me, majesty. I meant you no harm. I couldn't think of anything else to keep you safe from enemies and their speculation, not in the seconds we had." Contrition in his eyes, he rose to his feet. "It's better to be disciplined for fraternization than executed for treason."

My fury cooled. The thought hadn't occurred to me. "Oh."

"Your people need the rightful heir on the throne. We need *you*. Grakus is a bloodthirsty tyrant, bent on the enslavement of Delta. We are your army, Majesty. We will be your sword with which to smite the serpent's head."

Not only was he on my side, but on the side of all the people of Delta.

He picked up the drawing pad from the floor. "I'll take care of this. You can't ever get caught with anything like this. It's a death sentence."

I nodded.

"We'll have to be careful, but I will do everything I can to help you fly under the radar as long as you're here. I'll be there for you every step of the way." He gave my shoulder a pat as a faint chime sounded beyond the door.

We had a few minutes to report to our respective religious services. He grabbed a set of sheets to keep with his cover story, and neither of us wasted a moment. We made it to our seats in the chapel just moments before the service began. I heard little of the messages spoken while I digested the discussion in the linen closet. Sitting in the pew beside me was my battle buddy and my best friend's brother.

I wasn't here in vain. There was an army standing against Grakus. My people wanted what I did—freedom from the usurper's tyranny— and I wanted them to have the prosperity that my father provided during his reign. For the first time, my plan to assassinate my uncle felt short-sighted. Yes, he deserved to answer for lives lost in the massacre that took my family from me, but if there was a way to dethrone him without the bloodshed, I owed it to my people to try.

18

Any recruit found in possession of Caprician paraphernalia shall face court martial, which will be overseen by the presiding sergeant commander. All power to convict, sentence, and execute shall rest in his hands. The sergeant commander shall stand as a line of defense against Caprician agents infiltrating the military and will act as King Divo Von Grakus's hand. The king himself shall back any decision made by the sergeant commander, who shall be absolved of wrongdoing while acting in this capacity.

~Official Edict 6813: King Grakus

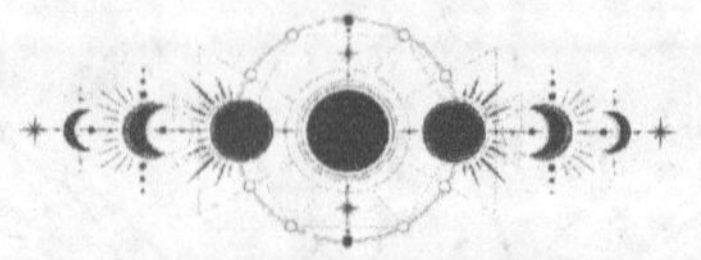

ELAURA

A bull horn's blare broke through the early morning cold, snatching me from sleep's embrace, and in no time, we found ourselves back on the grounds for more training. David remained at my side, but the other men whispered to one another in low tones. I couldn't hear what they said, but with the looks they threw our way, it wasn't hard to guess. I did my best to ignore them and kept my eyes forward.

One sergeant pivoted abruptly. "What is so interesting that y'all can't keep your filthy traps shut?"

After a few minutes, one man stepped forward, his hands clasped behind his back and a smirk on his face. "Drill Sergeant!" he shouted. "We were debating if Carpe is a good kisser or not. Sir!"

My fingernails pressed into my palm, and I chanced a glance at David. He gave me a quick shake of the head and returned his gaze forward. Taking a deep breath to keep my anger in check, I followed suit. From the corner of my eye, I watched the sergeant stalk up to the outspoken recruit.

"You think she'd want to kiss you, you disgusting parasite? Your mama couldn't contain her own vomit long enough to kiss your sorry face!" The sergeant turned and pointed at me. "Carpe! Here! Now!"

I marched to the sergeant's side. "Yes, Drill Sergeant!"

"Carpe, this worm wants a kiss. Let him have it."

The recruit leaned his cleft chin forward. For a fraction of a second, anger shot through me, but it only took one look at the wicked gleam in the drill sergeant's eyes to understand what he meant.

"Yes, sir!" I shouted back.

I turned to the waiting recruit and launched my fist into his waiting face. Tourelle would have been proud. The recruit stumbled, tripped over a rock, and landed on his backside with a thump. A stunned silence fell over the recruits while the fallen man's battle buddy helped him up. I didn't wait for the sergeant's orders, but returned to my assigned space and stood at attention like the rest of the company.

"Anyone else want a kiss? We could all share the love or get back to work. You disgusting pack of ingrates!" another sergeant shouted.

The company's response echoed off the buildings, and the morning's routine resumed. I couldn't be sure, but I could have sworn I noticed the sergeants smirking as they sent us off to breakfast.

After our meal, though, something felt off. There was a strain in the barked commands. I dismissed the thought, attributing it to my imagination, but when we left the mess, they ran us to the central courtyard, where every base sergeant stood in a straight line before the central building opposite us. They watched as each member of the company fell into place, standing at attention. Confusion echoed across every face, except for David's. He offered me a quick, reassuring smile, then fixed his gaze forward toward the central building.

When all was still, the sergeant commander emerged from the building, pulling someone behind him. My stomach twisted as the sergeant commander threw the young recruit who'd gone missing from our company, to the ground in the no-man's-land between the sergeants and our company. Hodges, the recruit from two beds over. His right eye was swollen shut, his hands were bound before him, and dark bruises shone where tears in his shirt exposed his skin.

A pregnant silence hung in the air while the dust settled around him.

"It would seem that we have a Caprician in our midst." The sergeant commander's strident tones echoed off the buildings while he paced back and forth before the assembled men. His voice grew louder with each word. "Someone joined these ranks with the sole purpose of treason against the King of Delta. *Our King!*"

A chill ran down my spine. Did he know who I was?

They'd clearly beaten the poor recruit on the ground for information, and his information must have led them to a traitor, but to whom? Had he seen me drawing my family crest? I hadn't thought to hide it until David pulled me out of the barracks.

"We found this in one of your racks." The sergeant commander pulled a piece of paper from his pocket and held it high.

My blood froze. *My drawing.* Where did they find it? How on Delta did this poor recruit get caught up in it all?

The sergeant commander continued, "This is proof that one of you is the enemy."

The recruit on the ground struggled to his feet, despite the rope binding his hands.

I stole a glance at David, who stared straight ahead. A reminder that I should do the same. Biting my lower lip, I fixed my gaze forward as well.

Hodges tried to straighten, but the sergeant commander kicked him behind the knees, knocking him back to the ground. Before Hodges could get back on his knees, the sergeant commander pulled his sidearm from his belt and shot Hodges in the back of the head.

Time stood still as Hodges dropped to the flagstones.

My own cry was swallowed by a chorus of horrified gasps and shouts. Hodges lie motionless, blood forming a shallow pool beneath him. Another shot rang out, snapping our attention from our fallen comrade to the sergeant commander, who held his gun aloft.

"I will execute any traitor found in possession of such paraphernalia," he said, his rant even louder in the deadly quiet. "If you so much as speak in favor of the Caprician enemy, I will execute you. Treason is treason and has no place here." He bent over and placed the paper on Hodge's back. "While you recruits are on my base, I am judge, I am jury, and God as my witness, I will be your executioner."

He stopped speaking long enough to shoot the drawing twice. He looked up at the rest of us, then, eyes narrowed, he asked. "Who was this traitor's battle buddy?"

A collective chill rushed through the ranks, freezing us all in our place. A single recruit from the last row made his way to the front, standing a foot in front of the assembled company, his chin held high.

"Sergeant commander! I was his assigned battle buddy, sir!" he said.

I couldn't shake the feeling I knew him as well. Not just for who his battle buddy was, but there was something else.

The sergeant commander waved him into the no-man's-land, where he marched to the sergeant commander's side and turned to face us. Then it clicked. Gibbings.

He and Hodges were the ones who walked in on us in the linen closet.

"What is your name, recruit?"

"Sir! Recruit Gibbings, number zero two three, Sergeant Commander!"

"Gibbings, do you feel for your traitorous fallen buddy?" The sergeant commander pressed.

Gibbings faced us proudly. "No, sir! The traitor got what he deserved. Death to all Caprician traitors. Long live King Grakus!"

The sergeant commander circled him like a predator stalking its prey.

"How much did you know of your buddy's affiliations?" he asked in Gibbing's ear, though his words carried through the square.

"Not a thing, Sergeant Commander. Hodges toed the line, far as I saw. I had no reason to suspect a thing."

"Did you ever leave your buddy alone, Gibbings?"

His eyes flashed over us, then to Hodges, then back to the man now at his side. "No, sergeant commander, sir!"

"Do you think I'm stupid, Gibbings?" the sergeant commander shouted. "We have video surveillance showing you leaving your buddy alone. More than once."

The desperation in Gibbings's brown eyes plead for help, but there was none to give. Words formed on his lips, but offered no sound.

"Sir, I only visited the mess as needed. I am diabetic and had to correct my blood sugar."

"Kneel!"

Gibbings complied.

The sergeant commander snarled, "I will ask you one last time. Did you know your buddy was a traitor?"

The deep gravel of his voice churned my stomach, which threatened an upheaval.

"No, sir. I should have..." Another gunshot silenced the words on his tongue.

I jumped at the sound, the hot-metal and gunpowder singed my nose, even at this distance. Recruit Gibbings fell to the ground, body writhing, blood pouring from the black hole in his chest. Aside from the light breeze, his gurgling gasps were the only sound.

Fear and horror hung in the air like a fog, so heavy and thick there was no escape. The sergeant commander stood watching the company while Gibbings stilled against the stones. A sheen of sweat coated my forehead, and I kept a firm hand against my mouth.

"All of you had better take measure," the sergeant commander said, breaking the silence. "You are responsible for your buddy. Your buddy is responsible for you. You'd better know everything about them by the end of the day. If they have any Caprician sympathies or any family or friends who oppose the king you serve, I'd better be the first one you tell." He looked down at the bodies at his feet, then back at us. "As you've just witnessed, if I find out from anyone else, it'll be the last mistake you ever make. Now get back to your racks. Dismissed!"

He holstered his weapon. The sergeants facing us disappeared into the compound, leaving us alone with our fallen comrades.

I stood there until the last sergeant disappeared, afraid to move for fear of reprisal. A touch on my shoulder launched my heart into palpitations. David's hazel eyes stared into mine, too calm. Not a single muscle in his body betrayed the fact that we'd just watched two innocent men murdered in cold blood.

How could he be so calm?

Behind him, Hodges and Gibbings lay dead in puddles of blood.

David took my arm and pulled me away. With every step, I fought the bile clawing its way up my throat, but that was a losing battle. I broke away from David's grip and raced headlong toward the nearest latrine, with him at my heels.

I barreled through the heavy steel door, stumbled into the first stall, and surrendered the contents of my stomach to the waiting porcelain throne. Resting my forehead on my arms, I tried to catch my breath, but the image of Hodges and Gibbings lying in pools of their own blood returned, and I heaved again.

A sudden hand on my back should have made me flinch, but I'd passed the point of caring. The hand rubbed my back up and down as I continued to retch. When at last I thought it might be over, David's voice broke the clammy silence.

"Laura, you okay?" His voice should've been comforting, but I only shook my head, barely containing my nausea. He whispered, "It wasn't your fault. Things like this happen with people like us. You've got to be ready for anything. This is what we are up against."

The door crashed open again, and David's hand stilled on my back.

"First execution," he said.

The only response was a grunt before rapid footsteps led to the stall next to mine, and the sound of retching followed.

I spat out a mouthful of bile-tainted saliva into the basin. David took my elbow and helped me to my feet. Three recruits stood against the far wall, their faces pale and green. It seemed no man would leave his buddy for any length of time, for both their sakes.

"C'mon," David said. "Let's get you to the medical officer."

There were too many eyes and ears, so I settled for a simple nod, even though I wanted to scream at him. He should have destroyed the paper. Instead, my drawing and his actions condemned two innocent men to death.

David held me against himself as we walked, as though he were afraid I wouldn't stand on my own. He wasn't completely wrong. We made our way across the grass from the latrine and turned toward the laundry building instead of the medical offices. The way my stomach still rolled, I wasn't sure which would be better.

A symphony of humming, whirring, and clicking enveloped us inside, and once more, we entered the first linen closet to the left. The moment the door clicked shut, I pushed away from him, but when he placed a hand on my shoulder, every fiber of my being flinched.

"Get away from me," I croaked, though the command emerged more like a desperate plea.

"Laura, you need to calm down. You aren't thinking straight. I told you it wasn't your fault, and I meant it."

"No, it's yours." He watched me quietly for a moment, his face blank, so I continued, "You took the drawing. You should've destroyed it. Burned it. Thrown it away. Anything. All you had to do…"

"Was to keep us alive." He rubbed his forehead, then lowered himself to the floor across from me. "I opened my mouth to argue, but he stopped me. "We're in the middle of a war, dammit. There are going to be casualties. Yes, innocent ones, too. Hell, there've been thousands of casualties on both sides, your family and mine included." I bristled at the mention of the massacre. "You're going to have to accept that if our people are ever going to be free… If you want to honor the dead and claim your birthright, then you're going to have to get over it." He rose to his feet and paced the width of the cramped room.

"If we're going to survive this, we are going to have to watch good men die and act like it's just another day. It is perfectly natural to feel and care for the lives lost, but you need to bury that deep, so deep no one can see. You owe your people a regent who'll make things right and look out for Delta's interests before your own. And don't think for a second that empathy for your enemy will win you any respect here. Grakus's men surround us. Hodges was your enemy. I'm sorry, but he was getting too close to destroying everything. Gibbings was an unfortunate collateral of a corrupt system. You can't trust anyone—"

"Not even you?" I interrupted. My heart sputtered.

"Well." The barest hint of a smile crossed his lips. "You're safe with me, but the other friendships you make here have to be for show.

If these soldiers knew who you really were, they would kill you without a second thought." He took a few deep breaths, then knelt before me.

His voice was calm and measured when he spoke again. "I don't want good people to die any more than you do, majesty. But you need to understand what we're facing here. Our racks and our lockers get checked. We're watched day and night. They listen to what we say, everywhere, and they even watch our trash. Did you know that?"

"How can they check our trash? The chute goes straight into the incinerator." I'd imagined nothing nefarious about an incinerator chute. They functioned the same everywhere. You dump the trash in and it burns. He shook his head, lips pursed.

"There is a sorting room at the bottom of that chute. They go through every piece of refuse from the barracks. I've seen it myself. It's one of their tools to root out traitors; like us." He let out a deep breath. "Yes, two people died today. Yes, it was terrible. But if you are going to have any chance of taking Grakus down, you've gotta take it in the teeth. Innocent people will continue to die while evil wins. Either a few good men die for freedom, or the whole world perishes under the thumb of tyranny."

As much as I hated it, he was right.

The weight that had settled on my shoulders when I started out had grown, pulling me down. Would I be enough to lead? If I couldn't keep my head through basic training, what chance would I have at leading a nation?

"What if I can't do it?" I whispered.

His eyes softened, and he rose. "You can do it. Just remember that you don't have to do this alone. No great leader ever does." Lifting my chin, he angled my eyes to meet his. "Mourning the loss of good men is a sign of a great leader. Respect for life is not a weakness, it is an amazing strength. You have the makings of greatness, even if you don't see it yet."

Closing my eyes, I could almost hear James in his words. The soft assurance, the encouragement. I'd forgotten how much I needed it to see through the fog I'd been living in. I smiled up at my new friend and let out a deeper breath than I'd realized I was holding.

"So, what now?" I asked.

"Well, I all but announced that I was taking you to the medical officer, so we should probably do just that. Then we'll get some food before they corral us and make us throw it up again." He offered me his hand with a half-smile, and I took it.

19

His majesty, King Divo Von Grakus, is pleased to announce the betrothal of his daughter, Princess Persephone Ellen Grakus, to Marquess Tourelle Alexander Breckenridge, the son of the Grand Duke of Breckenridge. The happy couple will make their engagement official at a ball in their honor on the fifth day of June, 5240.
~Official Deletian Palace Announcement

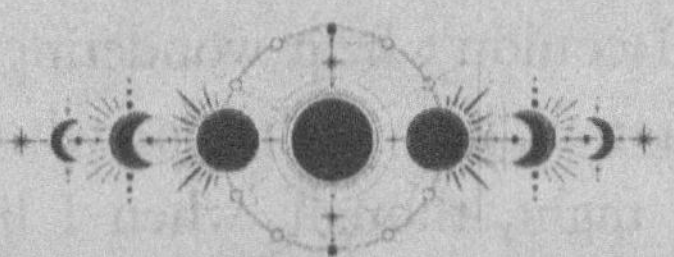

ELAURA

Executions changed everything.

Over the next few weeks, the recruits became suspicious of their buddy's allegiances, fought more with one another, and saw shadows everywhere. Team drills the following week became near impossible. Once they overcame their initial suspicions of another traitor, however, everyone fell in line. We moved more like a unit than like individuals.

David and I, who were both being trained in administrative/clerical work, often visited the laundry's linen closet to discuss our plans for after we graduated. He wanted to figure out how to handle my introduction to the men already undercover on base and to fill me in on how they arranged their meetings.

Of course, we faced discipline for our apparent fraternization, including two firm reprovals, individual smoke sessions with our sergeants, and countless announcements that I was to leave the base come morning. Nevertheless, I remained a member of the company. I took particular pleasure in how much it frustrated the sergeants that I was impossible to dismiss. At least the way they wanted me gone. True to his word, Tourelle stayed each frivolous complaint, which allowed me to succeed on my own merit.

By the end of twelve weeks, I was in the best shape of my life and had gained a new-found confidence. Tourelle's training proved invaluable not only for surviving physically, but also when handling the drill sergeants, especially with how to react to their insults. I lost track of the number of times the sergeants tried to get a rise out of me.

Making it to the finish line was nothing short of astounding.

Although I drew a degree of comfort knowing that I was following in James's footsteps, I couldn't help wondering if Tourelle would be proud of me, too. After all, he was the one who had trained me from the beginning. Every night, though, when I lifted my voice to the

Almighty, I prayed for my brother's wisdom. I certainly needed it if I was ever to lead our people.

My weeks on the base had made the muted footfall, hand signals, popping gunfire, and the gunpowder in the air as familiar as a family tradition. Our final drill had us raiding a mock Caprician compound, engaging combatants, rescuing the prisoners, and taking the 'leader' hostage. While I hated the idea of my family crest being portrayed as the symbol of villains, when Papa had been a fair and just ruler, I enjoyed the combat simulation.

The ballistic dummies reacted to being shot by falling to the ground, much like they would in reality. I half-wished I could study the ways they made them, but kept my focus on the task at hand. At the successful end of our drill, the sergeants fed us a generous meal, complete with respect and cake. Even I enjoyed the dessert, despite my usual aversion to it.

Our graduation wasn't what I'd expected. I had seen such ceremonies before, always with an on-stage speech before an audience of peers and loved ones, after which the graduates walked across that same stage to receive a certificate. Instead, the whole ceremony was handled without an ounce of pomp or circumstance. We donned our new, crisp, official uniforms and lined up through the offices. One by one, we shook hands with our sergeants, then received our certificates of completion, commemorative pins, and our orders. While I waited my turn, I did my best to suppress a grin. No one had expected me to do so well. Even I had my doubts. My presence in the line meant that I might actually have what it takes to lead my people after all.

When my turn came, the sergeant commander shook my hand and, right as I was about to take the certificate and leave, he held the certificate folder out of my reach and pulled me close enough to hear his quiet words.

"Congratulations, Private Carpe. It seems you have friends in some pretty high places." His whisper hissed in my ear. "Don't worry, though. Your luck will run out eventually, and when it does, I'll be there with a smile on my face." He released my hand and lowered the certificate enough I could grab it and released my hand.

Every hair on my arms stood on end. I snatched the folder away, snapped a salute, and added my own quiet reply. "I pray you're there when I prove you wrong, Sergeant Commander."

He sneered and leaned forward. "My dear, I'll see you fall if it's the last thing I do. Now get out of my sight," he snarled.

Turning on my heels, I marched to receive my official orders.

Once I reached my barracks for the last time, I set my folder down and rubbed the goosebumps from my arms. After they'd receded, I packed my belongings, which was a simple job, given that everything was military issue.

I shouldered the duffel and went to the main hall, where the rest of my company was saying goodbyes before boarding our transports. I smiled and nodded to several men who waved at me, but kept my eyes forward. I'd kept to myself enough during training that I wouldn't miss anyone. David's words had remained in mind since the execution: "None of these men are your friends. Every one of them would shoot you on sight if they knew who you really were."

Bypassing all of my fellow privates, I boarded my transport, settled into my seat, and closed my eyes. The long trip north would take several hours, which offered an opportunity to catch up on a great deal of sleep that I'd missed. I'd dozed off before the journey began until a bump in the road roused me. Someone asked the driver how far we were from Springfield. Tired, I clung to the dark and shifted in my seat.

As I moved, the arm draped over my shoulders moved as well. A heartbeat thrummed under my hand and the smell of cologne shattered the remains of my sleep. Wide-eyed, I bolted upright. David chuckled and removed his arm. I scooted as far away from him as the small seat allowed.

"Don't worry. You didn't snore much." One of David's dimples appeared. "I'm just glad I made a good pillow."

He laughed when I glared at him. My cheeks heated, and I trained my focus outside the window. I'd never been in a relationship before, real or fake. In training, our dating charade kept us safe. I wondered if maintaining the charade might be necessary on the base... I wasn't sure how comfortable I was with the idea. At least David sometimes reminded me of James, which made spending time with him easier.

When we reached our new home base, a team met us at the gate, gave us directions, and the bus delivered us to our lodgings. Once there, they gave us leave to settle ourselves before reporting to our C.O. the next morning. I was in C-Block, again.

When we met Captain Davis the following morning, he reviewed our orders and informed us of our assignments. David was to serve Major General Breckenridge, and I would take the slot Banks had vacated: General Schmidt. The interim assistants gladly walked us through our daily duties and everything we would need to know about our officers. They stayed on with us for a week before leaving us to serve on our own.

That first week, when I walked into the mess, I sometimes started toward the kitchen before I caught myself and went to the chow line instead. David stayed at my side whenever he wasn't at his station. It didn't take long for word to make it through the base that David and I were a "thing," so no one thought twice about seeing us together. We trained together, ate together, and often spent our rec time together. As it had in training, the charade worked to our benefit. No one blinked an eye at the amount of time we spent together.

Though I saw David every day, I hadn't seen Tourelle. Not since I'd left for basic, even though David was his assistant. Though, he'd seen that my box of belongings was delivered to the desk attendant of my building on my first day back.

Two weeks after I started working with the general solo, an envelope slid under my door as I was getting ready for bed. I opened it cautiously to find Tourelle's signature inside a celebratory card, where he'd written a lengthy congratulation note. As I read the words expressing his pride in me and how he'd believed in my success, I finally understood why I hadn't seen him. His position as my superior complicated our friendship. He wanted my success to be mine, without sullying it with whispers of special treatment on the base.

I traced his handwritten letters with my index finger. The fact that he'd taken the time to write me a card and hand delivered it made me smile.

Tourelle Breckenridge was a man of high morals, so avoiding the appearance of impropriety made sense, and for a split second, I wished I could be honest with him about my true identity.

Which was unwise, to say the least.

I stuffed the card in the bottom of my desk drawer. Having it out would be a distraction, and distractions like that could be dangerous when I had a great deal to learn.

My assignment wasn't the only thing I needed to figure out, either. I also needed to understand the ins and outs of the base's Caprician undercover cell.

I spent much of the next few weeks memorizing the precise codes we used on base with David, primarily in lost and found notices. The number of variations was overwhelming. If someone lost his wallet, it meant to keep a low profile. A lost set of keys with an asterisk in the corner indicated an emergency meeting at the time and place listed. Someone losing his girlfriend's camera meant all operations were a go, while a lost girlfriend or pair of pants served as a meeting reminder. And last, but certainly not least, the lost blow-up doll served as a warning that reports would be sent to Caprician leadership the following day. The military's senior officers never figured it out.

I also got to know the collection of men working as agents of the Caprician army, and was even more grateful as Major Brandon Jefferson stepped aside and walked me through how to lead meetings the Caprician way. After six months, he handed over full control of the cell to me, which I hadn't expected.

Working with the general was unpleasant. He thought his company was the only one capable of subduing traitors at all. I wouldn't have imagined that being assigned to General Schmidt might be fortunate, not with his constant advances, but as the year ended, I found myself grateful for it. As his assistant, I was privy to his communications and to meetings where they discussed raids. He often berated every other branch of the king's army for allowing the treasonous, traitorous snakes to slip through their fingers. I fed this information to the Capricians, and we thwarted many attacks on Caprician sites and sympathizers. It made his endless attempted advances almost bearable.

Months passed, and I slowly rebuilt a more professional friendship with Tourelle. Then, a month before David and I were promoted to lance corporal, Tourelle surprised David and I at lunch.

"Private First Class Carpe, Private First Class Wilhelm." He smiled, setting his own tray down and joining us at the small table. "How are you?"

My eyes widened, and I stopped chewing my mouthful of food. Had he heard our discussion as he approached? I nodded a silent greeting to him.

David took a long swig of water and smiled up at Tourelle. "Doing well, sir. Just enjoying lunch with my girl—Ow!"

My foot connected with his shin under the table. Even after over a year of this charade, I still didn't like being called 'his' girl.

Tourelle chuckled and picked up his fork. "Trouble in paradise?"

David joined in on the laughter. "Nah, she just doesn't like to be called mine. Says it sounds too much like a declaration of property. But I can't help it. She's just too cute!"

I glared at him, then turned back to Tourelle. "I'm well, Major General Breckenridge. How are you? I haven't seen you in a while."

He kept his eyes on his food. "I've been well. Working on preparations for the engagement celebration ball next month." His fork stabbed a chunk of beef, and he pointed it between David and I. "Are you two going together?"

My fork paused on its journey to my mouth, the food fell back to my tray with a splat. *Going to what?* I wondered, my eyes darting between the two men. *Did he just say there was a ball?* All at once, my mind swam through forgotten hopes and dreams. I'd always imagined wearing a gown like my mother's. My favorite was navy blue, with off-shoulder short sleeves. She and Papa were a vision together on ball nights. He was the very image of regality in his tux with medals and sash, his hair carefully gelled back, and his occasional whiskers shaved smooth. When they'd stop by to tuck me in, he'd ask me to dance with him first. Mama always watched with tears in her eyes while I danced on his toes in my nightdress.

"I thought you were going to ask her, Wilhelm."

Tourelle's voice ripped me from my memories. Confused, I looked first at Tourelle, then at David, who was blushing.

"Sir, I... I'd planned to do it tonight when I took her out to dinner."

Tourelle cleared his throat, and David's ears flashed scarlet.

Was I a subject of discussion when they were alone? The idea was an uncomfortable one. I wiped my mouth with my napkin and pinned them with a stare. "What are you two talking about?"

Tourelle leaned forward and rested his elbows on the table. "The king is throwing a ball to celebrate the official engagement of his daughter, Princess Persephone. There will be an assembly here on base to recognize the event." He turned to David. "Sod the plan, Wilhelm. Just ask her."

David groaned but turned obediently to me. "Laura, would you do me the honor of escorting me to the ball?" A vulnerability swam in his eyes, which made me want to either pat his head or give him a hug, but I knew better. His acting certainly made me feel unequal. The king would be in attendance, which meant I must be as well. It might just be the opportunity we'd been waiting for.

That and I'd have the chance to go to a ball, just like I'd dreamed of so much as a child. I grinned.

"I'd love to!" I smiled, then turned to Tourelle for more information, fully ignoring David's presence at the table. "So, is this a formal uniform event, or tails and gowns? I need to know what the dress code is going to be."

He chuckled, a deep and throaty sort of laugh that sounded almost musical. "Well, it's a bit of both, to be honest. It is a black-tie dress code. The men will wear the formal dress uniform, unless title and status dictate otherwise. I'll be wearing tails myself. Ladies wear gowns. Since you're the only female soldier to be in attendance, you are welcome to choose how you'll attend."

"Do you know where I can find a dress shop nearby, sir?" I asked.

"Not personally, but Lunette does. She knows every dress shop in a two-hundred-kilometer radius." He slid his chair back and collected his tray. "I'll let you two get back to your meal." He stood but met my gaze again. "Luna will be here at the end of the week. I'll let her know you'd like her help when she gets here." He nodded to both of us, turned, and left.

Biting my lower lip, I tried in vain to squelch my smile while Tourelle left. I shoveled a few bites of food in my mouth, hoping it might disguise my expression. It took a few minutes before I noticed David's eyes on me.

"What?" I took a bite.

His somber hazel eyes bored right through me. "You like him, don't you?"

I sputtered. After a few half-coughs, I took a large drink to wash down my food, set my fork down, and gave him my full attention. "Well, of course I like him," I stated matter-of-factly. "He's been a good friend, even if he is loyal to the enemy."

But... something felt off as the words passed my lips.

David's brows rose in question, as though he were trying to imply something more than I'd admitted. His voice dropped to a conspiratorial tone. "Not like that. I mean, you *like him* like him. Not as a friend. More than that."

For a moment, my heart fluttered. He... David was *right*.

My eyes widened, but I clenched my jaw to keep from giving myself away. But Tourelle... No, that match was impossible. How had I allowed myself to like a man who served Grakus?

Well, I wouldn't admit it!

I lowered my attention to the peas on my plate. "If you're escorting me, you'll need to get your formal blues dry cleaned and pressed before the ball."

"Don't change the subject, Laura. I'm right, aren't I?" he challenged.

Finally, I relented and met his gaze. "What do you want me to say, David? I don't have that luxury. I can't. He's loyal to Grakus. I've come too far to cloud my judgment with silly things like school-girl crushes." Moisture threatened my eyes, so I blinked rapidly as I stood. "If you'll excuse me, I think I lost my keys. I need to go report them missing."

With that, I turned and left, not waiting for his answer, and ignoring his protests. I needed a few minutes alone before I returned to my post.

It wasn't fair to him to have left like I did, but something in my heart bristled at the way he saw right through me. I could only hope Tourelle hadn't seen it as well. Was I so obvious to everyone else? I prayed that David was the outlier.

20

A King's Council shall judge any souls found to be employed in the act of espionage against the crown. Based on the severity of said espionage, the convicted shall face a minimum sentence of twenty-five years in a detention facility. The maximum sentence of death by firing squad shall be at the discretion of the King, himself. After the sentencing of those guilty of espionage, an investigation shall be launched upon their friends and family until the root of the insurrection is found.

~Monarchal Code 861343.69.59

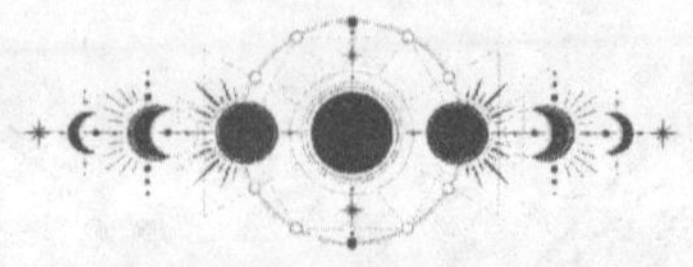

ELAURA

After dinner that Thursday, a knock sounded at my door, which was odd. No one bothered me at home, so the rapping had the hair on my arms standing on end. I smoothed my uniform jacket, drew a deep breath, and threw the door open.

"Truce? I brought cake." Luna smiled self-consciously and thrust the cake box out into the no-man's-land between us.

"Lunette, what a surprise." I smiled and waved her in. "I didn't expect you until tomorrow."

She darted into my room, spun to face me without hesitation, and took my hands once I'd closed the door. "Laura, I'm so sorry. First and foremost, I wanted to be your friend more than I ever wanted to help Rellie. He was a fool to do what he did. But I should have made it clear who I was when I met you. I really would like to be friends, if you'll allow it." Her fingers wove together before her as she pleaded her case.

I set the cake down and stepped away from the desk. "You know, I do have something in mind that would help me forgive you." I smiled.

She bounced on her toes before I could continue. "I'll do it! Whatever it is, I'll do it!" she squealed.

"Did your brother tell you what I need help with?"

"No, he just said that I should stop by." She tipped her head to the side, some of her curls swinging behind her.

I took a breath, hoping that I might one day trust her. "There's a ball coming up, and I find myself in need of a gown. I hear you know every dress shop in a one-hundred-kilometer radius."

Her eyes lit up as she grinned.

"It's actually a two-hundred-kilometer radius, but who's counting?" Her hands perched themselves on her hips. "I wouldn't bother with any shops on base. They are woefully lacking in femininity. They don't even account for a soldier's family."

"Oh." The thought had crossed my mind, but the idea of searching out a good shop was daunting. I was, at best, a novice at this.

She circled me, her eyes scanning me from top to bottom. "With your figure, you could pull off a Pemasheer gown with only minor alterations."

"I wouldn't know," I mumbled.

"Their quality is fit for royalty, if I do say so myself, but I don't have to. I believe the former queen was one of their best patrons before the attack."

Her mention of mama brought a huge smile to my face. Any shop she had frequented would be perfect. It would almost be like taking her with me to my first ball.

Two unwelcome thoughts immediately assailed me. Lunette had the freedom to go to any dress shop in Delta. I didn't. My assignments and tenuous spot as a soldier brought with it more restrictions than I ever imagined. And if Mother had been a patron, how expensive would it be?

Picking the least difficult obstacle, I asked, "How far is it?"

She pondered a moment, tapping her fingers against her lips. "Well, the original shop is in Lanira, but that's too far south for a day trip." My heart sank, and I resigned myself to the idea I'd have to go somewhere else, but she continued, "They opened a new shop in Springfield just last year. It may not be the flagship, but I'm sure it'll do." She smiled like a cat who'd cornered a canary. "We could go on Saturday, if you'd like. Or even tomorrow."

The following day was the last of the week, so General Schmidt would leave the office early. He always did. Once he'd gone, I could go when I pleased.

"Tomorrow would be perfect. I can meet you in front of the administration building as early as 1530. Do you have a car?"

Lunette giggled. "I didn't bring one, but we can use Rellie's. Normally, I have my horse and buggy, but poor Pepper was under the weather. Since the base is between our estate and the palace, Daddy just dropped me off."

The casual way she spoke of owning a horse, like it was nothing, surprised me.

"You drive a horse and buggy?" I asked. "Rather than a car?"

"When I can."

I, however, didn't quite understand. "As a primary means of transportation?"

She nodded. "Pepper is mine, and Duke is Rellie's. They were a gift to our parents when I was born. Now they belong to us. Daddy uses Duke more than Rellie does. It's not good for a horse to be neglected, so Daddy makes sure he gets his exercise."

Horses were not a native species to Delta and hard to come by. Very few could afford to own one, and even fewer bred them. Ownership was a symbol of status and wealth. I'd asked Papa for a pony once. He told me that it would be unfair to tax the people in order to import one from planet Betaris. My joy was not a price the people should pay. I couldn't help but whistle in astonishment.

"Must be nice." I muttered, unable to hide my jealousy. She just shrugged.

"The horses are nice to have, but they're also a lot of work. With Rellie in the military and never home, I end up with the lion's share."

"I'd better let you get back. Your brother is probably worried."

She giggled. "Sometimes he frets till he's crazy. Not that it takes much, mind you." She turned to leave, pausing just past the door. "By the way..."

"Yes?"

She smiled brightly, and said, "Don't forget, we're friends now. Please call me Luna."

She bounded away, disappearing around the corner before I could say another word.

***

When I left work the next day, Luna was waiting outside as planned, leaning against a sleek red convertible with the top down.

There weren't many men on the streets at this time of day, and yet I could still feel eyes on me. We both climbed in, and before I could secure myself, she stepped on the accelerator. The vehicle surged forward, pressing me into the seat.

"Woah!" I cried as I hurried to fasten the safety belt. "I'm not in that much of a hurry!"

Luna laughed. Her hair whipped behind her as she launched us around a corner, toward the gate.

"Come on, Laura! Live a little!" she shouted over the rushing wind.

The gate guards must have recognized the car because they dashed to open the gates in time for us to rush through them. It took a great deal of focus to keep my mind off of our speed and the wild driver in control of my fate. I couldn't help but wonder if someone had figured out who I was and sent Luna to assassinate me before I killed my uncle. A suicide assassination? Unlikely. Luna wouldn't throw her life away. She couldn't know who I was. If Tourelle hadn't put two and two together in the near eighteen months he'd known me, especially when I'd told him my given name, Luna wouldn't have figured it out. As far as I knew, the only people that wanted me dead were a few sergeants from basic training.

Neither of us talked during the rest of the nerve-wracking drive, which lasted about fifteen minutes. Luna pulled into a small parking lot, and I resisted the urge to kiss the ground after getting out of the car.

The simple store front boasted very little decoration. Instead, the mannequins in the large window announced the wares within, each premiering a different gown, displaying the shop's versatility. One gown, in particular, caught my attention at once. It was a darker shade of blue than my favorite of Mama's dresses, and yet I couldn't help imagining her standing there wearing it.

Luna materialized at my side, slipped her arm through my own, and pulled me into the store. "Let's go in and try some dresses on!"

A bell chimed above our heads when we walked through the doors to announce our arrival.

"Welcome to Pemasheer," a gentleman called from somewhere

behind a crimson curtain. "I'll be with you in just a moment. Please feel free to look around while you wait."

Racks of gowns lined the walls, leaving the space in the center of the room clear, save for multiple lounge chairs scattered throughout the room. Luna, of course, needed no invitation to drag me to the nearest rack of gowns and then to the ones on display on small stands throughout the space. Each gown seemed more extravagant than the last.

Carefully, she pulled a few dresses from the rack and turned their hangers so the beautiful fabric hung horizontally over the others. I cringed inwardly. The prices must be outrageous, considering the richness of the materials. As I browsed, I found myself drawn again and again to the blue gown in the window, as if pulled by an invisible tether. I reached out to touch the soft material of the skirt.

"It's been so long since I've felt anything like this," I murmured without thinking. I froze, panicking at the imagined assumptions that might be garnered from my simple statement. A quick glance over my shoulder revealed Luna inspecting a lavender gown. With a quick step, I moved two dresses over to a crinkly forest-green gown with a much rougher material before Luna could question me.

At last, the shopkeeper emerged through the curtain with a flourish and zeroed in on Luna, who clearly belonged in a shop like this one. He greeted her with a mock kiss on either side of her face.

"Luna, my darling! It's been much too long. Why do you keep me waiting all the time?"

"Charles. So good to see you. My friend would like to try on that gorgeous blue number in the window."

"Of course. And what can I get for you?"

"Nothing," she said brightly. "I'm not shopping today."

"Don't be a tease. When have you ever abstained from one of our signature gowns?" He glanced over at me with his lips pursed and looked me up and down.

"I'm afraid you don't have what I'm looking for here today. I need a little more coverage on the shoulders, and I already have the only options here in your showroom. But don't worry. Pema is working on my custom gown in Lanira." She smiled and patted his hand. "Now... The blue gown in the window?"

He gave an exaggerated pout, then sighed. "Well, if you insist. Can I at least bring in a few more for you to look through?" When she nodded, he led us to a fitting room with a dressing space to the side and a sixteen-centimeter circular pedestal in the center of the room. He returned a few minutes later with the gown draped over his arms. Resting the gown over a chair, he deposited a small paper bag of clips on the floor, bowed to Lunette with a smile, and left us.

She helped me into the dress, sliding the smooth material up into place and clipped the back so it fit. I stepped onto the pedestal and admired myself in the triple mirrors. The soldier I had become had disappeared and in her place a woman who looked like her mother in a gorgeous gown. On instinct, I touched mama's necklace, and wished she could have been by my side now.

Luna's reflection behind mine caught my eye. Her expression held a strange mix of knowing and success.

I blinked, suddenly self-conscious and nervous. "What's wrong? Am I making a funny face or something?"

Luna stepped closer and whispered, "I know your secret."

Ice crystallized in my veins, while my mind went wild. Had Tourelle told her my real name, or that I was the one who attacked him? That he let me go when I should have faced my death? It took some effort to keep my voice level. "What secret? I... I don't have any..."

She nodded her head with a smile. "I know who your mother was." When I didn't reply, she whispered softly, "You're wearing her necklace."

I stood, immobilized on the platform. My fingers curled around the locket, concealing it too late. *No! She can't know!* A thick lump formed in my throat. She stepped forward, grabbing me by the shoulder before I could retreat.

Luna continued talking, but my mind refused to process her words. Instead, my heart raced as though she'd threatened to kill me. I imagined her grin was meant to reassure me. As I focused on her expression, Luna's words finally reached me.

"I'm on your side, Majesty."

My eyes searched hers, and her smile grew. She stepped back, dropped to one knee, placed her right fist against her chest, and bowed her head. Pins and needles prickled across my fingers and toes.

"Luna...Wh-what," I stammered, "what are you doing?"

She looked back up and tears shone in her eyes. "I am kneeling before my sovereign queen, daughter of King Charles and beloved Queen Denna."

My hands rose to my mouth of their own accord. I stood as still as a statue in the heavy gown while the nearby air-conditioner blew across my bare shoulders.

Luna rose beaming. "Majesty, I gather intelligence for the Caprician army among the circles of the social elite. We have swayed many hearts and minds within our circle of influence against the Bloody Baron. Our goal is to remove him from power and grow your army."

"My army..." I whispered, my eyes fixing on nothing in particular as thoughts raced. Something about Luna's words caught me off guard. Yes, I'd known of the army before, but once more I'd found a new ally.

Luna touched my shoulder. "We're with you, Majesty."

Four simple words, provided the reassurance that reminded me that there was more at stake than me, than a ball, than avenging my family.

Then, unbidden, the image crept into my mind, giving my heart wings: Tourelle, joining the tight-knit circle of operatives on base.

"What about your brother? Is he with you? Does he stand against the..." I paused before saying aloud words I'd last said to James, "Bloody Baron?"

Her lips flattened to a thin line. "I'm sorry." Her brows knitted together. "Tourelle is too close to the false king. He doesn't even know what I do. He thinks I'm running a charity for the troubled. Mental health services and the like."

Every word thrust a dagger into my hopes. "How is he too close?

He's only a major general, not a full one or an Admiral. Isn't that what he'd need to be included in the inner circle?"

A shadow crossed her expression. "Hasn't he told you?"

"Told me what?" I tried suggesting the most impossible thing I could think of, hoping the truth might be kinder. "That he's secretly related to the baron... I mean, the king?"

The look in her eyes hinted that I must be closer than I thought. When the silence stretched on, my heart beat so loudly I thought it might explode.

"Luna!"

"Well," she began, then stopped to bite the corner of her lip. "He's not related to them yet. He's... he's betrothed to Princess Persephone Grakus."

The world around me came to a screeching halt. Not only was he unavailable as a friend or ally, but he would soon marry my enemy? Become my enemy? Even if her father was my true adversary, marriage to my cousin placed him so far out of reach that it took effort to pull in a shallow breath. I focused on taking another, and then on taking the next.

When Luna broke the silence this time, her words came out in a rush. "He doesn't want to. Daddy arranged the whole affair. Rellie has tried to get out of it so many times, but Daddy's agreement was the only thing keeping our family safe."

"I don't understand."

"Daddy was an admiral. He served in your father's inner circle. After the massacre, all the noble families loyal or connected to King Charles began disappearing. Many turned up dead, while others simply vanished without a trace. Daddy was ill the day *it* happened, and after the first family vanished, he retired from his position and arranged the betrothal. It was the only way to secure our safety." Her gaze fell. "I don't like the idea any more than Rellie does."

My heart ached for them both. Poor Tourelle, doomed to a loveless marriage. Poor Luna, watching, knowing all the while that he did it for her. They were as close as James and I had been. The desperation in her eyes mirrored my feelings whenever I thought of James. If fate had allowed me a way to spare his life, I would gladly do it. Luna clearly felt the same way for Tourelle.

I forced a warm smile and met Luna's gaze. "I understand, Luna. We do what we have to do to survive. Perhaps we can find a way to keep him from marrying Persephone and still keep you and your family safe." I pulled her into a hug.

And yet, my heart ached with more than simply witnessing the sting of a sister watching her brother suffer. It ached with the two-fold desire for something I could not have. I wished not only to have James with me, but also to have Tourelle at my side. I had told David that I understood that Tourelle and I couldn't be together, but had to admit the truth. In the innermost hopeful corner of my heart, that secret hope struggled and died. I'd wanted to believe that, perhaps, if he found himself on the Caprician side, I could even fall in love with him.

Once again, fate was not that kind.

No matter what dreams I might have, the reality was that my people needed me at the head of the army. I couldn't afford pining away after what couldn't be mine.

21

I, William Jasper Breckenridge, the Grand Duke of the Breckenridge estates, do hereby relinquish my position as Admiral to the Crown. As a symbol of fealty to King Divo Von Grakus, I hereby promise my eldest son, Tourelle Alexander Breckenridge's hand in marriage to Princess Persephone Ellen Grakus, if it pleases the king. This covenant shall stand as a witness to the fealty of my family. If I, or any of my family, shall breech this contract, may we all stand at the King's mercy.

~Breckenridge Estate Press Release

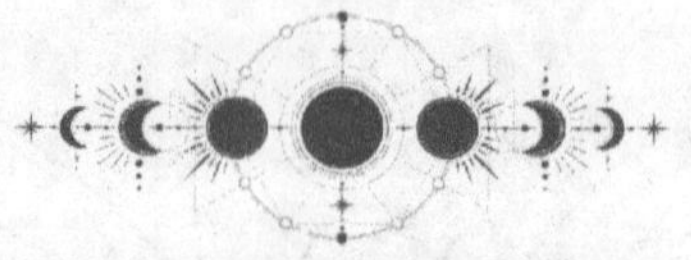

ELAURA

I should have asked more questions when Luna insisted I take dance lessons leading up to the ball. Not because I didn't need them, because I sorely did. The problem came with the instructor she arranged: her brother.

After I slipped into high heels she'd given me, Luna described the first steps before demonstrating them with Tourelle. Her hand all but floated to his arm, and when he took a step, she mirrored the motion. Tourelle urged her backward before pushing her away. Without breaking stride, she spun and returned to Tourelle's arms. As their advance curved through the room, I was mesmerized by the beauty of their movements and the sheer serenity on their faces. On *his* face.

I hadn't imagined him doing anything as graceful as dancing, but it seemed so natural.

They moved effortlessly in time to the music, floating as though the floor didn't occupy the same hemisphere. The way he twirled her and continued dancing without missing a beat took my breath away. When they came to a stop, inadequacy rose in my chest.

I was supposed to be paying attention to the steps being taken, not admiring the man dancing with his sister. Pressing my lips together, I walked toward them, trying to hide my chagrin.

"I didn't know you could move like that." My face heated the moment the words left my mouth.

Tourelle's half smile hung in suspended time. "You know, a man can be a skilled warrior *and* an elegant dancer. Not one of us is as one dimensional as we seem."

I opened my mouth, intending to respond, but I just stood there impersonating a fish. When Tourelle laughed, Luna smacked his chest with the back of her hand.

"You behave," she ordered, but her command had the opposite effect.

He laughed even harder, wiping a tear from his eye while she glared at him.

"Sorry, Luna." His laughter abated as he turned to me. "To be honest, it's more because of our father's social standing. Social niceties were a requirement of our education, as well as learning all of polite society dances. Besides, my looney little sister needs a good dance partner from time to time."

He'd barely finished speaking before Luna threw him a look of frustration and punched his shoulder. "Honestly, Rellie," she snapped. "How many times do I have to tell you—don't call me looney!"

He chuckled again and held up his hands in mock surrender.

She huffed, then spun to me, her easy smile back on her face. "Your turn!" When I didn't move, she marched to my side, grabbed my shoulders, and directed me to face Tourelle. "Now, get closer. Laura, your right hand goes on his shoulder, and your left hand will rest in his."

On cue, Tourelle lifted his hand, palm up. Following instructions, I set my hand on his shoulder. My mouth went dry. It seemed too intimate of a thing to place my hand in his, but there was no way around it. After the revelation at the dress shop, however, I didn't want to get close to someone who could be my enemy.

The world seemed to come to a halt.

What if I had to give an order that resulted in his death? It would be like killing him myself, and I couldn't—

Apparently frustrated by my lack of movement, Luna grabbed my other hand in Tourelle's. A civil war raged between my head and heart. One faction against another. On one hand, I needed to stay objective. I should hate him for what he represented. On the other hand, my heart soared at the pressure of his fingers coiled around my own, and the smell of his cologne set my heart to racing.

His hand slid down to the small of my back, leaving a trail of goosebumps in its wake. I took a deep and shaking breath, careful to blow it out as slow as I could, focusing only on my hand in his. I chanced looking up and found myself lost in those pools of blue. It would be easy to drown in them. Luna cleared her throat, startling out of the spell I was under. With a mumbled apology, I turned my attention back to her.

For the rest of the evening, I kept my eyes on my feet or on Luna, though my feet often needed more attention. Luna kept my mind on the dance, making it easier to forget about who my dance partner was. Over the next few evenings, they both tried to instruct me on the major dances I'd need to know.

I should have known these. I would have started dancing on my birthday after the murders, so I would have been ready when my parents would have presented me on my eighteenth birthday.

Luna left a few days later, leaving me to practice with Tourelle. I didn't mind when our practices shortened after Luna's departure: focusing on the steps was hard enough without thinking about who they were with. My heart raced every time he took my hand, mostly because he fit a little too well into the model of the good husband I'd imagined since I was a girl. Handsome, moral, kind, good to his family —a prince in all but name—Tourelle checked every box.

All but one. The most important aspect that negated the entire list. He belonged to someone else. Even if I could afford to find love now, which I couldn't, I refused to pursue a man who had already been promised to another.

My heart ached for what might have been if my family had remained in power. I would have been preparing for my own ball, one where I might find an eligible suitor. And in that scenario, maybe Tourelle would have been there. Dreams of what would never be whispered when I danced in his arms, and each time I had to chastise myself with a reminder that he wasn't my ally.

Daydreams were dangerous.

Reality was a cruel playwright, indeed.

***

After a full week of lessons, I felt confident enough not to step on anyone's toes, even though Tourelle joked about purchasing steel-toed boots to protect his feet during practices. However, on the day before the ball, anxiety robbed me of my hard-earned confidence. I needed to ask Tourelle for one last lesson. When the time came and I danced with the king, he couldn't know his end was nigh at hand. As soon as I found out the King would be at the ball and the following assembly, an emergency meeting was called. His attendance offered the greatest opportunity to strike we'd have in a long time. The plans had been made and confirmed with contingencies on every side.

Knowing the risks and despite my own common sense, I strode down the hall to Tourelle's office. I smiled at David, and a smirk pulled at his cheek as he rose from his desk to greet me.

"Hey, beautiful! Did you miss me that much?" He held his arms out wide for a hug.

Uncomfortable, I side-stepped his embrace. "I actually came to speak with the major general. Is he free?"

He eyed me for a moment, suspicion evident in his raised eyebrow. "He doesn't have another meeting for an hour."

When I took a step toward the door, he took me into his arms, and I stiffened. He held me a moment before he spoke, his breath tickling my ear. "What are you up to?"

"Getting ready for a ball. What else?" I sighed.

He pulled away but held my shoulders for a moment. "Be careful."

I nodded. I couldn't say much in public where someone might hear. David looked over my shoulder at someone passing behind me. When he let go, I stepped around him and knocked on Tourelle's door.

"Come in," he called.

I pushed open the door and found him hunched over his desk, pen in hand. His eyes never left the paper on his desk.

"I'll be with you in a moment," he mumbled. When he finally looked up, a smile lit his face. "Lance Corporal Carpe, what a surprise. Please, have a seat." He motioned to the chairs before his desk, setting down his pen and threading his fingers together. "How can I help you?"

I complied, but bit my lower lip. Dance lessons had officially ended, but I hoped he would grant me this last favor.

"Is there any chance I could talk you into one last practice?"

As I spoke, his eyes closed, and his jaw tensed. "Laura..."

"Please? I know how busy you are tomorrow. I only need an hour of your time. I just don't want to step on anyone's feet."

He pinched the bridge of his nose and drew a deep breath before answering. "Why don't you ask Wilhelm? Aren't you going with him? I'm sure his feet can take it."

I didn't answer as I studied the blank wall behind Tourelle. What could I say? That I wanted to dance with him one last time before I burned all of our chances to the ground? That I was planning to break up with my fake boyfriend? Or that I had no desire to dance with Wilhelm? With the assassination so close at hand, there wouldn't be another chance to let my heart have its way, and after the battle ended, he might just hate me.

Tourelle cleared his throat, pulling me from my thoughts. Perhaps my silence had spoken for me. His eyes met mine, a look of concern, or perhaps pity, on his face. "I suppose I could spare an hour." He sighed, "If Luna heard about me telling you no, it would be my head."

"Thank you." I stood, my fist at my side to resist the urge to reach out to shake hands. Instead, I delivered a crisp salute. "Same time and place?"

He nodded and turned his attention back to the paperwork before him. I slipped out as he picked his pen back up, ignoring David on my way out.

Five hours later, we were dancing across the wood floor in the gym. He twirled and pulled me close at the end of the revolution. We danced at a speed that gave me only moments to remember the next steps as he urged me across the floor to the music. At the end of the song, he used his leverage to tip me backward in a dip.

In the short time I'd been dancing, I found the dip to be the most uncomfortable part. Yielding to a dance partner's lead had been enough loss of control. Surrendering to gravity defied nature, and this time, my body rebelled against the action. Every muscle in my abdomen tightened, pulling me upright, contrary to the dip.

Our lips met, and electricity danced between us.

The shock in Tourelle's eyes mirrored my own. His hold slackened, and I slipped toward the hard floor. Panicked, I gripped his sleeve for dear life. At the last moment, he grabbed at my arms in an attempt to right me. Gravity, however, had the last laugh. In his attempt to stop me from falling, he compromised his own balance, and we both tumbled to the floor.

The music played on, mocking our misfortune.

Tourelle rolled away almost as soon as we'd landed.

My head hit the floor just as the impact knocked the wind out of me. It took me a few moments to pull in a deep enough breath to satisfy my lungs. I sat up and touched the back of my head where my scalp protested the touch. I winced and squeezed my eyes shut.

What had I done? Why on Delta's sandy hills had I straightened then?

"You okay?"

I nodded, afraid to speak, for fear of making a fool of myself.

Tourelle's blue eyes watched my every move. It only took him a moment to gain his feet again and offer me a hand up. I stared at his hand a moment before I relented and let him lift me to my feet.

A fire raged beneath the surface of my face. I had kissed him... Although I knew it was an accident and should mean nothing to either of us, somehow it mattered to me. He was betrothed, and I *couldn't* have feelings for a taken man.

Not good, Elaura, not good.

Tourelle cleared his throat, halting my internal self-reprimand. "Well... That was, um..."

Words, it seemed, failed him as well. An uncomfortable tension stretched on. His tight expression revealed nothing more than a rigid control over his emotions.

"I'm so sorry," I blurted. He half opened his mouth to speak, but I was afraid to let him. "I think that's enough for tonight. After all, you were right. David's feet should be fine." Anxiety made me chuckle more strangled than humorous. I looked at my bare wrist, retreating with every syllable. "Oh, is that the time? I'd better go. You've got a busy day ahead. I'll let myself out. Night."

Without waiting for his reply, I dashed out of the gym and across the base. Our cell would still be meeting to solidify plans for the next day. I'd almost crossed to the bunkhouse housing the theatre where I'd scheduled to meet with my team before I stopped to catch my breath. Being a service member on this base wouldn't exempt me from suspicion. Running into a building could give rise to questions I might not want to answer. Once I'd calmed enough, I strode through the doors with my head held high and made my way down to the basement theatre.

The empty room brought a sigh of relief. I'd arrived early enough to allow for quiet reflection before our meeting started. I dropped into one of the cushioned chairs to mull over the evening's events. Much as I wanted to banish it from my mind, the memory of that accidental kiss kept slipping back into my head like an unwelcome guest.

Focus Elaura! Focus!

Pounding my forehead with my fists proved useless. I needed to have my wits about me, not reliving the feel of his arms holding me close or his lips on mine. The way my heart leapt at the thought was almost enough to make me forget my goal. Almost.

Tourelle Breckenridge would make an excellent ally. Even as I wished for his support, I knew it would never come. I rapped my head with a fist again, trying to banish the traitorous thought from my head. Much as I would love to surrender to the feelings of a girl in love, there was a greater matter at hand. He was, in fact, the enemy.

All girlish fantasies of a happily ever after had died with my family, had been destroyed by a man I had the misfortune of calling great-uncle.

I hoped Tourelle didn't misunderstand that accidental kiss.

After all, my actions seemed suspicious. I'd been cold with David, insisted Tourelle dance with me once more, and my silence at Tourelle's question could have suggested that my relationship with David might not last much longer. I groaned. What if Tourelle thought I had turned my intentions to pursuing *him*? Though he had never told me about his betrothal, it would stand to reason that I might imagine him to be available.

My face fell into my hands.

It seemed fate would sooner mock me than allow me to escape unscathed.

22

Military personnel at formal events shall wear dress blues, freshly pressed and in good repair. All military personnel are emissaries of the king and are expected to behave accordingly. Public drunkenness and any manner of disorderly conduct are unbecoming of a king's soldier and shall not be tolerated. Any man in breach of conduct shall be demoted without opportunity for promotion for eighteen months or until a council of commanding officers shall find him repentant and worthy.
~Military Code of Conduct 12.5.3

TOURELLE

My dance with Elaura the night before crept through my thoughts at random intervals throughout the day. The memory of a flash of her smile, her hand in mine, or the twinkling of her eyes were bad enough, but external reminders came from everywhere. The shush of paper sliding against the desk summoned images of her twirling across the floor. Tapping my pen on my upper lip, a habit I couldn't break, resurrected the electricity that danced through me when her lips pressed against mine.

Every time memories stopped me only focused breathing and rubbing my face centered me enough to return to the work at hand. The day crept past. I should have finished hours earlier, but still a mountain of paperwork remained, with little to show for my efforts.

Glancing at the clock did little to ease my frustration. There wouldn't be enough time to finish before the ball. Squeezing my eyes shut, I pulled in a deep breath. In just a few brief hours, I would announce my engagement to the princess. Until that point, our betrothal had simply stood as a promise between two families. At the ball, it would become a promise between two people. Persephone would officially become my fiancée, and I could do nothing to delay the date, which even now loomed in the distance. I would have to learn to live with and hopefully, one day, love her. Everything rode upon keeping my family safe.

A knock at the door pulled me from my morose thoughts back to the present. A young private hung in the open frame.

"Sir, it's time. You asked me to remind you."

I stood, sliding my chair behind me, and nodded at him. "Thank you, Richter, was it?"

He returned my nod and disappeared.

Abandoning the pile on my desk, I straightened my uniform jacket and left the office. I'd kept the truth about my betrothal from the troops, for fear of changing their behavior around me. I had a reputation for allowing my moral compass to govern decisions. Being called major general goody-two shoes didn't bother me as long as they knew me for doing things right. After the ball, the official announcement would haunt my career.

I made my way through the base, which was oddly quiet, presumably busy with preparations for the ball. My apartment was empty.

Luna must have been helping Elaura get ready, and the thought almost made me smile. My sister was a master painter with a makeup brush and had an unhealthy obsession with shoes.

I stowed my weapon in the table drawer as always, then trudged to my bedroom and opened my closet. My dress blues hanging before me brought a pang of guilt. I wanted to be recognized for my service, not my lineage or my connections. Instead, however, I pulled out the tuxedo and sash from the farthest recesses of my closet.

As I dressed, I consoled myself that while my hereditary title might be a part of me, it did not define me. My betrothed—no, my soon-to-be fiancée—had sent word ahead that it would make her happiest to see me in tails and sash. Much as I preferred the dress blues, accommodating her request felt appropriate, considering I was pledging my life to her.

I had little doubt that it wouldn't be my last such compromise.

I finished fastening the cuff links and inspected myself in the mirror. The image of a nobleman and future prince stared back as I adjusted my bowtie and smoothed a hand over my carefully gelled hair. After checking the time, I noted the appointed time for me to meet my betrothed out front had come. I eyed the light blue sash draped over the side of my sink and slid the detestable thing over my head to rest on my shoulder. One last check, and I made my way downstairs to the limo.

Persephone waited in the backseat in her bright pink, single sleeve gown. Her lavender curls were piled on her head, with two strands hanging on either side of her face. She looked me up and down with an approving smile.

"You look so handsome tonight." She leaned forward as soon as I had settled into the seat and knocked on the roof of the limo, a signal to the driver to go.

"You look lovely yourself," I said, and we settled into silence.

The road to the ball was mercifully short. Neither of us spoke until we arrived. I climbed out first and offered my gloved hand to assist her out.

"Shall we?" I asked, lifting her from the low seats. She took my arm and held me where we stood while someone rolled a red carpet to our feet.

"Isn't it a nice touch?" Her violet eyes sparkled with excitement. "Loony wasn't sure you'd like it, but *I* think you deserve the honor."

"Thank you," I managed, though the carpet's assertion of importance went against so much of what I stood for, but I could live with it for now. It was, after all, an innocent attempt to express her endearment, so I held out my arm. She slipped her arm through mine, and I led her down the carpet and through the grand doors. "It's very kind of you to hold me in such high esteem."

"Of course," she said.

A grand spectacle waited past the impressive doors. No expense had been spared. Bushels of roses and lit candles lined the grand staircase and gold drapes clung to every wall. Gold chairs pressed against tables draped with crimson. Pure silver willow trees sat atop each table with diamonds hanging from each branch while crystalline stars hung from the ceiling. The Sight atop the staircase alone screamed extravagance and we'd yet to fully enter the space. I'd meant to remain cool and collected, but my jaw dropped.

"Wow," I muttered. "I'd marvel that they did all this for us, but I think the king's attendance may have something to do with it."

"About that." Persephone's soprano voice pulled me back. "Daddy wanted to come, but... well, something came up. He wouldn't tell me what." She bit her lip and looked away. "He promised he'd be here for the assembly in a few days for certain."

I gave her hand a pat. "I'm sure he'd rather be here."

Eyes glistening and turned down, she exhaled slowly before turning toward the staircase. "Might as well get started. We are the guests of honor, after all."

A smile appeared on her face before Persephone drew her shoulders back and stood a little taller. All traces of her prior disappointment vanished. We stepped in unison toward the stairs, and a chorus of trumpets split the air. All eyes fastened on us.

When silence permeated through the grand room, a man

announced in a loud voice: "Presenting, Her Royal Highness, Princess Persephone Ellen Grakus, and her fiancée, Marquis Tourelle Alexander of Breckenridge."

A chorus of applause echoed through the great hall and a path formed through the crowd as we descended.

When the cheering subsided, whispers and giggles took its place. I tried to ignore the sound and kept my head high. I'd never acclimate to feeling like a spectacle, present only for others' entertainment or like an animal in a zoo. It was best to get the performance over with and end the gawking. I drew Persephone closer, but I found it difficult to not compare the feel of my fiancée in my arms to the way it felt to hold Elaura close. The lack of electricity left me feeling a little cold.

It's just new. Affection takes effort.

The music swelled, and I took Persephone in my arms. Drawing a deep breath, we danced. At least the activity gave me something to focus on, even if thoughts of Elaura kept resurfacing.

When it finished, an older duke claimed Persephone's hand, so I searched the crowd for my sister, trying not to panic when I didn't see Luna right away. Yes, she'd promised to help Elaura prepare for the ball before she came, but I had no idea if she'd arrived early or if she would be late. Though my inability to find her in the crowd suggested the latter.

Another song started, and couples began filling the dance floor. Movement at the top of the stairs caught my eye. A stunning young woman I didn't know stood on the landing, watching the dancers in the hall. Hair scooped artfully upon her head, and a dark blue dress hugged every curve. The lady's hand drifted to touch the simple necklace at her throat, and then her face lit up when she spotted someone. She all but floated down the stairs, and I stood transfixed.

She met her escort at the base of the stairs, took his hand, and they disappeared into the crowd.

The officer waiting for her had been Lance Corporal Wilhelm? But that would mean—

The beautiful creature I'd just seen was Elaura? Laura had never worn much makeup. 'Too much hassle,' she'd said once. I shook myself. Lunette had certainly outdone herself.

I couldn't deny feeling an invisible tether pulling me to find her. The vision of her descending the stairs replayed again in my mind, but a tug on my sleeve returned me to terra firma.

"Tourelle? What's got you so distracted?" Persephone asked, raising up to her toes to see what I saw.

At her height, she didn't quite clear the heads of the crowd. If I could no longer see Elaura when I stood over six feet tall, there was no way my five-foot-two fiancée would be able to find her. I yanked my attention back to Persephone.

"Forgive me. It's just that... Well, I haven't seen Lunette today. I was hoping she might be here by now." I offered a smile. My statement did ring true, but it did not fully explain my distraction. I didn't want to bring Elaura into Persephone's crosshairs.

Fate had dealt my hand, and I would stay the course. I would not fold, not if I wanted my family safe.

My fiancée tilted her head to the left with a smile. "I wish I had a big brother like you to watch over me. Loony is so lucky." Ignoring the surrounding crowd, she wrapped her arms around my middle and held me tight.

Uncomfortable, I patted her shoulder. "I'll be there for you as well, Your Royal Highness."

She pulled back and looked up at me. "Please call me Persephone. After all, you'll be a Royal Highness yourself soon enough."

I smiled and took a step back. "It may take me some time, Your... I mean, Persephone. Old habits die hard. Especially in His Majesty's army." We'd not seen one another much in the time we'd been promised. A handful of lunches and base tours were not enough to properly acquaint two people enough to be friends, let alone spouses.

"As long as you try." She touched my cheek, a gentle smile on her face. "There is a lot for both of us to get used to."

A tap on my shoulder spun me around, blocking my fiancée from whatever threat awaited, but she shifted around to my side.

A young soldier blushed and cleared his throat. "Pardon me, sir. May I dance with Her Royal Highness?"

She nodded and accepted the young man's outstretched hand, and so began an hour and a half of her fulfilling her duty to dance with her subjects. I took a seat at the table near the front of the room and waited to be summoned. Once or twice, I spotted Elaura smiling up at Lance Corporal Wilhelm while they danced.

When at last my turn came to dance with the princess, my fiancée, a murmured protest made its way across the dance floor, beginning at the crowd's edge and making its way toward us. The commotion became audible enough that every hair on the back of my neck stood at attention. Someone must be shoving their way through the crowd.

Multiple scenarios raced through my mind, and I planned how I would keep my princess safe. I removed her hand from my shoulder and spun to face the disturbance, pulling Persephone behind me in a smooth motion.

Instead of a threat, however, Elaura stepped through the wall of dancers into the small open space before me. I opened my mouth to ask her what was wrong, but the fury on her face stilled my tongue. I released Persephone's wrist.

"We need to talk," Elaura said before turning to Persephone. "Please forgive the intrusion, ma'am." Without another word, she pulled me into the crowd, leaving Persephone alone on the dance floor, her mouth gaping.

I followed Elaura into an adjacent study, where she released me and closed the glass doors.

"Laura, what the hell is this about?" I demanded, pausing half a breath to check my emotions. "Do you have any idea who you just ripped me away from? Don't you think about the consequences before you act?"

"I don't care." She snapped. "Not with what I just went through." Her finger stabbed the air between us. She had always been an animated speaker, but now the movements of her hands as she spoke became almost frenzied with every syllable. "That piece of garbage general of yours just tried to force himself on me!"

I stilled. "What? Who?"

"General Schmidt." The name dripped with venom. Her skirts swirled as she paced. "I went to sit down for a minute somewhere quiet, and he comes staggering into the room, drunk as a skunk, and insists that I am his property. Bought and paid for." Her finger jabbed at the glass door. "I am no one's property! Least of all *his*."

It wasn't uncommon for an officer to cherry-pick his personnel, a practice that didn't sit well with me. Although I had heard rumors, Elaura had never reported his behavior, but at that moment, I had no doubts that Schmidt had directly requested her. Had targeted her. My jaw tightened as she strode back and forth.

"You are not." I managed after a deep breath. It took a great deal of control to hide the tremor in my gripped hands. "Where was your escort through all of this?" I'd decided to have a few words with Lance Corporal Wilhelm in the morning. He shouldn't have let her be alone with another man, let alone General Schmidt.

She put her hands on her hips and glared at me. "Oh, because I need a babysitter? Are you seriously suggesting... wait," she paused, eyes growing wide. "That's it! I need to transfer."

"Laura," I began, "transfers aren't whims, and I can't do much."

"Get me away from him." Anger painted her cheeks pink, and she folded her arms. "Transfer me away. Trade me with Lance Corporal Wilhelm."

My concern for her situation warred with the reality of my growing feelings for her and the idea of her in my office. I crossed my own arms, mirroring her, and even though I knew that I needed to help her, I heard myself argue, "You do realize a move like that is a demotion, don't you?"

"I don't care. It gets me away from him."

"Scuttlebutt will fly through the ranks, and it won't be flattering."

"What else is new? I can handle scuttlebutt, but I can't work for that man." She shoved a loose curl behind her ear, and my attention caught momentarily on her sparkling teardrop earrings. "Willhelm's been an excellent assistant, hasn't he?"

"Of course. He excels in every task I give him."

"Then give him the promotion. He's deserving, and I want the move. It's a win-win, wouldn't you agree?"

I exhaled. Like Luna, once she'd set her mind to something, there was little one could do to change it.

"Alright." I relented. "Report to my office in the morning. You'll function as my assistant until I can find a more suitable position for you. I'll promote Lance Corporal Wilhelm to the general's assistant until further notice."

Her shoulders relaxed, then she snapped a salute. The sudden movement made her teardrop earrings catch the light, which accentuated the elegance of her exposed neck and her necklace. The simple locket drew my eye to the uncharacteristic cleavage. After Schmidt's behavior, I certainly couldn't allow my attention to linger.

The reality was, however, that the way she held herself spoke of a regality one couldn't fabricate. Everything about her tonight screamed royalty, passion, and fire, but behind her, behind the glass doors, a crowd and a princess waited. And she was one of my subordinates.

"You look exquisite tonight, you know" I said.

Her mouth dropped open, and she blinked.

I stuffed my hands into my pockets and managed a smile, though my eyes fell to the hem of her deep blue skirt. "Ah! The lady is speechless."

When I raised my eyes to hers again, she looked away, her cheeks flashing a shade of crimson.

"Thank you," she said quietly. "For the compliment and for your help when I needed it." Her skirts rustled as she crossed to the doors. She paused with her hand on the glass knob, and then she left, disappearing into the crowd.

Standing there alone in the study, I lost track of time. I needed to banish Elaura from my thoughts, but she had a way of charging back in, persistent as ever. Her determination had impressed me from the moment I met her. A confident young woman, unwilling to wait for the world to change. Defiantly challenging the status quo.

The following days would be a challenge. Having Laura work so closely with me would force me continually to confront and deny my attraction to her. She had to be transferred to another officer sooner rather than later. Building my relationship with my fiancée was the priority. I drew in a deep breath and straightened my jacket so I could be present and afford Persephone my complete attention once I left the room. Any less would be unfair to both of us.

Before finding myself ready to leave, Persephone found me alone in the study.

"Tourelle, what's going on?" She asked, her head tilted to the side. "What did that girl want?"

"Nothing much," I replied. "Just a personnel matter. I have a few people to move around in the morning."

"If it was about personnel, why interrupt our evening? Surely it could've waited."

I shook my head. "It involved unseemly behavior."

Her brows pulled together. "Well, I think that the soldier should have come to you himself. It seems rather untoward to have one's escort retrieve an officer for him."

"She is the soldier," I admitted.

"Oh?" She scanned the room, looking anywhere but at me. "Do... Do you like her?"

For a moment, time stood still. I tried several times to speak, without success. She smiled softly and touched my arm. "It's okay if you do."

"Persephone, I—"

"Look, neither of us chose this," she said, her voice soft and contrite. "It's natural to have a life. To have wants and dreams. What is important now is that we be honest with one another."

A wave of guilt rushed through me. Here I had focused so much on concealing the truth from her in order to protect my family, while she offered the honesty I craved.

"Yes, I have feelings for her." The words turned my stomach as they crossed my lips. I hadn't wished for it, nor had I wished much of what happened in my life. I squeezed my eyes shut, unable to leave it unspoken. "She is not aware of them. I have not pursued those feelings, and have treated her as I would any colleague or friend of my sister."

She stepped closer, holding my gaze, and the delicate hand on my cheek warmed me. "Tourelle. It's alright. You are the most honorable man I know. If you tell me nothing has happened, then I believe you."

I covered her hand with my own, leaning into her touch.

My heart soared. I may have had no choice in whom I would marry, but at least she was a suitable match. Her invitation had lightened my burden and my anxieties relaxed as the truth came to light.

"Thank you." I pulled her hand from my face, slid my fingers in hers and kissed her hand.

Her smile grew wider, and a light blush stained her cheeks. She pulled her hand away with a gentle cough. "Well, we should probably get back to the party. It would be rude if the guests of honor hid for too long."

She slid her arm through mine and leaned her head on my shoulder as we returned to the dance floor. For another hour we danced together and with others, but then Persephone grew tired enough to leave. She declined my offer to walk her to the limo and I went to look for Lunette, who had been conspicuously absent.

I found her seated at a table, talking animatedly with Lance Corporal Wilhelm. Elaura sat between them, not paying much attention to their conversation, her gaze squarely fixed on the centerpiece before her. For a moment I wanted to ask what they'd done to make her look so dejected, but reminded myself that it should not be my business. I was there for Luna, not Elaura.

I walked behind my sister's chair and laid a kiss atop her head.

She pivoted in her seat to peek up at me with a smile. "Hey, stranger. I wasn't sure I'd see you tonight."

"You look lovely tonight Luna." I leaned over and set a key on the table in front of her. "I'm heading home. Let me know when you get there, so I don't spend all night worrying."

"I promise," she said with a smile. I patted her shoulder and made my way through the dance floor and out into the open air. I had little energy left to deal with much else, and wanted nothing more than to shower and crawl into bed. If I was lucky, I would sleep dreamlessly.

Though, I doubted fate would be so kind.

23

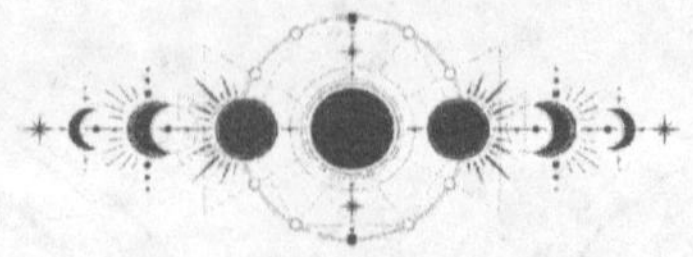

ELAURA

After the disappointment of the king not being in attendance the night before, as well as the fiasco with General Schmidt, I was grateful to see David seated outside his office in my stead. He acknowledged me with a nod but returned to working on his computer.

Things had grown tense between us during the ball. Lunette had turned his head. It didn't take a soothsayer to see that the meeting had left him more than a little conflicted. Though it wouldn't be for long.

After seeing them together the night before, I decided I would officially break off our fake relationship before the day was out. It would have to be a public spectacle. The base must speak of nothing else so that I cleared his name without undue hassle.

My steps slowed as I reviewed the plan, and to my chagrin, Tourelle was sitting on the edge of the assistant desk when I reached my new post.

He stood and folded his arms. "A few things to go over before you begin your brief assignment here."

I snapped to a salute. "Sir?"

"First off, I don't care what time General Schmidt allows you to arrive. I expect you to report to your station a minimum of fifteen early, which was half an hour ago. Any later and it will be a demerit. I have no problem demoting you further should you receive three such demerits." All signs of his jovial behavior from the night before had vanished with the setting of the moons. "I need you to understand that your time as my assistant will be short-lived. I cannot have you working directly under me for a variety of reasons. This arrangement will only last a couple of days, tops. Is that clear?"

"Yes, sir," I said, then bit my lip. When I'd approached him the night before, I'd let my anger forge my path against his advice. Now, in the light of day, I could see that while it got me away from the general, the transfer must've put him in a difficult situation. I had already relied on him too much. His goodness had made it easy to ask, even if asking was wrong.

He offered a curt nod and retreated to his office. I sat and familiarized myself with his schedule, noting the upcoming meetings with other officers and his usual routine. Within the hour, Tourelle was entertaining Major General Ancoupe. Ten minutes before the scheduled meeting's end, the young lady Tourelle had been dancing with the night before rounded the corner. She stopped short upon seeing me, and her eyes narrowed slightly, looking me up and down. Of course, I recognized my cousin, Princess Persephone Grakus.

Her pastel pink dress suit accented her curves while the miniature pink top hat contrasted with the lavender curls piled intricately atop her head. After sizing me up, she plastered on a genial smile, and her heels clacked in the small space as she approached my desk. "Is the major general free?" she asked, her soprano voice a little too sweet. "I need to steal a few moments of his time."

"I'm sorry, ma'am. He's in a meeting at the moment. Would you like to leave a message? I can give it to him as soon as the meeting ends." I offered the best smile I could. She was family, being my second cousin and all.

She giggled, her fingers covering her mouth. "You don't know who I am, do you?" She straightened with a smile, her chin lifting half an inch. "I'm Princess Persephone Grakus. Daughter of the king and the major general's fiancée."

Family or not, her use of my title still stung. I kept the smile on my face and nodded. "Of course, Your Highness. Please forgive me, but your fiancée *is* in a meeting at the moment. You are welcome to wait for him, or I can take down a message to give him when it is done." I motioned to the wooden chairs lining the hall.

Her lips pursed, but she took one of the open seats, smoothing her skirt beneath her as she sat. I'd hoped she would wait in silence. I had reports to finish. Those hopes died moments later.

"So, do you have a boyfriend?" she asked.

I glanced up to find violet eyes intent on me. I nodded and turned back to my work.

"Ooh! How long have you been together?"

I glanced up, my fingers paused in the middle of typing. "About a year and a half. We met in training and have been together since."

She squealed, clapped her hands together, then scooted forward in her seat. "Oh, that is so wonderful! I love to hear about how people fell in love. Who made the first move? You or him?"

I hadn't thought about how to answer a question like that. Frankly, I hadn't thought anyone might be interested in that much detail. Most of the people I interacted with were men, and it only took the mention of having a boyfriend since training to shut them up.

"Um, he did. We were battle buddies, and he found an opportunity for us to be alone and kissed me." There. That was enough truth to convince even Lunette, but it occurred to me that the princess might want the same questions asked to her. "How long have you and the major general been engaged?"

The way her smile grew, my guess had been right.

"Well, our parents betrothed us about six and a half years ago. We just made it official at the ball last night. I believe we invited the whole base. Didn't you go?"

"I did, but I'm afraid I arrived a little late. I must've missed the announcement. It was beautiful. I've wanted to go to one since I was a little girl." I paused, considering my next words. "It was like a dream come true."

"I'm so glad you liked it." She leaned back in her chair and studied her nails. "Have you been his assistant long?"

"Just today. His assistant got a promotion, and I'm filling in for a day or two."

She said nothing else, so I turned back to my work, grateful for the pregnant silence that followed. It seemed she had run out of subjects to ask about. Thank Kipp and Eira for that! The silence stretched on for a good five minutes before the door handle rattled. Persephone launched to her feet, handbag clutched before her, and her lower lip pinched between her teeth. The door opened to reveal Major General Ancoupe shaking Tourelle's hand.

"Thank you," Major General Ancoupe was saying. "I appreciate your help with the security for the—" Both men stopped short as soon as they saw the princess, who leapt forward.

"Your High... Persephone, what a surprise," Tourelle sputtered.

Major General Ancoupe clapped him on the shoulder and muttered, "We'll talk later." He bowed to the princess and left.

He had barely turned the corner when Persephone pouted, swaying her shoulder. "Tourelle, aren't you happy to see me?" She sounded so pitiful it almost made me sick. He crossed to his fiancée with only the slightest glance at me. "I am. I'm just... surprised is all." He smiled, though it seemed hollow somehow. "How about we go into the office and have a cup of tea?"

She nodded, her eyes glistening.

Was she *crying*? I'd never seen someone turn on the waterworks that fast. Perhaps she was overly sensitive. Without knowing her better, I couldn't be sure. I'd ask Luna later. She would know.

"Lance Corporal Carpe." Tourelle's voice ripped me from my thoughts.

"Yes, sir?" I said, looking up at Tourelle and Persephone, who was now staring at me, her brows knitted together.

"I asked you to go get some tea for Her Royal Highness, Princess Persephone." He said, his brow raised. I nodded and jumped out of my chair.

"Five minutes," he warned. "Don't take any longer."

I raced down the hallway.

I could feel her eyes following me until I was out of sight. The hair on the back of my neck stood at attention, as though she could read my thoughts, which was impossible. She'd have to be a soothsayer to do that. Still, I couldn't shake the feeling she didn't like me. Not the greatest of concerns, if I were honest with myself, since my time on base was to be short-lived.

I found David in the small alcove where assistants retrieved coffee, tea, or small snacks for our officers. He smiled when I arrived.

"David, thank goodness you're here. How is the promotion?"

He collected the small ornate coffee carafe and a few snacks onto a tray with an equally ornate cup and saucer. "Honestly? I'm on my third run of the morning. How did you handle it?"

I smirked. Working for Tourelle was more of a promotion than what the paperwork might suggest.

"Make a run to the mess hall after you drop this off. He won't notice you're missing till he finishes. That's when you give him the steaks he's really after. Then you'll have time to get some work done." I started on my tray, arranging the teapot and cups carefully to allow room for the biscuits and jams.

He bumped my elbow. "Are we still on for tonight? I got something fun planned this time."

The smile on his face turned my stomach. I didn't like what I would have to do tonight, and I doubted he would either. For a moment, I thought about doing it right away instead of waiting until we had an audience.

"Something new, huh?" My teasing fell flat in my ears, but he didn't seem to notice. "Did a new movie come out?"

"You know me too well." He balanced the tray with one hand and backed to the door. "But I'm still taking you to dinner tonight. Movie after."

"It's a date," I managed, forcing a smile while I hoisted the tray and edged past him.

I hurried back to Tourelle's office, knocked, and entered. Persephone sat facing Tourelle's desk, dabbing at her eyes with a tissue, while Tourelle knelt at her side, his arm around her. Something in me stirred at the concern in his eyes. I set the tray down on the desk before them and extricated myself as quickly and quietly as humanly possible. I didn't think they even noticed my presence. Only another twenty-four hours to go.

By this time tomorrow, I would be a fugitive of Grakus's current regime and far away from this place... and them. I closed the door as quietly as I could and returned to the stack of paperwork waiting for me.

Once I had the documents ready for Tourelle's signature stacked at the end of the desk, I printed the emails containing the lost and found notices for the base bulletin board. I slid one extra notice into the stack. This had to be the last meeting I would call. No matter what happened at the base assembly the next day, I could never serve in the same capacity again. Everything would change, and hopefully for the better.

Knowing the scene on the other side of the door, I didn't bother trying to knock. A quick glance at the clock justified leaving my post to get the lost and found cards posted before lunch. I posted the notices on the base bulletin board and ran to my building. I no longer cared what a passerby might think. Once in my small apartment, I collected all of my personal items and stuffed them in my military issue duffel. I paused at the gown hanging in my closet.

Touching the material, I considered taking it for just a moment, if only for the memories, both old and new, that it carried with it. I pulled away with a shake of my head. There would be time to find dresses in the future. Perhaps I would even be able to commission a closer replica of mother's gown. I slid the closet closed and turned to the last of my belongings in my desk.

It startled me how the room looked so much the same as it had when I moved in after training. I would miss nothing, yet part of me ached at leaving another home. True, it was nothing special. Not as grand as the palace of my youth, and not as homey as the cottage in Atha, but it was still a home. I stood at the edge of the unknown and would never return to this place.

The time on the alarm clock drew a curse from my lips. I'd already taken too long, and Tourelle would notice my absence. Pocketing my key, I raced to the front desk where Otto was on desk duty, as promised.

The thunk of my bag on the desk brought his attention out of the pages of his book.

"Hey, Sergeant Brays. Would you mind hanging onto this for me?" I asked with a wink. "I have to run back to my post."

The dimple on his cheek appeared when he grinned back. "Sure thing, Carpe. I'd be happy to. Have you posted the lost and found notices yet? I have a few items that need to be claimed." He offered me a sly wink, much better at the gesture than I was.

"Just posted them. Can you believe some guy lost his keys *and* a blow-up doll? Some of the stuff you guys lose baffles me."

He chuckled.

I rapped my knuckles on the desk. "I'd better get back. Thanks again."

I waved and jogged out the door, slowing my pace to a walk once I made it inside the administration building.

A new stack of paperwork took the place of the stack I had prepared for Tourelle. He had already noticed my absence. I took my seat and dove into the pile, hoping to make a dent before the office door opened. Hopefully, the princess was still in there, distracting him from the clock. I hadn't made plans to answer an inquisition about my whereabouts, which it would if the princess had left already.

The door opened, and a deep cough pulled my attention to Tourelle, who leaned against the frame and watched me with narrowed eyes. My luck was out. I wanted to shrink from the intensity of his glare.

"Where were you, Carpe?"

My mouth became a barren desert. What could I say that wouldn't lead to my execution? Neither "Sorry, my assassination plans took longer than I planned?" nor "I'm planning on abandoning you in the morning. What of it?" were suitable answers.

"Sir. I posted the notices to the board and then ran a personal errand."

His eyes might as well have been lasers for their unrelenting stare. One eyebrow crept up. "Did you go visit Lance Corporal Wilhelm?"

The question surprised me. Why would it matter if I'd gone down the hall to visit the man posing as my boyfriend? Then it hit me. Tourelle prided himself on honor. And a relationship between soldiers should not impede them from performing their duties.

Flames engulfed my ears. He imagined me so foolish as to shirk my duties in order to flirt with my boyfriend? Indignantly, I rose to my feet, my shoulders squared, and stared him down. "Since you insist on knowing, I am on my period and found myself without the supplies to deal with it. I returned to my bunk to retrieve adequate resources so that the desk outside your office didn't look like a crime scene by the end of the day." Slightly shocked at myself for the ease of the lie, I paused to let the words float between us. "I apologize for any inconvenience that my gender entails, sir."

All color drained from his face, then pink tinted his cheeks. He rubbed a hand over his mouth and nodded at me before retreating into his office and closing the door without another word.

I stared at the door between us for a moment, wondering what in the name of the founders had prompted me to make such a claim. My stomach twisted at the knowledge that I'd lied so easily and effortlessly. Papa would have held me to a higher standard. Guilty, I resumed my seat and began compiling notes from the paperwork on my desk. I'd never met a man as good as Tourelle outside of the palace before, and it hurt to know that even his treasured little sister lied to him.

Someday... someday, there would no longer be any cause for deceit, and I could be myself without guile, wherever I was.

***

My dinner with David was as explosive as I'd hoped. My behavior was necessary, but I wasn't proud of the things I said. I'd wounded his pride, and the cutting remarks had elicited the defensive reaction I'd needed. Things even got so heated that we were asked to leave the establishment before we finished our food. We rode in silence back to the base and made our way to the basement theater where the other five members of our team waited for us.

David stayed in the back while I took my place before the small group.

"I trust that you've all gotten your belongings to Sergeant Brays by now," I said, somehow keeping my voice steady after the disastrous, though intentional, dinner. "Tomorrow is the day we've been waiting for. We've had confirmation that the serpent will be in place come morning." Five heads bobbed in unison before me. "To be thorough, we'll go over the assignments one last time."

Save for David, the men before me smiled.

"Sergeant Warnock," I continued, "you'll feign illness tonight and in the morning. Being exempted from attendance, you'll be in charge of the extract vehicle."

Jeremy Warnock nodded, and I turned to Otto. "Sergeant Brays, have you finished loading the rig?"

Otto nodded, his curls bobbing above his glasses. "Loaded and ready to roll, Your Majesty." His attentiveness always impressed me, which was one of the many reasons he remained one of my favorites.

Jacob Ruiz and Jeremy both elbowed Otto and I chuckled. Their service and loyalty to Papa's legacy summoned a gratitude which wouldn't extinguish until my dying breath. Here I could be myself, and Papa would be proud I had such gallant friends on my side.

"Alright, let's bring it back, gentleman," I said, and they quieted. "Now, Major Jefferson and Major Rassier will sit on either side of me during the assembly. Major Ruiz will sit in front of me. You three will act as guards, if necessary. Sergeant Brays will sit near the door to assist in evac. We will wait for the signal before we make our stand. This should give Warnock enough time to get the jeep in place. Once the serpent has fallen, we get out and join the rest of our friends. Understood?"

Again, every head, save David's in the back, nodded in unison.

My eyes met his, and I knew he deserved an explanation. After my performance at dinner, he deserved it. We couldn't leave anything ambiguous. How could I find the right words to say that I needed him the most? I'd seen his goodness and dedication to the cause firsthand,

and his character made his presence on the base indispensable. With him here, I would have greater intel, but I also needed someone to watch over Lunette.

Even if the lengths I would need to go to fully exonerate him frightened me.

For a moment, I closed my eyes and imagined James by my side. "We owe them everything, Ella," he would have said. "We have a duty to fight for these brave men."

A lump rose in my throat, and tears sprang to my eyes. I cleared my throat. "No matter what happens tomorrow, I believe my father would be proud to know that such noble soldiers stand for Deletian ideals. I am proud to have you at my side."

I bowed to the men who had welcomed me as their leader. Their sovereign.

A muted thump sounded like a staccato beat as each man pounded his right fist against his chest in a non-verbal battle cry, offering their all to sovereign and people alike. As I rose, I couldn't stop the tears from racing down my cheeks. There was no way I could stem the wave of emotion washing over me.

"Thank you." I met each man's eyes in turn. "Now, it's time you all got to bed. We've got a big day tomorrow."

One by one, they rose, shook my hand, and left. All except David. He remained in his seat, elbows propped on his knees. I made my way to him and took the seat by his side. We sat in silence for a while, neither one of us wanting to speak first. At last, David spoke, his voice barely above a whisper, "So, how long have you been planning for me to stay?"

"Just after the ball," I admitted, detesting the way the words felt on my lips.

He nodded, almost mechanically. "You could have told me sooner, y'know. That break up thing you staged... I know you had your reasons, but... but I thought..." He pulled in a deep breath before he continued. "I thought we were partners here. Got each other's backs. I mean... I thought I'd be going to Charlesburg with you."

"Charlesburg?"

He chuckled dryly. "Well, that's what we call it. The founders named it Aberdeen, but we re-named it after your father when the rebellion formed... I just thought I'd be seeing it again soon."

I patted his knee. "I trust you more than anyone. Which is why—"

"—why you need me with you!" he interjected.

The hurtful things I'd said during our dinner floated through my mind along with a guilt I couldn't shake.

"Which is why I need you here," I finished. "I need to know that the reports I see are accurate. You've always given it to me straight, David. But... more than just the intel... I need you to look after someone."

At my mention of looking after someone, he rolled his eyes. "You want me to watch after the major general, don't you?"

With a deep breath to steady myself, I explained, "Actually, I'm not worried about the major general. It's his sister, Lunette." I knew without looking that his eyes were on me now, but I kept my gaze forward. "Believe it or not, she's a Caprician." I gave it a moment or two of silence before I met his gaze. Eyes and mouth wide, he took a few moments to form his thoughts.

"Lunette is a Caprician? What? I mean..." His hands covered his face with a rub before his palms turned out to the open room, trying to make some sense of the information. "Okay, okay. This is good. I mean... wait. How do you know?"

Reaching into the collar of my blouse, I lifted my locket from the confines of my shirt. "You recognized my family crest in a drawing. She recognized my mother's locket."

"Okay," he finally mumbled.

I sucked in a deep breath to ready myself, and touched his shoulder, bringing his eyes back to mine. "David, I need you to promise me one more thing... but you're not going to like it."

24

"Any base-wide assembly called by His Majesty, the King, shall be mandatory to all men, save those assigned to security of the base and those receiving medical exemption, both of which shall be reviewed following the assembly to prove validity. An invalidated exception shall count against a soldier as though he had voluntarily forgone the assembly. Failure to appear at such an assembly shall result in a sentence of three to six months in the brig. A third infraction shall carry with it the weight of treason."
~Military code 316861.48 Amendment B:15

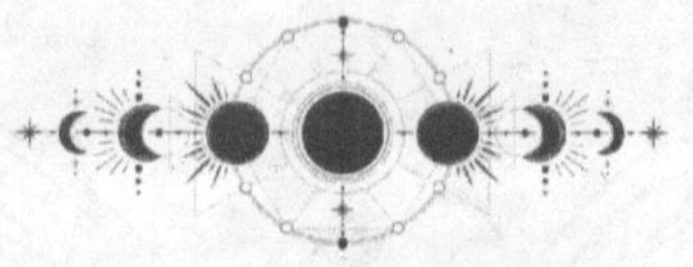

ELAURA

With everything in place, fear and excitement warred for supremacy with the coming assembly as I walked through the administration building for the last time. Once I'd reached my desk, I trailed my fingers across the glossy wooden surface, closed my eyes, and breathed deeply, committing the faint hint of musk in the air to memory. I never knew if the scent came from a cologne or aftershave, but it surrounded me when I was around him. I would miss that.

Like a shock of cold water, that longing froze me. He was my enemy. I understood his reasons for being loyal to my uncle. He had a family to protect. Not for one moment did I believe that he supported tyranny. I shook my head to banish the thoughts. No matter what his reasons might be, I would not allow him to be my downfall. Not when I was so close to my goal.

The offices were near empty due to the assembly, and only a short stack of folders contained paperwork awaiting Tourelle's signature. With my actual world finished, I'd run out of excuses to prolong what I actually came to do. Write a farewell note to Tourelle. After all, with the coming assembly, he wouldn't need to come to his office. It was a little risky, but the opportunity to leave my goodbye was worth it.

I'd wrestled long and hard with the idea of telling him, but given our history, the explanation needed to come from me. My heart needed to be honest with him. After today, they would know my name planet-wide, and he would see me through a different lens.

Once the incriminating words were inscribed in ink, I folded the paper and slid it beneath the documents. Anxiety churned my stomach as I entered his empty office. While I crossed the room with measured steps, the lone portrait on the wall to my right distracted me.

Tourelle, Lunette, and an older man, maybe Tourelle's father, gazed back. The older man's eyes and jawline had a remarkable resemblance to Tourelle, though his hair had been peppered gray. While both men's expressions reflected the solemnity of military zeal, Tourelle's eyes held more warmth and kindness than his father's. Lunette's smile elicited a smile of my own. With one last smile at my young friend, I turned my attention to Tourelle's desk itself.

Each stack of paper sat neatly aligned with one another, their corners crisp and symmetrical. Only one small picture frame disturbed the otherwise minimalist, functional surface. Tucking the folder under my arm, I picked up the frame, my fingers tracing the faces beneath the glass.

In this one, Tourelle's father looked a lifetime younger. The crisp and precise lines of his decorated uniform contrasted with the delicate pink dress worn by the dazzling, tall blonde at his side. Her eyes crinkled, but the chubby-cheeked little girl on her hip grimaced at the photographer. Both adults rested their hands on the shoulders of a grinning teenage boy, whose tousled hair was several shades lighter than his father's.

"That was taken a year before our mother passed."

Tourelle's voice in my ear made me jump and drop the folder. Its contents scattered across the floor. Terror gripped my stomach in its fist. My note lay mixed among the documents on the floor. I spun to face Tourelle.

How had I missed his approach and his scent, which enveloped my senses?

Instead of being upset at the invasion of his privacy, he smiled and took the frame from me, trailing a lone finger down the glass. "I was thirteen when she got sick. Luna was just four. She prayed every night for her mama to get better and be able to play with her again… but she only got worse." His countenance fell as he spoke. "I tried to make up for her absence when she passed. Lord knows I was a poor substitute."

The pain in his voice brought tears to my eyes. The papers littering the floor forgotten, I touched his arm. His eyes met mine for a moment. He cleared his throat, and his gaze dropped to the documents scattered around our shoes.

"Here, let me help," he offered.

He set the frame back on the desk and bent over to pick up a sheet from atop his boot. The blood in my veins froze. Where was the note?

"I've got it, thanks," I blurted as I dropped to my knees and snatched every paper I could lay my fingers on. In my frenzied haste, I crumpled several before I found it.

My heart slowed its pounding.

With a slight nod, Tourelle handed me the folder and, grabbing my elbow, lifted me to my feet before retrieving the last of the documents on the floor. "I'm sorry for startling you. I thought you heard me come in."

"It's alright. Need to stay on my toes anyway," I joked before reassembling the folder, taking care to keep the note out of it. Sliding the folder to the center of his desk, I chanced speaking my mind. I kept my back to him, afraid of his reaction. "What are you doing here, anyway? Don't you have your hands full with the King's assembly after formally announcing your engagement to the princess? I mean... I didn't expect to see you here today."

"Yeah, I hadn't planned on it either, but I... I wanted to apologize for my behavior yesterday. I was short with you when I shouldn't have been." He paused for a moment, and I dared to turn around to face him. "Being engaged to the princess... All of this is new to me. I don't know how to behave when she's around, and..." He rubbed his fore-head absently. "I've been out of sorts the last few days trying to prepare for this thing that my father arranged. It isn't fair for you to bear that burden. I was wrong to behave the way I did."

His eyes met mine and held me captive in their watery depths. Words, like shadows, remained unspoken, and in that moment, my heart nudged me to tell him the truth. To put an end to all the lies that instant.

If only.

If only I could take the chance and speak from my heart. If only it was just my life hanging in the balance. If only I had the courage to be completely honest.

Instead, I would leave him a note like a coward. A coward with lives on the line.

He cleared his throat and looked away. At least one of us still had a shred of propriety.

I blinked a few times and donned a grateful smile. "I appreciate the apology. Your friendship means a lot to me." It was as close as I would come to the pure truth before my betrayal.

He responded with such a wide smile that the corners of his eyes crinkled. "Maybe I'll take those documents and get them finished during the assembly. Then I might have enough time that we could meet up afterward. I could introduce you and David to Persephone as my friends."

He reached for the folder on the desk, sliding it to the edge of the wood. I smiled, but slapped my hand atop the folder, keeping him from pulling it further. His eyes went wide at the loud thwack.

"Nice as that sounds, sir," I said, my mouth suddenly dry, "It wouldn't be prudent. I don't recommend you work on these documents until after your fiancée leaves. It wouldn't be fair to her if you divide your attention at such an important event."

"You're probably right." He withdrew his hand and, with a half-hearted smile, said, "Thanks, Elaura. And sorry… again."

He disappeared through the doorway, leaving me stunned.

Elaura.

He'd not used my given name since we'd met. Once I told Schmidt my name was Laura, he followed suit without deviation. I'd almost forgotten that he ever knew. I stared at the open door for what felt like an eternity, though the clock on the wall only marked a few minutes passing.

At last I came to my senses and went back to work. Rounding the desk, I placed the folder in the center of the wood before the chair and pulled a pen from the cup, setting it parallel to the documents. Thankful he hadn't seen the note in my hand, I slid it under his keypad and made sure the corner of the paper stood out.

I stole one last look at the family photo atop his desk, memorizing the joy of a young man unburdened by life's cares. I wished I had met Tourelle when I was just as carefree. I wrenched myself away, praying that God willing, I'd find a measure of happiness...someday.

It took only six strides to cross the room and leave the office and its memories behind. The clock on my desk informed me that the men would gather for the assembly soon. I needed to claim my seat in the hall. I'd heard from multiple sources that the higher-ups would not tolerate tardiness in the king's presence, so I tidied my workspace, trying to push past the idea that someone might read the note before the assembly. At least attendance was mandatory, save for the security forces, which would have no cause to investigate small pieces of paper on an officer's desk.

With a deep breath, I made my way through the hallway, down the elevator, and out of the building. Once the sunlight touched my skin, I jogged the few blocks to the assembly hall. I wanted to get to my seat and have my men at my side. Once inside, I didn't have to look far to see Brandon and Cade in the crowd. Cade waved me over with a cheerful grin. His easygoing demeanor, even in the circumstance, calmed the butterflies in my stomach. Brandon leaned over as I sank into the cushioned seat between them.

"Where were you?" he asked in a hushed tone. "I thought you'd be here before us."

"I had to take care of something," I whispered, then turned my attention to the empty stage.

Brandon shifted a little in his seat. "You ready?"

I glanced at him, then back, before nodding.

He continued, "Good. You'll need this."

Without looking, he slid a weighty, wrapped object onto my lap. I curled my fingers around his, glancing at him for no longer than a moment. He pulled his fingers free, allowing me to tuck the package under my thigh.

"Thanks," I muttered. "You ready?" I leaned my head on his shoulder in hopes the action would add to the gossip about my break-up with David the night before.

"Yeah," he said.

I raised my voice and said, "It's a big day."

"Careful, Carpe." Brandon chuckled. "Your boyfriend might get jealous."

"So what? We're not together anymore," I stated.

"What do you mean?" Cade exclaimed on my other side.

I expected that the news would come as a bit of a shock to those within earshot. Even to the men at my side. I had told no one but David about this part. Their organic reactions were critical to re-enforcing David's innocence. His safety depended on it.

Brandon pulled away from me, his brow furrowed. His sudden motion forced me to sit back up. "You guys have been thick as thieves since you got here."

"He wanted more than I did," I said offhandedly, "so I ended it. That's all there is to it."

He stared at me a moment before nodding slowly and allowing me to replace my head on his shoulder. I sneaked a glance at Cade, whose jaw was tighter as he stared at the stage, as though I'd said nothing.

A murmured hum rippled out around us. Hopefully, word was spreading to any who hadn't already heard the news about my split from David. It never ceased to amaze me how fast rumors spread among men. Old ladies got a bad rap for gossip when men in close quarters had the loosest lips. No doubt news would travel the base before the assembly started.

I chanced a look around the assembled soldiers and found David sitting a few rows back on the other side of the aisle. Our eyes met, and he looked away just as fast. He didn't like the plan. He'd said as much the night before, but his expression screamed it now. The man to his right tapped his shoulder, then said something. David gave a half-hearted smile, said something, and glared at me. It was my turn to look away. It offered a small amount of comfort that now the entire company might know about our messy break-up.

As the assembly's start drew closer, I slid my hand within the folds of the fabric of the wrapped object Brandon gave me and reveled in the feel of cold steel against my fingers. Everything was about to change. Everything.

25

Without respect of person, any soul convicted of the assassination of a sitting sovereign, either by his own hand or by the hand of another, shall be put to death by firing squad. Whether the subject of the assassination survives the attempt on their life or not, the sentence shall not change.
~Deletian Criminal Code 35630.58.23

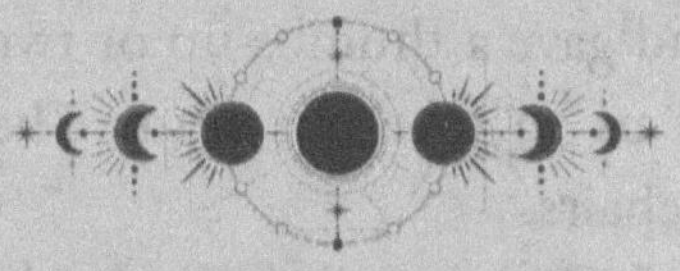

ELAURA

A hush fell across the men as, one by one, the base officers took the stage. Princess Persephone and Lunette followed close behind Tourelle, and ahead of the other major generals. Lunette walked tall with her chin held high and her arm linked with Princess Persephone's. She didn't even glance at the princess, but kept her gaze on her brother before her. They all waited in front of their seats as the last officers joined them.

A low buzz of activity began at the back end of the hall, growing steadily louder and moving its way through the crowd. Every officer on stage saluted the company. The men before me all turned and saluted the source of the commotion.

When at last I turned myself, my great uncle Grakus, the reigning king of Delta, walked down the center aisle, shaking every hand thrust at him, smiling, winking, and patting the backs of the soldiers he passed, as though he were a celebrated performer. He caught my eye as he passed, pointed at me with both hands, and gave me a very deliberate wink. The hair on my arms stood on end. Papa had been right about hiding us from him.

Brandon elbowed me, reminding me to show proper military respect. I brought my fist to my heart, taking great care to keep my elbow pointed at my side. Thankfully, every soldier along the aisles had been slow to salute as well, having been more focused on touching their sovereign like he was a prophet sent to cure them. My stomach churned.

With a brilliant smile upon his face, Grakus took the stage before the cheering crowd of Deletion soldiers. His arms rose above his head as he pointed, waved, and gave a thumbs-up or two. At last, he took the podium and signaled us to take our seats. The officers behind him finally sank into their chairs.

"Deletian soldiers," Grakus called. "I thank you for your tireless service to the crown and to the good people of Delta! Nowhere in the known expanse of universes is there a more loyal and faithful bunch than you!"

The men cheered, and Grakus's smile grew wider. While he waited for the assembly to quiet down, I bit back the bile threatening to claw its way to freedom. My fingers tightened around the handle of the gun under my thigh. How long would the signal take?

We needed to get us out of there as soon as possible.

"Now we still have some work to do wiping those treacherous Capricians from the map," he continued once the crowd's roar settled. "Rather than hop a shuttle to another world more aligned to their views, they remain to torment the good people of Delta with their treachery. This is a battle for the very soul of our planet. In our proud history, since the landing of the founders, not even those who deny the very existence of the creator, God, have dared so great a perversion of what it means to be a Deletian."

Applause thundered, then died again in the space of Grakus's pause.

"I receive regular reports of these criminals trying to infiltrate your ranks."

The men around me booed the news.

He shook his head. "Yes. In the last few years alone, we have executed many of these would-be spies in our training camps. Our vigilant sergeants have gone to great lengths to single out every Caprician who tries to sneak among your ranks."

His mention of executions in the training camp brought back the images of those two innocent men who had died for a doodle. The memory made me sick. I dared a glance at Brandon by my side. He clapped along with the rest of the company, his back straight, the very image of a dutiful soldier.

Applauding those deaths as though they were a good thing made my blood boil.

My heart pounded in my ears, drowning out the noise around me. I'd never wanted power, had been happy to leave that to my father and brother. Power, however, was all that my great-uncle had ever craved.

My jaw clenched. The man at the podium presented himself as a loving leader, but he was evil. His speech was nothing but the crafty words of a dictator, poisoning the hearts of his men, turning them against one another.

I squeezed my eyes shut and called upon the memory of my family for strength. As the applause died away, warmth swelled in my chest, emboldening me. I sat a little straighter, lifting my chin and resting my hands on my lap, ready to clap if necessary. Opening my eyes, I focused on the stage.

Grakus had taken a seat, and General Schmidt approached the podium, waving someone onto the stage. Confused, I looked at Brandon. I had missed something. This was an assembly to announce the engagement between Tourelle and Persephone, wasn't it? Brandon's eyes never left the stage, but the white pallor of his knuckles in his lap did not bode well.

A pair of MPs dragged a young private to the center of the stage in front of the seated dignitaries and officers. His unbuttoned shirt flapped with the motion of their movement, revealing a bloodied white tank top. His face was discolored and swollen from a beating. The MPs shoved him down to a kneeling position, facing the audience.

Grakus looked on, reclined in his chair, his ankle resting on his knee.

I didn't care if anyone heard anymore. I leaned toward Brandon and asked in a hushed whisper, "What's going on?"

"They'll read some bogus charges," he hissed back, "and then whip the kid. They make an example of some poor green private every time the king visits. Schmidt has to prove how tough he is. It's his way of 'weeding out' the traitors."

Shocked, I turned my gaze back to the stage. They'd discarded the private's torn button up on the floor, and the MPs held his arms out to the side, preventing him from falling to the ground. Red seeped in a jagged trail from the right shoulder to his waist. Major General Ancoupe cut the man's undershirt off. Bruises of black, purple, and older green covered his back, and his ribs showed. The half of his face not swollen from brutality testified that he was barely old enough to enlist.

Rage simmered in my chest. This boy didn't deserve treatment like this. No one did.

General Schmidt stepped forward. "Private Justin Ostler stands accused of assaulting Her Highness, Princess Persephone, during her time on base. She has graciously declined to press any formal charges, but I will have justice and order in my ranks. Private Ostler, you will receive another twenty lashes and spend the rest of the month in the brig."

Private Ostler begged, his voice hoarse and ragged, his words incomprehensible, but when his pleas to the general fell on deaf ears, he turned tear-filled eyes to the princess.

The first lash split the air. Ostler cried out, his back arching away from the blow.

I hadn't even seen Major General Ancoupe retrieve the whip.

A second and a third lash, and the poor boy sagged between the MPs. I winced with every crack. Every cry resonated in my chest as if they were my own.

Between cracks, someone behind me muttered, "Poor bugger. Spilled his drink on the princess, leaving the ball. She must've taken it pretty personally."

"Naw, not her," another soldier said. "She's too nice for that. Wouldn't get that mad over a spilled drink."

"But he spilled it in front of Schmidt. You know how behoven to the king the old fart is. Anything happens to the princess on his watch, it's a one-way ticket to a body-bag."

The first cleared his throat. "A few lashes and a couple of weeks in the brig aren't that bad."

"I wouldn't count on it. If the kid survives, you can bet he'll never see duty again."

At my other side, Cade growled out, "Shut up, the lot of you!"

They fell silent, though the whip continued. Fire ignited in my veins. This wasn't discipline. Such a callous disregard for human life had to be stopped. Again, the image of the two recruits executed in training came to mind. Their lifeless eyes turned to me, a silent plea for justice.

As if my hands moved without my permission, they slid into the folds of the fabric on my lap. The cold steel of the handle welcomed my fingers like an old friend. My index finger traced the outline of the trigger.

The whip snapped again.

My fingers ached as they clenched the grip.

I can't act. Not yet. I can't ruin the plan.

Every cry dug a deeper trench in my heart.

We hadn't received the signal yet, but I couldn't sit idly by as they snuffed out another innocent life in the name of tyranny. I had seen enough.

I jumped to my feet, aimed the gun to the ceiling, and fired.

Debris cascaded down. Ancoupe's whip dropped. The boy fell as the MPs froze in alarm. Every eye—even the king's—focused on me.

"Uncle Divo," I called through the stunned silence, "your reign of terror has gone on long enough."

His eyes narrowed, focusing on me like lasers, and his bodyguards closed in on him.

A rustle and footsteps sounded behind me, and Brandon leapt to my defense. Out of the corner of my eye, I saw his fist slam into the offender's face. Cade and Jacob rose, their weapons drawn. I stood a little taller with my allies around me, lifted my chin, and pulled my shoulders back.

"I am Elaura Delphine Caprice, second child of King Charles Andrew Caprice and Queen Denna Ellen Harraldine Caprice, rightful heir to the throne of Delta."

Several officers on the stage started toward me, but Grakus shoved past his bodyguards and held up a hand, halting them, an amused smile on his face.

"My nephew's children were lost to the Ages," he began. "You cannot possibly—"

The color from his face drained, and his jaw went slack.

"Your reign of terror is at an end." I leveled the gun at him and pulled the trigger.

Time slowed as the bullet left the chamber. Schmidt leapt to put himself between Grakus and the speeding slug, but the bullet struck the podium and Grakus crumpled to the ground.

Near the stage, Tourelle crouched over Lunette and Persephone; his eyes never leaving me. Everything in his expression screamed betrayal.

Brandon pushed me toward Cade, who was already in the aisle, his gun at the ready, aimed at the stage. Cade led the way down the aisle with Jacob at his side, their firearms trained on any threats from the audience.

Another shot rang out, this one from behind. Cade crumpled backward to the ground before me, a crimson trail forming from a hole between his unseeing eyes. Looking to the source of the sound, I spun around. David trained his gun on me, and my heart pounded in my chest. I had planned it, but the sight still chilled me to the bone.

Brandon hauled me away from Cade, toward our salvation.

Another shot rang out, and my right bicep erupted in fire. The shock of the pain stunned me, I faltered, and crashed to the ground past the door. Gravel biting into my skin.

With a surge of energy I couldn't explain, I fought past the blazing inferno beneath the skin and stood. I ran, and my right arm pulsed steady thrums of pressure. After a few strides, Brandon's arm circled me, pulling me around the corner.

"What were you thinking?" Brandon shouted, while practically pulling me with him.

"Faster," Jacob panted. "Our extract might be burnt now!"

I swallowed a groan, gripping my arm.

The screech of tires pulled my attention up as the jeep pulled up beside us.

"Get in," Jeremy cried, noting our conditions with wide eyes. "Where's Rassier?"

Brandon lifted me into the backseat before answering. "Dead." He climbed in next to me and smacked the back of Jeremy's seat. "Go, go, *go!*"

Gravel spit from the tires just as a handful of soldiers rounded the corner. Bullets hit the back of the vehicle. Brandon pressed me down into the seat, while Jacob and Otto returned fire over the back of the vehicle.

"What happened to Cade?" Jeremy asked over his shoulder as he sped through the base.

"Wilhelm opened fire on us. Shot both Cade and Laura."

Jeremy slammed his palm on the steering wheel. "Traitor!"

A siren split the air as the jeep lurched around a turn, smashing the three of us together in the backseat. The pain in my arm exploded, and I cried out.

Brandon cursed. "Warnock! Mind those turns! This ain't no joyride!"

Otto rose in his seat, turning enough to shout, "Gate ahead! Get down! They'll be expecting us!"

Jeremy pulled a heavy blanket over himself, while Otto followed his own advice. Brandon helped me slide down to the floorboard and took his place atop me. The weight crushed me when Jacob climbed atop Brandon. Seconds later, bullets bit into the vehicle's sides or ricocheted into the seats. A massive shadow passed over us as we raced through the gate, and the front bumper shattered the stop arm.

Despite the cold air whipping around us, my eyelids felt heavier than they should. The bullets sounded more like rainfall than projectiles. When the sound vanished and Jeremy called out that we were clear, Brandon and Jacob helped me back up into the seat.

I let go of my arm, and when I glanced at my hand, the large amount of blood coating my fingers made the lack of pain surprising. I needed to look at the injury. With trembling fingers, I tried to work on unbuttoning my jacket, then my shirt, but the tremor in my right hand made it useless. Seeing my struggle, Brandon swatted my hand out of the way and ripped the buttons free, revealing the gray tank top beneath. He pulled my good arm free, and I whimpered as he helped peel the fabric from the wound. The pain steadily grew as the wind whipped around us, biting at the exposed flesh.

"No exit wound. Bullet's still in there," Brandon said, though I couldn't tell if he meant the words for me, or if he was thinking aloud. He grabbed my discarded shirt from the seat and wrapped it around my arm. "Brays, tell me we got a first aid kit on board!"

Despite the sunlight, my fingers and toes felt frozen, as though I had soaked them in ice, and the chill slowly crept up my extremities.

Otto handed the box back to Jacob, who began digging through it and handing supplies to Brandon. "It took a few bullets, but should still be good."

"Long as the gauze is still sterile, we'll be fine," Brandon said as he donned a pair of gloves. Using his teeth, he ripped open a few packets and stacked small squares of gauze, one on top of the other. He pulled the shirt away and dropped it before he slid a strip of gauze beneath my arm and met my gaze.

"Laura, this is going to hurt. It's going to hurt a lot. There's no way to get the bullet out now, but we have to stop this bleeding." He positioned the stack of square gauze pieces above the bullet wound. He nodded at Jacob, who braced me on the other side. "Get ready. On the count of three. One... two..."

Without giving a third count, he pressed the gauze square stack into the wound.

No amount of preparation could have prepared me for the sheer agony that flooded my arm and shoulder all the way to the tips of my frozen fingers. I cried out, tears racing down my face unrestrained. The world shifted to a shade of white while Brandon wrapped the long stretch of gauze around my arm. I struggled to focus on anything other than the sound of the rushing wind. It wasn't until a blanket wrapped around me that I realized how badly I was shivering.

"How... long... until..." I managed as Brandon pulled me under his arm. I didn't know if he meant to comfort or warm me, but I didn't care.

"Not long, Majesty," he said, anticipating my meaning.

Even with the blanket, I still couldn't get warm. The chill continued to creep through to my bones. I tried to smile, but the effort was more than I had the strength for.

"Thanks," I muttered, surrendering to exhaustion.

A stiff jostle woke me enough to look into Brandon's eyes. "Hey! I need you to stay awake for me, okay? I know you're tired, but you can't sleep yet."

"How's she doing back there?" Otto asked from the front.

At least, I think it was Otto. The air had a strange hum to it.

"She's hanging in there, but she needs a doctor ASAP."

"You used the Hemostat, right?" That voice—Jeremy?—sounded far away

Brandon scoffed in my ear. "No, I want her to bleed out before we meet the chopper. Of course, I did, you moron! Who's the field medic here?"

"Calm down."

"Yeah, well, you do your job and get us there in one piece, and I'll do mine. Brays, ping the chopper. Let them know we're coming in hot with wounded."

I stopped caring who was speaking. Even Brandon's voice felt distant after a while. Opening my eyes between blinks became more and more difficult. My head lolled onto someone's shoulder.

Brandon shook me again, snapping me from the lurking dark. "Hey, I need you to stay awake. Talk to me. Tell me something. First thing that comes to mind."

"Tourelle is gonna hate me," I mumbled.

Even then, I couldn't forget the pain of betrayal etched on his face as he crouched over his sister and fiancée. Even in my memory, his blue eyes burned into mine.

"That's expected. He's the enemy. Always has been."

"I like him, though," I admitted, the words tumbling from my lips unbidden.

"I like the guy, too, but you have to face facts. He's engaged to the bloody baron's daughter, and you are the rightful heir to the throne of Delta. He can't be trusted."

It was getting harder and harder to keep my own thoughts straight. I tipped my head forward but couldn't banish the cobwebs forming in my mind. "I hope David's okay."

Brandon made a noise. Something like a snort. "I wouldn't worry about that traitor. He can burn for all I care."

I shook my head, but the cobwebs were getting thicker. David followed... What was he following?

"He's still a... a..." What was the right word? "...still a friend."

"Laura, friends don't shoot each other. He shot you, and he killed Cade. Friends don't do that." Why was Brandon's voice so far away?

"He wasn't trying... didn't want to... had to keep their trust..." My tongue didn't want to cooperate.

"Laura! Hey!"

"Keep her awake, man!"

Pain flashed as hands shook me. The weight in my eyelids made it too hard to open them all the way, but I could make out Brandon's form beside me.

"Stay with me. Why does he need to keep their trust? Tell me."

Darkness reached out, its embrace inviting me to forget everything for a moment, but I had to tell them, had to make certain that they understood. "He's... my mmmmm..." The word didn't want to form. "Mole."

Brandon said something, but the words escaped me. He might as well have spoken across a crowded room. I was just so tired that I didn't care anymore.

As I surrendered to sleep's warm embrace, one image haunted my mind: Tourelle. The hurt and betrayal in his eyes demanded retribution. Without the strength to speak, I could only offer one parting thought as I slipped into the dark.

I'm so sorry.

At the joyous announcement of the engagement of Princess Persephone, a rebel by the name of Elaura "Laura" Carpe sought to assassinate his majesty, King Divo Von Grakus claiming to be the only surviving child of the former king.
We will not tolerate these baseless claims. His majesty King Grakus has offered the sum of three million dillerens to any soul to deliver her, dead or alive, to his majesty.
~ Royal Press Release

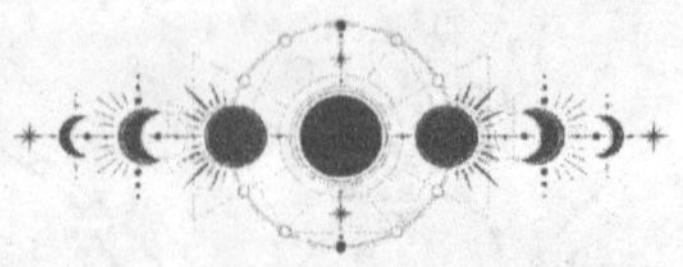

ELAURA

A soft, rhythmic beeping pulled me from the edge of the shimmering fog. My dreams, troubled as always, shifted between images of my loved ones to the hurt in Tourelle's eyes and the guilt that followed. As the haze slipped away, so did the images of Tourelle. All that remained was the steady beep.

When I opened my eyes, an unfamiliar ceiling greeted me, and sunlight poured through a large window to the left of my bed. Soft blue panels along the lower half of the walls did little to soften the yellow pallor. My sluggish mind failed to recognize where I was and why I was here. Nor could I imagine why my mouth was a barren desert, while my limbs had a weight I couldn't place.

Bit by bit, clues came to mind.

I had gone to an important assembly to do something, but what? I saw Tourelle's face, his eyes like sapphires, like deep pools of pain, fury, and betrayal. Who hurt him like that?

Pushing against the cobwebs, I fought through images of a ride in an open-air vehicle and bullets flying. I was... hurt? Yes, the memory of the white-hot pain was both vivid and out of reach. I swallowed against the gravel in my throat, already weary from the struggle to remember.

The click of a door latch interrupted my search, and I turned my head on the pillow. A muscular man in pale blue scrubs stood in the doorway, holding a data-pad. His dark curls swayed with the motion. He closed the space between us in two strides, adjusting his glasses as he did. Confused as I was, I knew a doctor when I saw one.

"Ah! Good, you're awake. How are you feeling?" His smile exposed a dimple in his right cheek.

"Fuzzy," I managed, my voice hoarse. I coughed, and he lifted a glass of water, touching the straw to my lips. After taking a sip or two of water, the gravel softened a little. "Thank you."

The doctor returned the cup back to the side table. "Of course. So, you said you feel fuzzy. How do you mean?"

"A little... I can't find the right words."

He scribbled something on the data-pad with a stylus. "That is to be expected. Waking from anesthesia can be rather jarring. I'm Dr. Ruben Martinez. I've been overseeing your care. Let's start with an easy question. Do you know where you are?"

The memory of the long, painful trip suggested we'd traveled a long way, but is that what he meant? "A hospital, I think, but I... I don't know where."

He met my eyes and smiled. "It's alright. You weren't conscious when you arrived. I wouldn't expect you to know what city we're in. What is the last thing you remember?"

"Someone was shooting. My arm," I said, then licked my lips. Brandon held me close, begging me to stay awake. I was sad about something, but what? The more I tried to reach it, the memory concealed itself like a ghost shrouded in linen. "I think something hit me? Brandon helped, but," I swallowed. "that's all I can remember."

Even what I could recall felt like a dream: I could picture it, but somehow it didn't seem real. My eyes darted side to side as if I might find the answers around me.

But even as I reached for the memory, alarms sounded in my mind.

Then, I found the information I sought. Great-uncle Grakus had murdered my family and stole the throne, and I was in the way of his claim.

Don't say anything else, Elaura.

"Sounds like you had a pretty rough time." The doctor's voice brought me back to the hospital room, where his stylus hovered over the data-pad expectantly. "Do you remember how you got shot?"

Panic surged, and the beeping beside my bed sped up with my heart rate, as all at once, the memory flooded back. I shot my great-uncle. We ran. We lost Cade. David fired a second shot, and it hit me. We fled, but Brandon had been with me. Who else? Flashes of the escape rushed back. Jeremy. He was driving, and Otto sat in front with him, while Jacob sat in the back seat at my side. Where were they now? Why was I alone? Where were they? In a detention center waiting for their coming executions?

Danger splintered like ice through my veins. Brandon wouldn't willingly leave me. Neither would the others. I had tried to assassinate my great-uncle, and whether or not I succeeded, someone would be looking for me. Even if my men had been forcibly removed, I needed to protect them.

The soft-spoken doctor seemed suspicious, dodging my questions as deftly as any investigator, making notes on every answer I gave. Was he really even a doctor? He glanced at the screen displaying my vitals, then back at me.

I shook my head. "Sorry, doctor, it's really hazy," I lied.

He nodded and scribbled something on the pad. This time, his smile didn't reveal his dimple. "Can you tell me your name?"

I opened my mouth to speak, but what name should I give? If I was on the run from the usurper, Grakus, I couldn't use my alias Laura Carpe. I couldn't give this stranger my real name, not without knowing where this hospital was and where his loyalties lie.

"Lucy Breckin," I said, blurting out the first thing that came to mind. "My friends call me Luce."

The doctor set his stylus down. "Really? Your friends gave me a different one." He looked down at his data pad and then back up at me. "Which one should I use?"

What name had they given? Where were they?

I tried to sit up, wincing against the pain in my arm and the wave of nausea that crashed over me, but a lethargic weight pinned me down.

Doctor Martinez leapt forward and pressed my shoulders back into the bed. "Hey, you need to rest. I don't want those stitches splitting. If you'd like to sit up, all you gotta do is say so." He let me go, leaned down to the side of the bed, and pressed a button. "You need to give your body more time to heal." The bed raised me into a reclined sitting position, allowing me to see the empty chairs in the hallway. I looked back at the doctor.

"Where are they?" I demanded, my voice cracking.

"Where are who?"

"My friends," I croaked. "The ones who brought me in. Where are they?" My attempt to sound stern sounded more like a desperate plea, even to my own ears.

The doctor's brown eyes searched mine, and a moment later, the realization crossed his face. Without any explanation, he began to laugh quietly, the dimple on his cheek mocking my confusion. The shift in atmosphere unbalanced me, and my cheeks heated.

"What's so funny?" I croaked.

He shook his head, and his humor subsided. "Forgive me, Elaura. Your friends are fine. They're talking with Admiral Markes, the head of the Caprician army." He bowed slightly. "*Your* army."

Relief washed through me like cool water on a hot day, washing away fear and doubt. I was finally free to be myself. Still, I had to ask, "How did you know my name? The men I was with, they only heard it once. They knew me by my alias, Laura Carpe. I didn't think they'd remember it after the assembly."

"I remember you." He ran a hand over his short, dark curls. "But first, forgive me. I forgot to tell you where you were earlier. You are in Charlestown, well behind the Caprician lines." His smile, warm and quick, comforted me like an embrace. "Perhaps you might recognize me later, though it's been a long time and you've been through hell and back since last we met." He took my hand and gave it a gentle squeeze. "I was the royal family's physician before the coup. I delivered you and your little brother. You've changed so much since, have grown into a beautiful young woman. You have your mother's beauty and your father's eyes. It's a miracle no one else saw it."

I swallowed against the lump growing in my already raw throat. "You knew my parents?"

He nodded, patting my hand in his. "I did. I knew them very well.

They were the best of people. I'm so sorry for your loss, Elaura. I can't even fathom what you've been through." He pressed his lips together.

"Thank you," I whispered, afraid to say anything else for fear that I might cry.

Clearing his throat, he released my hand and retrieved his data pad. "How about I tell you what we did after you got here? The bullet nicked your artery, but thankfully, it stayed to plug the hole it created. If it hadn't, you may not have made it. Major Jefferson's bandaging also helped a great deal." He rubbed his nose with the stylus still in hand. "When you got here, you'd already lost a lot of blood. Another hour, and we likely wouldn't be having this conversation. We repaired the artery and removed the bullet. You are going to be sore for a while. I don't want you lifting anything heavier than a pen with that arm quite some time."

I tried to listen, but knowing where I was and that I was safe, there wasn't enough room in my head for more information. We'd made it! I don't have to hide anymore. The people around me that wanted me to succeed, to have my family legacy celebrated rather than scourged. I didn't realize what a weight I'd carried until it lifted off my shoulders.

When I choked back a sob, Doctor Martinez stopped, eyeing me carefully. He rose halfway. "Elaura, are you alright? Are you in pain? I can—"

"No," I choked out, halting him a stride from his chair. "It's not pain. It's just... I... I don't know what to say. It's real. I'm here."

He sank back into his chair as I wiped at my face, avoiding the plastic box attached to my finger. His fingers slid around my free hand with a squeeze.

"Yes, Elaura, it's real. There are many people here who believe in you. Especially those young men. My nurses had quite a time getting them out of the room so I could treat you. Admiral Markes had to threaten them with a court martial to get them out of here." He shook his head.

"Sounds like them alright." The mental image of them causing a ruckus over standing guard brought a smile to my face.

Dr. Martinez released my fingers and rose, giving my hand a pat.

My eyes met his, and I had to know one more thing. "Doctor? Were we successful? Is my uncle dead?"

He patted my hand. "I'm afraid I don't know. I'll let you get a little rest. The admiral will be here later today to speak with you. I'm sure he'll let you know." He turned to leave, pausing at the door to say, "It's wonderful to see you again, Elaura."

I sat alone in the quiet room with only the rhythmic beeping of the medical equipment to keep me company.

There was so much to absorb. I made it to Charlestown. My childhood doctor was still alive. I could lead my people once I recovered. Though if Grakus lived, he would be determined to stop me. But thinking about the usurper brought Tourelle to mind. The way he'd crouched over his sister and fiancée after I'd shot my great-uncle, the king. If only I could have trusted Tourelle with the truth. To have been able to be honest with him about who I really was before it was too late. My chest ached with the thought that I'd hurt him. I hoped against all hope that I would not be the one to send him to the Ages now that we stood on opposite sides of the war. I couldn't be sure of my ability to do that just yet.

I hated my great-uncle even more for the way Tourelle had been trapped into his betrothal. Tourelle stayed to protect his family, and that was a bitter thought. He would honor his duty and keep his family safe.

If I could lead my people to free Delta from Grakus, then I would also release Tourelle from any obligation to marry my cousin.

I needed to be strong for my people; I reached for my mother's locket, but my hand grazed the oxygen hose hanging from my face. Exhausted, I let my hand fall to my lap and tried to relax against the pillow.

My family's faces emerged in my memory. Mama's smile radiated pride, as did Papa's. Greggie beamed with his arms outstretched. James wore a knowing smirk, the kind I used to want to smack from his face when I was young. Now I saw it for what it really was. He'd always believed in me... Always.

Mama, Papa, James, Greggie.

I closed my eyes and promised, "I've made it. We will have justice for our people. They will be free from tyranny, if it's the last thing I do."

AFTERWORD

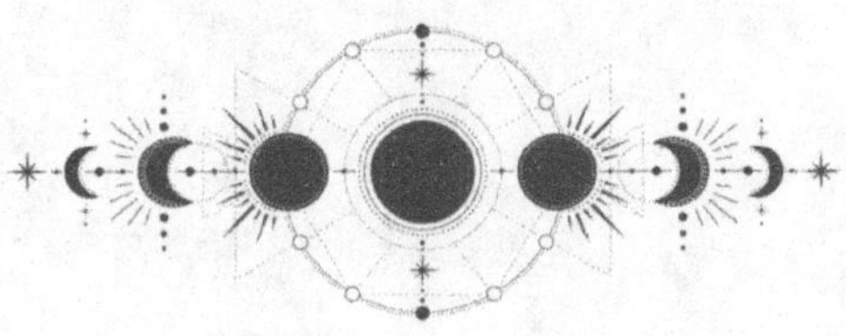

I hope that you have enjoyed exploring the world of Delta with me. As you return to Earth, I hope Elaura and Tourelle's stories resonate with you enough to look forward to the sequel: Ashes of an Empire and the coming completion of the Trilogy: Rebirth of an Empire.

Your support as a reader means the world to me!

ABOUT THE AUTHOR

Since she was small, April Fellows has had an affinity for spinning stories. Childhood games of pretend were never a simple affair. When given a writing assignment in school, she discovered her love of writing. That began a pursuit of sharing stories with the world. She describes herself as a walking Disney Princess, a classification many of her friends and associates agree with. She finds great joy in her family, her husband and children, and in serving her community as she is able. She adores sharing the stories that flood her dreams and hopes that they may allow you, the reader, an escape to have many adventures you might not otherwise have.

ALSO BY APRIL FELLOWS

Book 2 : Ashes of an Empire

Book 3: Rebirth of an Empire